Annie Burrows has been writing Regency romances for Mills & Boon since 2007. Her books have charmed readers worldwide, having been translated into nineteen different languages, and some have gone on to win the coveted Reviewers' Choice award from Cataromance. For more information, or to contact the author, please visit annie-burrows.co.uk, or you can find her on Facebook at facebook.com/AnnieBurrowsUK.

Also by Annie Burrows

A Mistress for Major Bartlett
The Captain's Christmas Bride
In Bed with the Duke
Once Upon a Regency Christmas
The Debutante's Daring Proposal
A Duke in Need of a Wife
A Marquess, a Miss and a Mystery

Brides for Bachelors miniseries

The Major Meets His Match
The Marquess Tames His Bride
The Captain Claims His Lady

Discover more at millsandboon.co.uk.

THE SCANDAL OF THE SEASON

Annie Burrows

MILLS & BOON

ISBN: 978-0-263-27285-7

MIX
Paper from
responsible sources
FSC C007454

This book is produced from independently certified FSC™ paper
to ensure responsible forest management.
For more information visit www.harpercollins.co.uk/green.

Printed and bound in Spain
by CPI, Barcelona

Oliver James.
Although I don't think Mummy and Daddy
will let you read this until you are eighteen!

Chapter One

Cassandra pressed her nose right up to the window pane as the carriage containing Miss Henley of Henley Hall went lurching past the front gate.

'You can come away from the window now,' said Aunt Eunice, from the cutting table where she was working. 'She's gone.'

Along with all the beautiful clothes Cassandra and her aunts had spent the last few months, often late into the night, creating.

Would Miss Henley wear the white muslin with the periwinkle ribbons and spangled over-dress, with which Cassandra had fallen half in love, to a ball? Or, once she reached London, would she discard it in favour of something created by a fashionable town modiste? The way she'd so easily discarded Cassandra the minute she could, apparently. Miss Henley hadn't even leaned out of the window to wave as she'd gone past just now, the way Cassandra would have done had she been in the coach, and Miss Henley the one whose fingers had developed calluses as she'd sat up till all hours, making sure everything was finished on time.

A heavy, invisible cloak seemed to settle over Cassandra's shoulders as she thought of how much effort she'd put into making each and every garment that comprised Miss Henley's wardrobe for her Season. She'd wanted them all to be perfect, because of the way Miss Henley had stood up to her mother, who'd wanted her to take her custom to a more reputable dressmaker with a shop in Exeter.

'I want nobody but my dear, dear friend, Miss Furnival,' she'd said, 'to make the clothes I'm going to wear in town. Because every time I put on something she has made for me, I will feel as if she is with me in spirit and then I shall feel less alone.'

The statement had touched something so deep inside Cassandra, she hadn't quite known how to deal with the feeling.

'You won't be alone,' Lady Henley, her mother, had said tartly enough to dispel it. 'I shall be with you. And so will your papa.'

'Yes, but I shan't have any friends my own

age,' Miss Henley had objected, with a pout. 'And everyone will be so…sophisticated and they are bound to make me feel like a mere country miss, and…'

Her big blue eyes had swum with tears. And Lady Henley had promptly capitulated.

'I suppose at least it will save us a deal of expense,' she'd said, looking round the front parlour of the cottage where Cassandra's aunts carried on their business. 'Which will please your papa. And we shan't have the fatigue of travelling up to Exeter whenever you need a fitting, either. Very well, my puss. You may have your way.'

'Spoiled madam,' Aunt Cordelia had muttered. After the Henleys had left, of course.

'Still, it is a big order,' the ever-practical Aunt Eunice had pointed out. 'And at least Sir Barnabas will pay promptly.'

'That is the one advantage of having a vicar with evangelical tendencies,' Aunt Cordelia had replied. 'He would rain down fire and brimstone on anyone who brought hardship on any of his flock by neglecting to pay what they owe.'

'Especially two spinster ladies of genteel birth, who have fallen on such hard times that they are forced to earn their living by the needle,' Aunt Eunice had said, her tongue most decidedly in her cheek.

Cassandra felt her lower lip wobble as Miss Henley's coach swept round the bend in the lane, taking it briefly out of sight. Would its youngest occupant ever really think of her when she was driving round the park in a curricle tooled by some handsome young buck? Or when some dashing blade was rowing her down the river to a grassy bank where dozens of dazzling young people would be gathering to take a picnic?

Probably not, she reflected, heaving a sigh.

'I'm just going to watch,' she said with a sniff, in belated answer to Aunt Eunice's comment about getting back to work, 'until they've gone over the bridge.' It might take her a while to shake off this fit of the dismals and she had no wish to show a glum face to her aunts, since it would smack of ingratitude.

'You won't be able to see them going over the bridge,' Aunt Eunice said, before Aunt Cordelia shushed her.

'The girl might be able to glimpse the trunks strapped to the roof when they get to the brow of it,' she said.

Yes, the trunks. And there they were! She could see them now as the coach crested the narrow bridge over the River Teene. Each and every one of them stuffed to bursting with outfits she'd helped create, outfits which were going to London, a place she had never been, nor would ever be likely to go, not now, even though it was an experience most girls of her age and station considered their right.

Because she'd committed a Fatal Error.

'Leave her be, Eunice,' said Aunt Cordelia. 'It can't be easy watching a stuck-up little madam like that swanning off to town when our Cassy...'

Had been stupid enough to trust in a handsome face and a scarlet jacket, and a kindly demeanour...

Oh, dear, there went her lower lip again.

She dug into the pocket of her apron for a handkerchief, and surreptitiously dabbed at her left eye, which was, in spite of her resolve, starting to leak. She had no intention of letting the aunts see that she was on the verge of tears. It might make them think she was unhappy with her lot. Which would be terribly...disloyal. Because if they hadn't taken her in and given her honest work, she could easily have ended up lying dead in a ditch somewhere. Or, worse, staying alive and earning her living by...

She pulled herself up short with a sniff. She

hadn't had to endure such horrors. Because the aunts *had* taken her in. Even though her own mother and stepfather had refused to do as much, claiming she would bring shame on them and blight her younger brother's reputation, as well.

It was true that Aunt Cordelia, who was not really an aunt but only some sort of cousin of her mother's, had only opened her door grudgingly. But that hadn't been anything to do with Cassandra's actions.

'We don't mix socially any longer,' she'd said gruffly. 'Not since we've set up house together. And if you come to stay the rest of the family will turn their backs on you, because they will consider you've been…er…contaminated by our sort of…'

'Eccentricity,' Aunt Eunice had concluded when Aunt Cordelia had floundered.

'Yes, that's the *least* unpleasant way they have described our arrangement,' Aunt Cordelia had mused.

Cassandra hadn't understood what they'd meant, not then. So she'd simply said that it wouldn't make any difference, because none of her immediate family would have anything further to do with her anyway. Her stepfather had warned her that he would see to that.

'Well, he has no say here,' Aunt Cordelia had said firmly. 'I've never had any time for that old lecher who married your mother for her money. And as for the rest of them...well, they all washed their hands of me many years ago, when I refused to marry some oafish male, and set up home with my good friend instead. But...that's why you came to me, isn't it?'

Cassandra had nodded.

'Then you can stay for a while and see if we can all rub along together.'

And they had. They did.

Cassandra blew her nose. She had become, if not exactly happy, then at least content with her lot. Her aunts never made her feel she was a failure, or a disappointment, or a burden. On the contrary, they made her feel that she was making a valuable contribution to the upkeep of the household, since she was such a swift and neat stitcher. Which was, ironically, thanks to her stepfather's insistence that she and her mother make all their own clothing rather than pay a dressmaker to do it.

However, on days like this, when the clouds looked as though they might part and let the sun through at any minute, and spears of daffodils were nosing their way through the frosty ground, bringing a sense of hope to everyone else, she was always particularly susceptible to suffering from regrets.

So Cassandra didn't think she'd better attempt to converse with her aunts until she was in better control of herself. Therefore she stayed where she was, gazing out of the window that overlooked their front garden and the lane which led, eventually, to the road to London. And kept her handkerchief at the ready.

She had blown her nose for the fourth, and positively the last, time when she saw the top of a carriage driving over the hump-backed bridge.

'Oh,' she said. 'It looks as though Miss Henley has forgotten something. At least…no, actually, I don't think that is her carriage coming over the bridge. There are no trunks on the roof. And, oh! You should see the horses. Four of them. All greys.' And all of them a distinct cut above the mixed team of chestnuts and blacks that Sir Barnabas occasionally put to work on his home farm.

Cassandra heard the clatter of scissors falling to the table an instant before feeling the presence of Aunt Eunice at her back.

'She's right, Cordelia. A spanking team. And, oh, my word, a crest on the door,' she said as the coach drew level with the cottage.

'A crest?' Now it was Aunt Cordelia's turn

to toss her work aside and join them at the little bow-fronted window. 'What on earth can somebody of that rank be doing in an out-of-the-way place like Market Gooding? Especially up this end.' For the lane on which their cottage stood only ran between Henley Hall and the London Road.

'They must have got lost,' said Aunt Eunice as the carriage drew to a halt by their front gate. 'Look, that fellow,' she said, as one of the pair of footmen, who'd been perched up behind, jumped down and opened their gate, 'is coming to ask for directions.'

'Then why is the other one opening the carriage door and letting down the steps?' asked Aunt Cordelia.

All three ladies fell silent at the first glimpse of the passenger, who was clearly a very grand lady to judge from not only the crest on the door, but also the air of reverence with which the footman held out his arm to help her alight.

'A lady like that wouldn't get out to ask her way from the inhabitants of a cottage like this,' said Aunt Cordelia.

'She must be a new customer,' said Cassandra as her footman deftly caught the lady's muff and the furs which must have been swaddling her, before they scattered in all directions.

'Not she,' said Aunt Cordelia. 'No lady decked out in a carriage dress that fine could possibly want to mar her image by buying anything from a provincial dressmaker.'

Cassandra felt Aunt Eunice swell with indignation at the slur on her creative talent. For she was the one with the eye for seeing just what would suit those who consulted her, as well as the skills of measuring and cutting. Cassandra did the rough basting, and plain stitching nowadays, while Cordelia added the finishing touches. 'I could turn her out just as fine,' she growled.

'Well, yes, you *could*,' Aunt Cordelia acknowledged. 'If you were able to get your hands on that amount of velvet, in just that shade of blue, and if she were to ask you to, but she wouldn't, would she?'

'Well, we're about to find out,' she retorted, as the footman who'd been stalking up the garden path rapped imperiously on their front door, causing all three ladies to cease their perusal of the vision of sophistication, who was finally ready to take the arm of the second footman, and rush to adopt various industrious poses around the room while Betty, their maid, went to answer the door.

Although Cassandra strained to make out

the conversation taking place in the hall, the thick oak door to the parlour kept it frustratingly muffled. Her aunts, who were merely holding the tools of their trade, while leaning in the same direction, were looking equally frustrated.

But at last the door opened and the lady in blue velvet came floating into the room on a cloud of exotic perfume. It was as well they'd watched her arrive, otherwise they would all probably have sat there gaping at the vision of fashionable elegance, flanked on either side by two footmen whose heads almost brushed the ceiling.

As it was, all three of them managed to rise to their feet and drop into suitably deferential curtsies, with an air of aplomb that conveyed the message that they were used to entertaining titled ladies practically every day.

The lady stood there for a moment, looking them over, then abruptly flung her arms wide and headed straight for Cassandra.

'Darling,' she said, enveloping her in a highly scented hug. 'I have found you at last!'

The aunts shot her looks of enquiry, which Cassandra had to return with a shrug. For she had absolutely no idea why this lady was hugging her and calling her *darling*.

'I beg your pardon,' she said, disentangling herself from the lady's perfumed embrace. 'But I think you must be mistaking me for someone else.'

The lady cocked her head to one side, and gave her what Cassandra could only think of as a twinkling look. 'You are Miss Cassandra Furnival, are you not? Daughter of Julia Hasely, third daughter of the Earl of Sydenham?'

'Er…yes, I am, but…'

The lady gave a rueful shake of her head and heaved a melodramatic sigh, making Cassandra suspect the lady never did anything without considering the effect it would have upon an audience. 'I suppose I should have been prepared to find you had forgotten me. Because you were, after all, just the tiniest babe when last we were in the same room together.' She drew off her gloves and held them out in midair. One of the footmen sprang forward just in time to catch them as she let them drop. 'Which was at your christening,' she finished saying, looking around as though searching for something. 'Your mother was a great friend of mine,' she said, making for one of the chairs reserved for customers. 'A very great friend,' she said, disposing herself upon it gracefully.

'I,' she announced, with a dazzling smile, 'am your godmother.'

'Your Grace,' gasped Cassandra, collapsing on to her own chair as she finally realised that this lady had, indeed, come to visit her. The Duchess of Theakstone, her godmother, was the only person from her past life who still corresponded with her. Even though it was only ever in the form of a note at Christmas and her birthday—hastily dashed off, to judge from the handwriting—she had treasured each and every one. For it was more than anyone else had done.

The Duchess laughed at this expression of Cassandra's shock at finally meeting her in person. 'I can see that I have taken you by surprise.'

Surprise? That was putting it mildly.

'You have never once asked me to help you, but I have often wished I could. While Theakstone was alive, of course, it was impossible.' She twisted her mouth into what, on a less beautiful woman, would have been called a sneer.

This statement only served to puzzle Cassandra even further. For one thing, the Duke to whom her godmother had been married had died several years ago. For another...

'Oh, my dear, how perplexed you look,' said the Duchess of Theakstone, with a challenging sort of smile. 'As though you never expected me to lift as much as a finger.'

'Ah…' Well, no, she hadn't. But the Duchess was making it sound as though somehow that view offended her.

'Well, no,' stammered Cassandra, 'I would never have presumed so far. How could I, when not even my own mother was prepared to acknowledge me after I committed my Fatal Error? But it wasn't only *that*…'

'Oh? Then what was *it*, precisely?' asked the Duchess, rather frostily.

'Only that you don't look…that is… I suppose that my mother must be considerably older than you. Well, she looked older than you last time I saw her, which was more than half-a-dozen years ago. So I don't see how you could have been such friends.'

'Oh, my dear, how clever of you to say just the right thing,' she crowed with delight. 'I am sure we are going to get along famously,' she said, untying and removing her bonnet to reveal a mass of gleaming golden curls, not one of which had been flattened by the cleverly constructed confection.

Aunt Eunice sprang forward to take the exquisite bonnet before either of the footmen could crush it in their meaty great paws, and carried it reverently over to a hatstand, currently occupied only by a swathe of sprig muslin.

'Thank you,' said the Duchess. 'Not only for taking such great care of my hat, but also of my goddaughter. I am *so* glad she found a safe haven with two such compassionate ladies.' She looked at each aunt in turn and then at Cassandra in a way that somehow made her aware that she hadn't effected a proper introduction.

'This is my Aunt Cordelia,' she said. 'Er… Miss Bramstock, I should have said,' she added, blushing.

'Ah, so *you* are the one who caused such a stir by spurning Hendon's offer and running off to set up home with your schoolfriend,' said the Duchess, before turning to examine Aunt Eunice, who lifted her chin to stare back with some belligerence.

'And this is, well, I call her Aunt Eunice,' Cassandra said, hoping that this was not going to turn into the sort of confrontation that would send her godmother flouncing out in a huff.

'Because you are so fond of her,' the Duchess concluded for her. 'Which is not surprising, when she has clearly done far more for you than any of your blood relations.'

Aunt Eunice subsided at once, murmuring her thanks and protesting that it was nothing.

'Is there somewhere that my boys,' said the Duchess, waving a hand at the two enormous footmen, 'may take refreshments?'

'Of course,' said Aunt Cordelia with a touch of chagrin at the reminder she was forgetting her duties as a hostess. Once she'd sent 'the boys' off to the kitchen with a message for Betty to not only look after them, but also to bring tea and cake to the parlour for their guest, Cassandra and both her aunts took to their chairs and gazed at their visitor in an expectant silence.

'Now that we are alone,' said the Duchess, 'we may get to the point. As I said, I am sure nobody could deny that you ladies have done my goddaughter a sterling service, up to this point. But now she needs someone with social standing to bring her out, wouldn't you agree?'

'Bring me out? That is not possible. Not when I am ruined. Socially, that is, if not in fact. For I'm sure that Stepfather must have made everyone aware he would not let me set foot in his house when I went back to try to explain...'

'Yes. *And* that he cut you off without a penny

to your name, as though it was something to be proud of,' put in the Duchess grimly.

'Yes. And I don't suppose even my mother has ever said one word in my defence...'

'The poor creature was so browbeaten by that bully she married I don't suppose she dared,' said the Duchess.

'No, she wouldn't,' said Cassandra, marvelling at how clearly the Duchess saw what had happened back then. She wondered if perhaps her mother had written to her, explaining, and asking her to help her only daughter... No, no, that couldn't be it. Stepfather would never allow any kind of missive to leave the house without scrutinising it carefully.

'But if I,' continued the Duchess, 'were to spread a rumour that it was all a plot he made up to swindle you out of your inheritance, plenty of people would be ready to believe it nowadays. Because, let me tell you, my dears, since the time he turned you out of doors he has shown his true colours often enough that he is generally held in aversion.'

'But, Your Grace, that is not true! I mean, yes, I'm sure he did leap at the chance to get his hands on what money should have come to me, because he is that sort of man. But he didn't have to make up any scandal about me.

I did run away with a soldier, you know, and I did return home unmarried…'

The Duchess held up her hand to stop her saying anything further. 'I am glad that you are being so frank with me. But you cannot restore your reputation if you go round blurting out the truth to all and sundry.'

Cassandra's heart gave a little lurch. Could it be possible? Could she really slough off the cloud of disgrace she could always feel hanging over her head, even when everyone was polite to her face these days? Could she find a place in polite society again? Become respectable once more?

But at what cost? 'I won't tell lies to try to persuade people I am something I am not,' she said firmly.

'There will be no need,' said the Duchess after a pause. 'From what you have just said, it sounds as if your so-called scandal was little more than a brief escapade, which could have been brushed over if your mother had not married such a monster.'

'Well, yes, but…' she clasped her hands at her waist as another barrier to the Duchess's scheme sprang to mind '…am I not too old to make a come-out?'

'Not at all. You cannot be more than twenty years of age?'

'I am three and twenty.'

'You look much younger. Besides, there are plenty of men who do not want a bride right out of the schoolroom. Someone more mature, with a bit of sense. And you are so pretty that I am sure there will be someone who is willing to overlook all that other business,' she said, waving her hand to dismiss Cassandra's Fatal Error as though it was no more than a bothersome fly.

'But… I'm not at all sure I wish to marry,' said Cassandra with a guilty look at her aunts, whose views on marriage she had begun to absorb. 'I am very happy here.'

'I am sure you are,' said the Duchess soothingly. 'And if you don't find a husband and wish to come back here after your Season, why, of course you may. But there's more to having a Season than catching a husband. There are all the balls and parties, and picnics and shopping, and visiting the theatre, and galleries and exhibitions. I vow and declare you deserve to enjoy all that has been so long denied you— through, I'm sure, no fault of your own.'

'That's true, Cassandra,' said Aunt Cordelia. 'And even though we both turned our backs on society, at least we had the luxury of *choosing* to do so.'

'You see?' The Duchess turned to Cassandra with a smile of triumph. 'Your aunts would love you to be able to find a husband, if that would make you happy, even if it wasn't for them,' she declared with a candour that was slightly shocking.

'And even if your experiences *have* put you off men altogether, that is no reason not to come to London with me. Wouldn't you like to go to balls and see the sights, Cassy darling?'

Cassy twisted the hands she still held clasped at her waist. Because not five minutes earlier, she had been wishing for just that very thing. And to be honest, if she could find a man like her real papa, a man who'd been kind and jolly from what she could remember of him, then she wouldn't mind marrying, either. For one thing it would mean she wouldn't have to work for her living any longer. And for another, she might have children. Adorable little chubby babies, who'd grow into people who would love her.

'You know,' pointed out Aunt Eunice, gruffly, just as Cassy had begun to get a real pang of longing to feel a warm little bundle in her arms, while another pair of youthful arms hugged her knees, 'it wouldn't do you any harm to go up to Town just to see the latest fashions being worn.'

'And visit some of the silk warehouses and see what's on offer,' said Aunt Cordelia.

'There, you see? These dear ladies are in agreement. Even if you cannot find a husband, there are plenty of other useful things you can do in town. And we shall have such fun,' said the Duchess, clapping her dainty little hands in delight. 'Oh, I knew this was going to answer.'

'Well,' said Cassandra, wondering why she was bothering to argue when everyone in the room, including her, thought that a trip to London was just what she needed. 'It is very good of you, Your Grace…'

'Oh, don't start off calling me that. I am your godmother and it will be of the utmost importance to remind everyone of that fact. So you had better get into the habit of calling me Godmama right away. And as for being good,' she added with a rather mischievous grin, 'that is not altogether true. Since you have been honest with me, my dear, it is only fair that I return the favour by being completely honest with you.' She cleared her throat. 'You see, although it is true that, for a while, at one point in our lives, your mother and I were great friends, that is not the *only* reason I have offered to bring you out.' She tilted her head to one side, setting her golden ringlets dancing, and smiled in what Cassandra thought of as a positively coaxing manner.

'It is my stepson,' she said, her smile fading. 'He has practically ordered me to leave Town and go to live in the Dower House. Which I shall never do! I have such horrid memories of my years at Theakstone Court that I vowed never to set foot anywhere on the estate ever again. But when I told him so, he said I would have no choice if he were to turn off all the London servants. Well...' she leaned back as both aunts gasped in outrage '...that was all he knew! For the moment I warned the staff of his threats, they all swore they would stay on without wages, if necessary. Isn't that loyal of them? The dears. Which meant that of course I could not abandon them, either. And so I started cudgelling my brains for a solution which would mean that we could *all* stay on in Grosvenor Square. Which,' she said, holding out her hand to Cassandra in a way that looked like an appeal for help, 'is where you come in...'

Chapter Two

Colonel Nathaniel Fairfax stood for a moment just inside the doorway of the ballroom, scouting the terrain. Dance floor directly ahead, full of couples performing complicated manoeuvres at the trot. To his right, a dowagers' bench, fully occupied by well-fed matrons. Beyond them, a trio of fiddlers sawing away industriously. There were two exits, he noted, apart from the doorway in which he was standing. One led to a refreshment room, to judge from the tables he could spy through the crowds gathered there, and the other led to the outside. A terrace, probably. Most houses of this size had them.

There was a sort of corridor between the terrace door and the dance floor, formed by a set of pillars, and several strategically placed urns stuffed with foliage behind which sharpshooters could crouch, should they wish to prevent uninvited guests getting in through any set of doors.

Not that he was expecting to encounter sharpshooters in a ballroom. Though he was scouting the terrain for something potentially far more dangerous.

A woman.

She wasn't one of the ladies cavorting about the dance floor. Only a couple of them had dark hair, but neither of them were anywhere near as pretty as he recalled her being.

She was not on the dowagers' bench. Not unless she'd aged a couple of decades and put on several stone in weight during the six years since he'd last clapped eyes on her.

Was she among the crowd loitering in the corridor by the terrace doors? That was where a lot of young females were standing, watching the dancers, and fluttering their fans. He ran his eyes along the rank of them. A tall thin blonde, a short squat ginger piece, a medium-sized brunette with…

Good God. His sister, Issy, had not lied. She *was* here. Cassandra Furnival. Brazenly pushing her way back into society when by rights she ought never dare show her face. But then he should already have known she was brazen. Why hadn't he learned his lesson when it came to her behaviour? She was the kind of girl who could entice a man to follow her out into a moonlit stable yard and almost make him forget the moral code by which he lived. The kind of girl who could, not one month later, entice an entirely different man to elope with her.

And that when she'd been scarce out of the schoolroom.

Back then she'd been pretty enough to cause two officers within the same regiment to lose their heads over her. Since then she'd only grown lovelier. To look at, that was. According to Issy, all that loveliness concealed the heart of an avaricious, designing baggage.

'Nate,' Issy had wailed, with tears trickling down her face, 'if you don't do something about her I don't know who can.'

'Do?' He'd flung down his pen in exasperation, since not only had she burst into his study unannounced, but had also taken a chair even though she could see he was busy. And the tears meant she was not going to leave until she'd said her piece. 'What do you expect me to do?'

'Stop her! Before she gets some other un-suspecting male in her clutches and wheedles his fortune out of him, the way she did to poor Lady Agatha's brother.'

Typical of Issy to use such emotionally charged words, in such a biased manner when, from what he'd observed of Lieutenant Gilbey and Miss Furnival, they'd both been equally culpable.

'And just how,' he'd said rather irritably, 'do you think I could do such a thing? Even if you could convince me it was any of my business, which I don't believe it is.'

Besides which, he had no wish to browbeat any female. It was not behaviour befitting an officer of His Majesty's Army.

'Of course it is your business! Lady Agatha's brother was one of your junior officers. You can't have forgotten poor Lieutenant Gilbey, can you?'

No, he hadn't forgotten the lovelorn young man. He hadn't forgotten any of the men who'd died while serving under his command. His life would now be far less uncomfortable if he only could.

'Surely,' Issy had persisted, 'you can see that you owe it to his memory, to…to his family, too, who are all devastated to learn that Furnival girl is trying to worm her way back into society.'

He did owe the fallen a great deal. And their families. But surely not to the extent of coming the heavy with Miss Furnival? Not the Miss Furnival he recalled, anyway. She'd seemed a rather timid little thing, not this brazen harpy his sister was describing.

'If she is as bad as you claim—' and he wasn't totally convinced of it '—I hardly think anyone is likely to receive her. You are probably making a fuss over nothing, Issy.'

'It's not nothing! Not to Lady Agatha. She was so cut up when she heard that girl had been taken up by that pea goose the Duchess of Theakstone that she left Town for fear she might accidentally come face to face with the designing baggage who cast her spell over her poor deluded brother.'

There had been a good deal more of the same. About how she'd brought some friend with her, too, who was from a background of trade and had no place in society ballrooms at all. Until, seeing that the only way he would be able to get his sister to leave him in peace to get on with his work would be to say that he would see what he could do.

Even though he had suspected much of what Issy claimed as fact would probably turn out to have no substance. He'd been certain that nobody would invite the girl anywhere, after what she'd done, even if she had taken up residence in London.

And so he hadn't got as far as working out what he could really *do* about her, even if he did run her to ground.

So, for a moment, all he could do was stand stock still, staring at her. Just staring at her. Until she bent to listen to something the short, ginger girl was saying, and laughed.

Laughed!

As though she hadn't a care in the world. When he…

He flinched as a series of stark and dreadful images surged to the forefront of his mind. Images he kept firmly locked away behind a sort of door in his memory. A good portion of them relating to Lieutenant Gilbey.

Gilbey sitting with his head in his hands. Gilbey pacing back and forth, his face tortured, after reading one of those damned letters she'd sent him. Gilbey's shattered body staining the snow scarlet…

He found himself stalking across the room, dazed to discover that Issy had been right. And, that being the case, he did have to do something. Even though he didn't know exactly what. Because, even though the hostess,

Lady Bunsford, was hardly a leader of society, if the Furnival girl had got in here she would not stop until she'd gained the objective Issy had painted in such lurid colours. And *that* he could not allow.

The very moment he began to stalk towards her, she turned, as though sensing his interest. Looked at him. Frowned a bit, as though trying to work out why his face looked familiar.

And then her face lit up. As though she was delighted to see him again.

The power of that smile almost, *almost* made him falter. It was so warm. So welcoming. And promised so much. For a moment or two it felt as if she'd cast some kind of net, formed from invisible gossamer threads, and that she was reeling him in rather than him marching across a crowded ballroom to challenge her because that was his choice. The same way she'd done the very first time he'd met her, at that assembly near where the regiment had been based for a time. All she'd had to do, that long-ago night, was to look over her shoulder at him, wistfully, as she went through a door that would take her to the stable yard, and he'd trotted after her like a…like a dog called to heel. Even though he'd resisted the temptation to ask her to dance before that moment. Even though she was too young for him. For any man, so he'd thought. She'd been all promise. Blossom. Not ready to be plucked. And yet, oh, so damned alluring.

It was her mouth. The way the top lip pouted, as though inviting a man to suck it into his own mouth and...

No, it was her eyes. The liveliness that danced in them, making a man yearn to drown in their greeny-brown depths...

No, it was her skin. Which wasn't blandly perfect like that of so many debutantes who reminded him of brittle porcelain. It was creamy and warm, and dotted here and there with moles which made his fingers itch to trace the course of their intriguing pattern...

'Colonel Fairfax,' she said, holding out her hand with the practised grace of a seasoned seductress.

No man could have resisted taking it, bending over it and bestowing the kiss she demanded. Least of all, as it turned out, him. Which infuriated him.

'How delightful to see you again,' she cooed, 'after all this time.'

He straightened up and dropped her hand. Just because he acknowledged her beauty, her allure, it did not mean he was going to fall under her spell. Thanks to Issy he knew what she was, now, what she was capable of. Saying she was delighted to see him again, for instance. Making him believe, with the radiance of that smile, that she meant it when he knew it must be impossible. She was too young, too lovely to genuinely have any interest in a dried-up husk of a man like him.

'Miss Furnival,' he said, his wounded pride smarting so much that his voice sounded harsh, even to his own ears. 'Still up to your pretty little neck in mischief, I see.'

The hand he'd just kissed flew to that neck, as though inviting his eyes to follow. Inviting his lips to do the same, at some later date. Or perhaps his teeth. If she was everything Issy had said, then she wouldn't care which.

Even though he'd just thrown down the gauntlet? Perhaps *because* he'd challenged her. Perhaps it was a declaration that she would fight back, with all the weapons in her arsenal. And a fight it was to be, now, he realised with a pang of what felt like loss. The warmth had gone from her smile. From a distance it probably looked the same, but this close to her, close enough to smell the floral fragrance she was wearing, he knew different.

'Mischief?' She gave a little frown, as though

she could not understand what he could possibly be implying. 'Whatever do you mean?'

For a moment, he wished she really didn't have any idea what he meant. That they were not on opposing sides. That he'd been able to bask in the warmth of that first smile, rather than having to make it freeze in place. That he could have taken her hand without reservation and begun to converse with her the way any man would talk to a pretty woman he'd met and felt drawn to.

But that outcome had never been possible. When they'd first met, he'd known he would shortly be going abroad and that he might be away too long to even suggest, let alone hope, she might wait for him. Known that she'd been too young for him and now…now his mission made fraternising with her an impossibility.

He tore his eyes from her before her loveliness gained sufficient power to weaken his resolve and focused on the girl next to her. The girl Issy had told him was the daughter of a mill owner. 'To begin with, foisting a girl like that,' he said to Miss Furnival, though he kept on looking at the ginger girl, 'on to a feather-brained creature like the Duchess of Theakstone.'

The ginger girl flinched. Scowled. And, as

he'd regained command of his wayward tendency to wish for the impossible, he turned his head to address Miss Furnival directly. 'I don't know how you have managed to persuade her to take part in one of your schemes, but I do know that you are encroaching upon her good nature.'

'One of my schemes?' Miss Furnival added a shake of her head to the mystified frown she'd manufactured for his benefit. 'What schemes?'

'Don't think you can fool me by that look of innocence,' he snarled at her through a mixture of bitterness and disappointment that she had, apparently, already done so once. 'Nor anyone else, not for very long. There are those who know what you have done, what you are...'

She flung up her chin. 'And what am I?'

Where to start? 'An adventuress. A heartbreaker.' Not that she'd broken *his* heart. He'd only got as far as wishing she was older, wishing he could get to know her better before the regiment left England, wishing he could ask her to consider waiting for him...

Thank goodness. Otherwise, when she'd turned up on the quayside, clinging to Gilbey's arm as the lad stammered out his intention to marry her and carry her on board with them like so much baggage...

But then, according to Issy, she *was* a baggage, wasn't she?

'Do you think,' he said, 'I could ever forget what you did to Lieutenant Gilbey?' According to Issy, that was. Although he still wasn't completely convinced. And it wasn't just because she was acting so surprised. Part of him really didn't *want* to believe she could look so lovely, yet be so hard-hearted. Perhaps, if he flung her supposed crimes in her face, she would refute them in such a way that he could go back and inform his sister she'd been mistaken. 'You cajoled him to make a runaway match of it,' he ventured. 'And then when I believed I'd managed to extricate him from your clutches, you still managed to wheedle his fortune out of him.'

'You...*got him out of my clutches*?' Her eyes widened, briefly, then turned hard.

His heart sank as she revealed a side of her he'd kept on hoping, right to this very minute, had been a figment of Issy's imagination.

But then wasn't that always the end result of hope? Shattering disappointment. Nothing ever lived up to a man's expectations. Not military glory, not social preferment and most definitely not, he'd just discovered, a woman.

'If that is your opinion of me,' she said frostily, 'then I fail to see that we have anything further to discuss.' She turned aside as if to cut him. He prevented her from doing so by simply stepping sideways and so maintaining his position directly in front of her.

'On the contrary,' he said, bitterness and disappointment driving him further than anything Issy could have provoked from him. 'I have come here tonight specifically to warn you that I have received intelligence as to your manoeuvres. I suppose you have run through Lieutenant Gilbey's fortune by now. That is why you have come to London. You are hoping to be able to dupe some other gullible fool into loosening his purse strings.' That was certainly what Issy believed. And, believing it, had not been able to sit back and watch Miss Furnival get away with it all over again.

'I have no intention of doing any such thing,' she denied hotly.

'Why else would you be using the Duchess to parade you about town, if not to catch yourself a husband?'

She frowned. Glanced at her companion. Took a breath. But before she could utter a single excuse, he said, 'You will not get away with it. I will not allow you to get away with it.' Issy had been right. He owed it to Gilbey, and Gilbey's family, and every other vulnerable male of marriageable age in England, to put a stop to her scheming before she could really get going.

'Get away with it?' Her eyes flashed with fury. 'And just how, pray, do you intend to stop me?'

If he'd had any doubts about her plans before, that statement exposed them. Because he could not very well hinder non-existent plans, could he?

'For a start,' he said, thinking on his feet, while wishing he'd taken the precaution of forming some kind of contingency plan, 'I shall inform the poor woman you have deceived into giving you house room exactly what you really are. And then I will make sure everyone knows that she,' he said, indicating the ginger girl, 'the one you claim is your friend, has no right to appear in decent society, either.'

'Cassy...' The ginger girl took hold of her arm, a look of concern on her face. He turned to address her.

'My quarrel is not with you, miss. If you withdraw from society quietly, I shall pursue you no further. And if you—' he turned to Miss Furnival once more '—confess your crimes to the Duchess, before any harm is done to her, and leave Town, I shall not expose you, either. I am, after all, a man of honour.'

'A man of honour?' Miss Furnival turned up her nose in scorn. 'Men of honour go about interfering in matters that are of no concern to them, do they? Flexing their muscles and threatening defenceless females?'

He hadn't flexed any muscles, in a literal sense, but somehow by referring to them he suddenly felt aware of several. One in particular that had been lying dormant for some years.

If she'd really been defenceless, that reaction might have given him pause. But she wasn't. The ease with which she could arouse a man who'd been practically dead in that department just went to prove it. So he gave a bitter laugh.

'Defenceless? You are about as defenceless as those sirens were, luring all those sailors to their deaths.'

She looked taken aback. It was a small victory, but one he was prepared to accept. And on the principle that it was better to withdraw while he had the advantage, he turned on his heel and quit the ballroom.

Chapter Three

Cassandra watched the Colonel stalk from the ballroom, her heart pounding and her limbs shaking. She couldn't believe she'd spoken so sharply to him. She never stood up to anyone, or lost her temper, ever. But then he'd dragged her through so many strong emotions in such a short space of time. Perhaps that was what had made her lose self-control.

To start with she couldn't believe he would turn out to be so…unkind. She'd had such fond memories of him. He'd been the first man she'd ever looked at with any sort of romantic interest. And although he'd been far too mature and important to return that interest, she hadn't held that against him. On the contrary, when he'd come to her rescue, several weeks after their initial meeting, he'd gone up in her estimation even higher. So much so that ever since, she'd thought of him as her hero. Her saviour. She'd never had the chance to thank him properly for what he'd done. And so she'd been really pleased to see him when he'd marched into the ballroom.

Only to learn that he hadn't done what she thought he'd done at all. Far from stepping in, and rescuing her from her folly, he thought he'd been rescuing Guy from her *clutches*. Those few curt words had shattered the bubble of pleasure in which she'd been floating, during these last few weeks since she'd come to London. No, come to think of it, he'd punctured her pleasure the moment he'd reached her side when he'd accused her of being up to her neck in mischief just as she'd been thinking how wonderful it was to be able to renew their acquaintance. Now that she was old enough to hope he might see her as a woman and not a silly schoolgirl.

'What,' said Rosalind, breaking through the turmoil of her reactions, 'was all that about? Who was he? And aren't you supposed to be smiling? Her Grace says we are always supposed to have a serene smile stuck to our lips no matter what, when we're out in society.'

Cassandra blinked. 'Yes, of course, you are correct. Thank you for reminding me,' she said, fixing the required smile in place.

'Who is he? An old flame, or something?'

'Not an old flame, no. But I did believe he'd been my friend. He was the only person, during the whole sorry episode, who did anything practical.' He'd been like a rock. Standing firm in the midst of all the confusion on the quayside, the only one who seemed to know what was going on and having some control over it.

'What sorry episode? And what did he mean about you scheming? Are we done for?'

'I am so sorry, Rosalind,' she said, turning to the girl, rather than continuing to gaze blankly at the door through which he'd just gone. 'I did warn Godmama that things from my past might come back to haunt us, but she assured me that she could scotch all the rumours about the indiscretion, particularly since I committed it when I was scarcely more than a schoolgirl…'

'Indiscretion?' Rosalind's eyes grew round with wonder. 'You? And you always being held up as a pattern card for me to follow.'

Yes, well, Cassandra had spoken to Godmama about that, too. But she'd brushed Cassandra's concerns aside, reminding her that Rosalind needed to learn so much in the way of deportment and etiquette that advising her to mould herself on Cassandra would be the quickest way to effect the necessary transformation in the short time they had available.

'After all, it is one of the reasons I brought you to Town, darling,' she'd said. 'So that you could help me school Miss Mollington into behaviour fitting someone who could marry a titled man.'

Of course, Cassandra had felt that it was the least she could do to repay Godmama's generosity and hard work in attempting to restore her reputation.

'I am so sorry,' said Cassandra. 'You must be so disappointed…'

'The only thing that will disappoint me is if you don't, immediately, tell me all about it. What kind of indiscretion did you commit when you was a schoolgirl that could get a man like that in such a pother that he'd threaten to expose you?'

'Not here,' said Cassandra, who'd noticed that several people were looking their way, then looking at the door through which Colonel Fairfax had just marched, and then back at them again and then whispering behind their fans. 'Come.' She linked her arm through Rosalind's and sauntered along until they reached the door to the terrace. There were a few people outside taking the air, but there was still plenty of places where they could talk without risk of being overheard.

'Well?' The moment they were out of earshot of the ballroom, Rosalind leaned back against the parapet, demanding an explanation. Cassandra rubbed her hands up and down her arms. She hated to have to let Rosalind down. Over the last few weeks, they'd become friends. Or the closest thing to friends that Cassandra had experienced for many years. Even though Rosalind was a bit rough around the edges, she had a generous nature and a warm heart. But now their friendship would all come to an end. The way friendships did at the first hint of trouble.

But where to start? With the first ball she'd ever attended, where she'd first met Colonel Fairfax?

No, for if she talked about that, she'd also have to go back further, to explain the complicated reasons why she'd gone there without her mother, and she didn't want to go into all that right now. It would take too long to relate the story of how Lady Agatha, her closest thing to a friend back then, had decided it was high time she had a little fun and persuaded her own mother to let her join a party of local young people attending a benefit ball at the White Hart.

Her stepfather had been not only too mean to wish to purchase three tickets to raise funds for the parish alms houses, but when Agatha's father, the Earl of Spendlow, had offered to collect her in his own carriage and convey her home in it, too, Mama had timidly suggested that it would be a splendid way of helping her prepare for her eventual come-out, by experiencing a ball in unsophisticated surroundings, without incurring any expense whatever.

She sighed as she thought of her younger self, walking into that ballroom arm in arm with Lady Agatha and being immediately besieged by a corps of scarlet-jacketed officers from her brother's regiment. Guy, Agatha's brother, had seen how wary she'd been of all those boisterous young men and had taken her under his wing. And she'd felt safe with him, for he'd treated her exactly the way he treated his own sister.

There had been only one officer who hadn't joined the mob, who hadn't teased and flattered either her or Agatha. And that had been Colonel Fairfax. There was nothing frivolous or false about him, she'd decided, as the evening had progressed. He was fully in command of himself, unlike other men who became increasingly intoxicated the closer it drew to midnight.

She'd begun to wish he'd ask her to dance, but he never did. She'd danced with the squire and the grocer's son. And then, after a particularly energetic reel with the young blacksmith, she'd gone outside to get a breath of fresh air and cool down. He'd followed her outside. And told her that she was being foolish to do so, alone. And had escorted her inside, having made her feel wretchedly guilty.

Especially because, for a moment, in the moonlit inn yard, he'd looked at her, or she'd thought he'd looked at her, or she'd *imagined* he'd looked at her, with a sort of admiration tinged with longing. As though he had been considering kissing her.

Wishful thinking, obviously. Ah, well. She knew better now. About a lot of things.

Including how much information to impart to someone she didn't, really, know all that well.

'When I was sixteen years old,' she therefore told Rosalind, cutting right to the heart of the matter, 'I eloped with a soldier.'

'No!'

Far from being outraged, Rosalind looked positively enthralled.

''Andsome, was he? 'Andsome as that Colonel?'

'No,' said Cassandra at once. She'd never

met anyone who could hold a candle to Colonel Fairfax. Not even considering the changes the years had wrought in him. He'd been taller than most of the men at the dance, so that he literally stood head and shoulders above them all. And he'd also had an air of self-containment about him, so that he'd seemed far more dignified than the rest of the laughing, sweating, roistering crowd.

Tonight, he'd looked like a pared-down version of himself. As though he'd been ill and was still recovering. Although the biggest change had been in his eyes. Or, at least, in the way they'd looked at her. No longer with kindness and understanding, but with a cold, implacable hostility. Like two chips of ice. She gave an involuntary shiver.

'A good kisser?'

What? She'd never kissed the Colonel, or come anywhere near it. Oh, but Rosalind was still harping on Guy. 'He only ever kissed me once or twice, to be honest,' Cassandra explained. 'And only on the cheek, or the hand...'

'Then why on earth did you elope with him? Was it money?' She frowned. 'Nah, because you don't have any. Or you wouldn't be taking Pa's wages to introduce me about to titled people.'

Cassandra flinched. She didn't think she'd ever get used to the blunt way Rosalind spoke about money, nor did she appreciate the reminder that she was being paid to be her friend.

'No,' she said. 'It wasn't about money.'

'Forbidden love, then? Ooh, how exciting! I never knew you had it in you. You always looks so prim and proper.'

'Well, if I am a bit prim nowadays,' said Cassandra defensively, 'it is because I learned my lesson back then. Guy was trying to rescue me from an unhappy home, as a matter of fact. My mother, who was a widow, was deceived into marrying a horrible, horrible man who made my life an utter…hell.' She shivered as she recalled those dark days. Darker than anything that had happened since. 'And Guy, well, he was my friend's brother, or, to be completely accurate he was only one of them, she had several. They lived in the neighbourhood where we went to live when my mother remarried. At least, some of the time. You see, Lady Agatha's father was an earl, who had several properties dotted all over the country. When they came to stay, they were the principal family in the area, which made it hard for my stepfather to refuse to let them in when they came calling.

Even though he wouldn't allow Mama or me to pay any social calls in return.'

'What? That's…that's…'

'Mean, yes. And when, one day, things had become particularly unbearable and Guy saw how things were, he, well, was overcome by a fit of chivalry, I think. Said he couldn't bear to leave me and begged me to run away with him. He promised that we'd get married. That his regiment was going abroad soon, but that as an officer's wife, I could go with him. He made,' she said sourly, 'living in a billet in a war-torn country sound terrifically exciting—'

'I'll say!'

'But the reality was anything but. When we got to Portsmouth, Colonel Fairfax—'

'The one who just called you a siren?'

'Yes. He…he really shouted at Guy. Said he'd ruined me because we were both under age and that I couldn't get married without my guardian's permission, and the permission of his commanding officer, as well.'

'He was your Guy's commanding officer?'

'Yes. And he ordered Guy to send me back to my family. But Guy couldn't, because he'd spent every penny he had getting us that far.' Guy had been all chivalry and no sense, she reflected sadly. Insisting on separate rooms when they'd had to stop overnight on their journey, to preserve her virtue. Hiring a chaise he could ill afford rather than mounting her on horseback where she'd be exposed to the elements...

'In the end, it was the Colonel himself who provided the fare home. And arranged for one of the other soldier's wives, one who didn't get picked to go with the regiment, to act as my chaperon, because,' she explained, seeing Rosalind's puzzled frown, 'only a certain number of the common soldier's wives are allowed to travel abroad and they draw lots to see who can go. And I was that grateful to him,' she said, running her hands up and down her arms again, in agitation. 'I thought he was sorting out the awful mess Guy had made of rescuing me, was being kind, when all the time...'

'He was rescuing Guy from *your clutches*,' said Rosalind, with a giggle.

'It isn't funny,' retorted Cassandra, recalling the way she'd felt when he, her hero, had said he thought her neck was pretty. It had taken a moment or two to realise he wasn't paying her a compliment. A few more insults before she'd seen that all these years, he'd been blaming her for the mess Guy had led her into and thinking she was some sort of siren who lured unsuspecting men to their doom.

'Why are you giggling?'

'That Colonel. Thinking that anyone would need rescuing from your *clutches*. At that age! And you not even knowing as much as that you were too young to obtain a special licence…'

'We were so silly. The pair of us. If I hadn't been so desperate to escape my stepfather, and of course in those days I thought marriage was the only way a girl could escape…' She shook her head. 'Well, it's all water under the bridge now. I *was* desperate and I *did* trust in a foolish boy, and ended up ruined.'

'Ooh.' Rosalind sidled a bit closer and leaned in. 'What was it like? Being ruined?'

'Cold and uncomfortable.'

Rosalind frowned. 'Cold? Didn't he…you know…snuggle up when he was doing it?'

'Doing it? Oh!' Cassandra suddenly saw that they'd been talking at cross-purposes. 'No, I thought I told you, we never did…*that*.' She lowered her voice to a whisper. 'It wasn't him, or anything he did that made me cold and uncomfortable. *He* was always a perfect gentleman. It was after. When I got home again. That was the worst bit. My stepfather refused to take me back. Said I was a…well, I don't want to repeat any of the names he called me.' She shuddered, recalling the look of glee on his face when he'd said that her behaviour obliged him to wash his hands of her. That from now on she was dead to him and to her mother, and to her brother. That she must never return and not a penny would she ever have from either of them.

'Betty and I had no money left and nowhere to go.'

'Betty?'

'The soldier's wife I told you about. The one who came with me, to lend me respectability on the journey. Fortunately, my stepfather hadn't seen her, since he'd been too busy shouting at me and forbidding me to enter the house. She had the sense to sneak round the back and ask the servants if any of them knew of anywhere else we could go. And the cook, who'd been with the family from before my mother's second marriage, let her know about an aunt of mine who was supposed to be living in a scandalous manner. I'd never heard of her before, because, well, nobody talks about scandalous aunts to young girls, do they?'

'I don't suppose they do, no,' said Rosalind, enthralled. 'And they took you in, did they?'

'Ah, eventually, yes.' It had taken weeks to reach the house in Devon. She and Betty had to walk all the way, foraging for food from the hedgerows as they went. They must have looked like scarecrows by the time they knocked on the front door of the cottage in Market Gooding, so she supposed it wasn't so surprising the two older ladies had been reluctant to let them in. It was only when Betty had broken down in tears, saying they had nowhere else to go and threatening to lie down and die in their front garden, that they'd said they supposed the pair could stay for a while until they thought of something else.

They hadn't been there long before discovering why the two ladies had been so reluctant to have them stay and also why they didn't have any live-in servants already. Although the house was relatively spacious, they shared a bedroom. Betty had explained to the puzzled young Cassandra that the pair of them were in love with each other, in a romantic way, and were probably worried about what people would say if they found out.

'For my part, Miss Cassy,' the pragmatic Betty had declared, 'I don't care what they get up to as long as they give me houseroom. And nor should you.'

And she didn't.

'Betty gradually took on more and more of the household chores,' she said, 'and I became an apprentice in their dressmaking enterprise.'

Rosalind frowned. 'You had to work with the needle to earn your living?'

Cassandra nodded, maintaining the fiction that her aunts used to disguise the real reason why they chose to live together, without a husband between them. People accepted the story of them being indigent females, throwing in their lot together and plying their needles to eke out a living, assuming that neither of them had managed to find a husband to support them. And the aunts, and now Cassandra and Betty, too, took great care to conceal the fact that they loved each other in a way that society would find shocking. As Rosalind might. Which was why she wasn't going to tell her about it. Or, at least, not right now.

'So what was all that about running through Guy's fortune?'

'I don't really know. I mean, he did leave me some money in his will—'

'Oh, did he die, then?'

'Yes, in the retreat to Corunna. Along with Betty's husband, which actually settled her position in my aunt's household. She is their cook-housekeeper now, with a proper wage to reflect her status.'

'And Guy left you a fortune…'

'No. I mean, he didn't have a fortune to

leave. I receive a small annuity, that is all. Though even that took me by surprise.' She gave a bitter laugh. 'Even though he kept in touch, after the way things had ended, I didn't really believe a word he wrote.' She wouldn't even have written to let him know where she was and what had become of her, if her aunts had not insisted, saying that he was responsible for it and should shoulder the blame. 'I mean, he said that he considered himself betrothed to me and that he would carry through on his promise to marry me as soon as we were old enough. And that he would always take care of me, no matter what. But…'

But Rosalind had clearly lost interest in Guy.

'So that Colonel was blowing a lot of smoke, then? He really has no reason to threaten you, or force me to go home?'

'Well, no, not exactly. But,' she said, lowering her voice and leaning in a bit closer, 'if he decides to make trouble for us, people might feel obliged to look a bit deeper into the reasons Godmama is giving everyone for our, um, relationship. And rumour can be terribly damaging.'

'So what are we to do?'

Cassandra had no idea. 'We will ask Godmama,' she said. 'I am sure she will come up with one of her clever notions.' And if not, well, at least she'd had a few weeks in London, which she'd thoroughly enjoyed, before having to pay the piper.

It was just such a shame that Rosalind's plans, too, would come to nothing.

Chapter Four

'Godmama,' said Cassandra, the moment they stepped through the front door of the house on Grosvenor Square which the Duchess called home. 'We need to speak with you, Rosalind and I.' She glanced at Captain Bucknell, who had been their escort as usual that night, and who was still loitering in the hall. 'In private.'

'Yes, yes, in the morning,' said the Duchess, as the butler reverently removed the cloak from her shoulders.

'I am afraid not, Godmama,' said Cassandra. 'We shall neither of us be able to sleep for worrying. Could we not just step into the drawing room for a while? I am sure you will excuse us, Captain,' she said, forcing herself to smile at him sweetly, 'won't you?'

'Oh, ah, I suppose I could do that,' he said, looking a bit annoyed. Which didn't surprise her. For usually, after acting as their escort for the evening, he would stand in the hall, arm in arm with Godmama, watching the girls go up to bed. Cassy suspected that he never left the premises before he'd spent several more hours with Godmama. 'That is, I mean to say...'

'Dear Captain Bucknell,' said Godmama, tripping across the hallway and extending her hand for him to kiss. 'It was so kind of you to escort us to the ball. How lucky I am to be able to rely on you so very often, for the most tedious of favours.'

She meant, Cassandra supposed, all the times she'd put him to use as a partner for the girls to practise on. He'd nobly allowed them to tread on his feet during the dancing lessons given by the wizened little dancing master Godmama had employed. And sat through many dinners during which Rosalind had learned how to carry on the kind of conversation considered appropriate in polite society— just in case anyone ever invited her to dine in such company. Given the fact that he'd never treated either girl as if he regarded them as nuisances, Cassandra couldn't really understand why she didn't like him.

But she felt a definite frisson of revulsion when Godmama reached up, on tiptoe, to whisper in his ear. Especially when whatever it was she'd whispered brought a smile back to his face. A rather devilish smile.

'Come, girls,' said Godmama, once she'd appeased Captain Bucknell. 'Let us go to the drawing room so that you can tell me all about whatever it is that has put you both in such a pother.'

While Godmama and Rosalind chose seats by the fireplace, where a cheerful blaze was crackling away, Cassandra hung back, listening out for the sound of the front door opening and closing. However, just as she'd suspected, instead of hearing anything to indicate Captain Bucknell was leaving the house, she heard the tread of heavy footsteps going up the stairs. She knew it! Godmama and Captain Bucknell *were* lovers.

The fact that there was a fire lit in here and that a decanter, two glasses and a plate of the Captain's favourite biscuits were set out on a little table beside the *chaise longue* was even further proof.

Even though she had no right to criticise a single aspect of Godmama's behaviour, she couldn't help feeling a bit annoyed, for Godmama had lured Cassandra to London with promises of restoring her reputation. And had also undertaken to find a titled husband for Rosalind. How on earth did she think she was going to accomplish either feat when she was carrying on with the big Guardsman so brazenly?

It wasn't as if he was irresistible. The best she could say about him was that he was easygoing. Many people said he was handsome, but Cassandra didn't find all that facial hair of his the slightest bit appealing. Nor the way the blackness of his whiskers made his lips look unnaturally red. What was more, he was one of those officers who had his uniforms tailored to fit so tightly that his breeches, in particular, left nothing to the imagination.

'So, girls,' said Godmama, thankfully interrupting Cassandra's train of thought before it could dwell too long upon Captain Bucknell's skin-tight breeches. 'What is so urgent it cannot wait until morning?'

'Colonel Fairfax was at the ball tonight. He—'

'Colonel Fairfax? Was at the ball? Gracious heavens! Lady Bunsford must be in alt.'

Cassandra frowned at her godmother, wondering what on earth she could mean.

'In alt? But he was only there for about five

minutes.' Nearly all of which he spent glaring and growling at her.

'That makes no difference. He was *there*, when he is famous for never wasting his time attending anything so frivolous as a society ball. Not unless someone from High Command hints that it might be of use to Wellington's plans. And I'm sure nobody in command would have thought any such thing about a function arranged by the likes of Lady Bunsford!' She laughed. 'But now Lady Bunsford will be able to claim the cachet of being the first hostess to succeed where so many others have failed.'

'Be that as it may,' Cassandra persisted, having learned by now that if she didn't pull the conversation back on track very swiftly, Godmama would find some other way of diverting it in the direction she wished it to take. 'He approached us and threatened to tell everyone about...' she swallowed '...my past.'

'No!' Godmama, at last, looked suitably shocked.

'Only, he had things all muddled up. He seemed to think that I had deceived you into launching me and Rosalind into society and insisted I confess all to you.'

'He said what? Oh!' Godmama burst out laughing.

'Begging your pardon, Your Grace, but I don't find it very funny,' said Rosalind mulishly. 'He said I wasn't fit to mix in polite society and would force me to leave.'

Godmama produced a handkerchief from somewhere and dabbed at her eyes with it. 'But don't you see? He has spiked his own guns by insisting you make a confession to me. Because the next time he challenges you, you may say, perfectly truthfully, that I know all and that I am very happy to continue to sponsor you. Both of you,' she added, sending one of her charming smiles at each girl in turn.

'Yes, but...'

'And anyway, what can he really do? He does not have the power to physically eject either of you from my home. He may spread rumours, but, really, I shouldn't think that he will. It would not be the act of a gentleman to speak ill of a lady and he is one of the most rigid, principled men you are ever likely to meet.'

That had, Cassy reflected, been just what she'd thought of him, before tonight. That he was noble and upright, and...*solid*. Like a rock, actually, when she'd seen him standing on the quayside, ramrod straight and clearly in command of all the soldiers scurrying about like so many ants. Even after he'd dealt with Guy, her belief in him hadn't wavered, because he'd seemed like the one man upon whom she could rely.

But now…well, he'd been so beastly earlier. He'd even made her question her initial impression of him. She'd thought, back then, that he'd been angry with Guy. Only now it turned out that he blamed *her* for everything.

But that was a topic to mull over another time.

'So…you don't think he will do or say anything to hinder Rosalind's chances,' Cassandra asked, 'until he has made sure I have confessed my supposed crimes to you?'

'No, I don't. What's more, he is so busy with his work for, oh, some general or other who organises supplies for the army, or something of the sort,' she said, waving her handkerchief about in a vague manner, as though working for the defence of the realm was neither here nor there, 'that he probably won't even remember to check up on you for some considerable time. And when that time comes, you may tell him whatever comes into your head that will serve the purpose.'

Oh, dear. Godmama appeared to have forgotten Cassandra's insistence that she was not going to sink to the depths of telling lies to explain her presence in London. She didn't even seem to think that telling lies was sinking to any sort of depths at all.

'But what,' Rosalind objected while Cassandra was still trying to come up with a polite and respectful way of expressing her reservations, 'if he thinks he can speak ill of *me*, since I ain't… I mean, I am not a lady?'

Godmama shook her head. 'He cannot say anything about you without making himself rather unpopular. Because, darling, everyone knows, or at least, suspects, that Cassandra never met you before she came to my home. Everyone knows, or thinks they know, that your father is paying me to find you a titled husband. But everyone is perfectly happy to go along with the story we have put about, that I am launching my goddaughter and graciously extending hospitality to her friend. That way, they can invite you to places where you can meet their sons without looking as though they are being mercenary about it. It is a fabrication that suits everyone concerned. And if Colonel Fairfax goes about trying to put a spoke in your wheel he is going to upset a lot of very influential families with younger sons to provide for.'

'Papa don't want a younger son for me,' Rosalind reminded her. 'He wants a title.'

Once again, the Duchess made play with her handkerchief. 'Yes, yes, but you know what I mean.'

'So, you don't think,' put in Cassandra before Rosalind could start really quarrelling with Godmama about the terms of their agreement, 'we have any reason to worry about what he may do?'

'There is never any point in worrying about what a man may do, darling. What matters is how you two deal with the threat. Trust me to know of which I speak,' she said darkly. 'Any sign of panic and people will say there is no smoke without fire. But laugh it all off as a piece of spite and people will…well, let us just see how it plays out, shall we? He has fired a shot across our bows, that is all. Given us a warning. Now, if that is all?' Godmama gave them one of her charming smiles, gathered her things together and got to her feet.

And, since there was nothing Cassy could do about Colonel Fairfax that night, anyway, she accepted her dismissal and went upstairs to bed.

She didn't sleep well, though. Her dreams were uncomfortably crowded with images from the darkest time of her life, all muddled up with the things she feared might happen in the future. First Stepfather would be shouting at her and thrusting her from his doorstep. Then Colonel Fairfax would be shouting at her and dragging her out of this house and along the streets of London, where people she'd met over the past few weeks were staring and jeering, and throwing rotten fruit.

She woke with what felt like a dark cloud hanging over her. A cloud that was all too familiar from years before, but which had been slowly dispersing ever since she'd gone to live with her unconventional aunts. The cloud comprised of the opinions of people who thought she was *no better than she ought to be*. Who had branded her a hussy and a slut for running away with an officer and coming back unmarried. Before reaching her aunts' house, nobody had blamed the officer concerned. And even when the aunts had come down on her side, she'd always felt it had been more from habit, since they hated all men on principle, rather than from having any faith in her. Betty didn't count, because she'd always claimed she had no right to judge anyone, considering the things she'd got up to when she'd been Cassandra's age.

And now it turned out not even Colonel Fairfax had believed in her when all these years she'd thought he had been the one person who had tried to protect her.

For a moment or two, when she first woke up, all she wanted to do was pull the covers up over her head and…and what? She couldn't hide from her own life. And to be honest, thanks to Godmama's effervescence and Rosalind's open manner, she'd been enjoying it immensely of late. Right up to the moment Colonel Fairfax had accosted her and robbed her of all her joy.

Well, to the devil with Colonel Fairfax, she shocked herself by thinking, as she thrust aside her bedcovers and got out of bed. She wasn't going to let him make her feel ashamed of herself. Because she hadn't jolly well done the half of what he'd said. Even the things she *had* done were only the result of being gullible and naive. Or, to put it another way, young and foolish, and so desperate to escape her stepfather's tyranny that even Guy's offer of marriage, and going off on campaign, had sounded perfectly acceptable.

But now she was older and had learned the folly of allowing some man to divert her from her plans. If only she'd waited, patiently, as her mother had counselled her to do, her stepfather would have had to allow her a Season in London, however grudgingly. Now she was here, she was not going to let anyone, not even Colonel Fairfax, ruin her pleasure in it. Not when she'd been dreaming about having one for such a long time. And what was more, she wasn't going to let him spoil Rosalind's chances of finding a husband. Why shouldn't Rosalind marry a man of rank? She was as lovely a person as many of the better-born girls she'd met in Town. She'd make any man an admirable wife. Nobody had the right to look down their long, thin, aristocratic noses at her just because her father had pulled himself up by his bootstraps rather than having his wealth handed to him on a plate.

Golly. She'd worked herself up to such a pitch that she needed to go to the window and fling up the sash to get some fresh air blowing over her heated face. She leaned on the windowsill and gazed out over her view of the mews at the back of the house, where the grooms were just starting to amble about, scratching various parts of their anatomy. The sun was already shining from a cloudless sky. It was going to be a lovely day. And she would enjoy it.

She *would*.

Because she wasn't in disgrace and shunned by society any longer. Nor was she alone and unprotected. Godmama didn't care what she might or might not have done. And it was thanks to her determination that she was here. And the generosity of Rosalind's papa, she would not forget that.

She bit down on her lower lip as she watched the grooms working the pump in the yard. She was going to stop finding fault with Godmama's motives and her flexible attitude to the issues of right and wrong and remember what she owed to her generous heart and that flexible attitude towards those suspected of great sins. It wasn't as if Godmama had tried to hide anything from her, was it, not after she'd made her own confession? And hadn't both her aunts agreed that, in certain circumstance, a *tiny* bit of subterfuge was justified? And who would know better than they?

Cassandra went to her washstand and lifted the ewer, which was empty. Because not quite all of Godmama's staff had been as loyal as she'd claimed. One or two of her more junior employees had defected during the period between the Duke making his threats and Godmama's coming up with the solution. In the form of Rosalind Mollington, whose father was willing to meet all the expenses of a London Season providing the Duchess could bring her out just as if she was a real lady and find her a titled husband while she was at it.

However, those who'd stayed with God-mama all pitched in to fill in the gaps. And, since Cassandra was awake before any of the staff had decided to take on the task, she had no objection to going down to the kitchen and fetching her own hot water for washing.

It was funny, she reflected as she covered her nightgown with a modest wrap before venturing from her room, how Godmama had manged to make her rather rash and impetuous stand against her stepson sound like taking up a noble cause. Even her aunts had applauded her determination to defy the man who was threatening the livelihoods of so many working people. And that was the thing about Godmama. Even though she would do just about anything to get her own way, no matter how unethical, she could always make it sound as if it would be no worse than having a bit of a lark. And to be fair, coming to London and meeting Rosalind, and going to see the sights, and attending a few routs, and balls, even if they weren't in the homes of people from the very best circles, had all been tremendous fun.

Until Colonel Fairfax had come storming over, accusing her of all sorts of bad things. Of being a *siren*, for heaven's sake!

She paused to check her rather dishevelled reflection in the mirror before leaving the room, to make sure nothing about her appearance would offend the servants. She was no siren! She had nice hair, she supposed. Or at least, it would look passable once she'd run a brush over it. The hairdresser Godmama had hired had raved about it, actually, saying what a pleasure it was to style, since it had a bit of a curl to it. And Godmama had declared that her lashes were long enough and dark enough that she would have no need to employ cosmetics to make her eyes stand out. But nobody had said anything about her mouth. Well, they couldn't, could they? Her lips were too full and the top one stuck out a bit, making it look as though she might have buck teeth.

She stuck her tongue out at her reflection and opened her bedroom door. She was no siren! She was no saint, either, or she would not have got herself tangled up in Godmama's schemes. She was just a girl. A girl who'd been punished enough for stepping out of line. A girl who, she decided, clutching her ewer to her chest like a shield, was never, ever, going to let some…*man*…some buffle-headed *delusional* man…spoil things for her again.

Chapter Five

Nathaniel slept little better than Cassandra for the first part of the night. But instead of pulling the blankets close round himself, he kicked most of them to the floor as he tossed and turned.

The subsequent chill permeated right through to his dreams, taking him back to the worst of his memories, memories he refused to visit when he was awake.

He was back in the mountains of northern Spain. But, unlike the reality, there was a wall of frozen corpses right in front of him. To get to safety, he was going to have to clamber over them all, the men, the women, the children and Lieutenant Gilbey. Who, though just as dead as the rest of them, was watching his struggles with reproachful eyes. And then, in the manner of dreams, the dead soldier spoke.

'You might have let me have those few months with her,' Gilbey complained. 'But you didn't want to let anyone else have her, did you, if you couldn't? That was why you sent her away...'

'No!' It wasn't true. Was it?

No. Anyway, if he'd let her marry Gilbey, she might have ended up here, in this pile of frozen, half-naked, ragged bodies.

'No, she wouldn't,' said Gilbey, even though Nathaniel had not voiced his excuse out loud. 'I would have taken care of her. *You* would have taken care of her...'

'I couldn't,' Nate protested. 'I couldn't even take care of my men, or the horses, or these children... I couldn't take care of anyone...'

And then he heard the boom of a cannon and, in spite of his revulsion, he was scrambling up the mound of dead, desperate to save his own skin, only he couldn't get a purchase and the mound was tumbling all around him, then his foot slid and he was falling, falling, down the mountainside to the very edge of an abyss...

His foot met with empty air and jerked him awake. It took a moment for him to understand that his leg really had jerked and it was that movement that had woken him.

His mouth was dry, the way it so often was

after one of these hellish dreams. He sat up and reached for the water jug he kept beside the bed every night, just in case it turned out like this. His hands shook so much, as he reached for it, that he thought he'd better sit up and place his feet on solid ground.

The floor was cool beneath his bare feet. But at least the wooden floorboards felt better than the horrid, frozen mass he'd been treading in a few moments before. Not that any of it was real, not exactly. He took hold of the jug with both hands, reminding himself, as he always did, that he hadn't clambered over anyone in order to save himself. That on the contrary, his unit had retreated in good order, fighting a rearguard action against pursuing French troops practically the whole way across the mountains. That it had been the collapse of discipline in other units that had resulted in so many of the needless casualties from cold and starvation.

He splashed some water into a glass as well as over the dresser top before setting the jug back down with a thump. Gilbey had certainly never, at any time, accused him of wanting Miss Furnival for himself. Because he hadn't. Not back then. She'd been too young for a man like him, or so he'd thought. Too innocent. The way she'd wandered out into the stable yard, he'd thought at the time, had been the act of a green girl. He'd wanted to protect her. From himself as much as any other of the men who'd been watching her with hungry eyes that night.

It was only after she'd shown up on Gilbey's arm that he'd wondered if she'd deliberately lured him out there. What did he know of women, really? he reflected, lifting the water glass to his lips. He lived in a man's world, for the most part. The only thing he knew about women he'd learned from his sister, Isabella…

He drained the glass, wondering if there was any truth in Gilbey's accusation. Had he put a stop to the marriage because he'd wanted her himself? Was he that kind of man?

He didn't know. Not any more. He'd always prided himself on being fair and just, and honourable. But there was nothing honourable about waging war on a woman. No matter what she'd done.

He rolled the empty glass between his hands, forcing his mind back to that day on the quayside. He'd been angry, certainly. Had given Gilbey a stern dressing down. But then, wouldn't he have done the same if any officer had turned up with any other girl that young?

Eloping was wrong. It was not acceptable behaviour for an officer.

But in this particular case, hadn't he also wanted to show the girl the difference between the brash impulsive behaviour of a lad and that of a mature man? Hadn't he wanted her to think he was dependable, yet dashing? Two completely contrary characteristics!

He shook his head at the folly of a man trying to impress a woman.

And began to get the glimmer of an idea as to why, in his dream, Gilbey had accused him of wanting her for himself.

It was because he'd seen her earlier that night and had been so attracted to her, just as she was now, and he'd fallen asleep comparing her to the way she'd seemed back then and wishing, wishing...

He slammed the empty glass back down on the dresser. Nothing altered the fact that Gilbey had died feeling cheated. Had died with a belly full of regrets. And that he, Nathaniel, had played a part in it.

He leaned over, his shoulders aching with the weight of guilt pressing down on them, and buried his face in his hands.

In order to come out of her next encounter with the Colonel with her head held high, Cassandra decided, as she made her way back to her room with her jug of steaming hot water, she was going to have to shore up her confidence. She wanted to be able to snap her fingers under his nose and tell him he was welcome to do his worst. To inform him that she had friends now, loyal friends, who would stand by her and defend her right to be in London making the most of everything on offer. And one of the easiest ways a woman could make herself feel good, she knew, from her years with her aunts, was to dress well.

So far she hadn't been choosing her clothes with that in mind. She'd been considering the expense and how well each item would fit into her life when she returned to Market Gooding and took up her occupation as a seamstress. She pursed her lips as she flung open the door of her wardrobe and surveyed the meagre selection she had allowed Godmama and Rosalind to purchase for her so far. Her walking dress was dowdy, her carriage dress looked like something a governess would wear on the stage to her latest posting and as for her ballgowns… She sighed. Insipid, that was the best she could say for them. She didn't even bother looking at her bonnets. Practical to the point of being ugly, every one of them.

If the Colonel confronted her in the park, or

walking along the streets, he wouldn't credit her for trying to be economical with other people's money. He'd take one look at her and think she was doing penance. Which, she realised, she had been doing. Even though Godmama had kept urging her to try to look the part of a wealthy young debutante and Rosalind had kept assuring her that her papa wouldn't care about the expense, she hadn't felt as if she deserved such treats as pretty clothes.

Well, no more! She was not going to wallow in guilt any longer, not when she hadn't done anything wrong. So there, Colonel Fairfax! Far from making her run away from London, he'd only succeeded in making her determined to cast off the clouds of her past and make the most of the life she now had.

She pulled out the least dowdy of her walking dresses and, at breakfast, surprised Rosalind by being the one to suggest they go out shopping, rather than making excuses for not doing so when anyone else suggested it. She had fabric to buy and modistes to consult. She was going to revel in the luxury of having someone else make up gowns for her, when back home she was the one making up gowns for everyone else. She needed to try on and purchase several utterly frivolous bonnets, too, as well as choose gloves and ribbons and whatnot to set everything off.

'Hurrah!' Rosalind clapped her hands when Cassandra told her about her change of heart. 'We're going to have such fun now you won't be hanging round disapproving of my spend-thrift ways,' she said.

'I am sorry. Have I been doing that? It was not my intention. I just—'

'Cassandra is used to having to practise the strictest economy,' put in Godmama. 'It is a hard habit to break, when one has got into it. But I do agree with Rosalind. You will have much more fun now that you have put aside your silly scruples.'

Which statement had the effect of making Cassandra experience a fleeting pang of guilt. But only a fleeting one. Because there were more important things than being economical with Mr Mollington's vast wealth. For one thing, if the Colonel did somehow manage to bring her Season to a premature close, which she still feared he might be able to do in some mysterious manner, in spite of Godmama's reassurances, then she would have a marvellous collection of outfits to take home to Market Gooding. Outfits that would be the envy of all their usual customers, which would bring new orders flooding in.

With that in mind, Cassandra began ordering three times as much cloth as she actually needed, so that she could give the remainder to her aunts to fill those potential orders.

Pretty soon boxes and parcels began arriving from the most expensive shops in London, until her wardrobe scarcely had the room to contain all her lovely new clothes. Every time she put on one of her pretty new outfits, she kept her eyes peeled for the Colonel, just in case he should leap out at her from behind the bushes in the park, or the tea urn at a supper party, to confront her.

But the days dragged by, with no sign of him. She was starting to feel a bit disappointed that he seemed to be, as Godmama predicted, too busy to bother chasing her down. Although she was jolly glad she'd started to take more care over her appearance when, almost a week after she'd made her vow to snap her fingers at the Colonel and all those who thought they had the right to look down their noses at her, two ladies who claimed to have been friends of her mother paid a morning call on Godmama.

'Such a shame, all that unpleasantness,'

said Lady Bradbury, eyeing Cassandra with a mournful shake of her head.

'Dreadful, dreadful,' said Mrs Cornworthy, dabbing at the corner of one dry eye with a little scrap of lace.

Cassandra looked to Godmama for her cue, which Godmama promptly supplied.

'Well, of course, that is why I was so determined to do something for Julia's daughter. That man she married…' she said, then pursed her lips and took a sip of tea as though she disliked even mentioning him so much that she had to wash the taste out of her mouth.

'And not a word of truth in it, I don't suppose,' said Lady Bradbury, lifting her own cup to her lips.

'Not one word,' said Godmama firmly. 'As if I would sponsor a girl who had…' She looked at Cassandra. 'Perhaps, dear, you would be so good as to run up to my room and fetch my shawl.' She eyed Rosalind. 'You can help her carry it down, dear.'

Both girls got up and curtsied, then left, trying hard not to giggle at the implication it would take two of them to carry one of the Duchess's delicately woven shawls. But they both knew it was just a ruse to get rid of them so that Godmama could speak privately to her mother's former cronies. And, knowing her, tearing her stepfather's reputation, or what was left of it, to shreds.

Cassandra supposed she ought to be concerned about what slanderous things Godmama might tell the ladies about her stepfather. She also wondered why these ladies had, after all this time, suddenly decided to unbend. But both concerns went out of her head when, as they returned after a suitable interval, Godmama leapt to her feet, holding out gilt-edged invitations to the kind of select soirées where so far they'd signally failed to be able to take Rosalind.

'I knew I could do it,' she declared in triumph. 'After all, if I managed to fire off both my daughters with such success, with all the disadvantages we...' She pulled herself up. 'I was *sure* people would accept you, darling,' she said to Cassandra. 'After all, you are the granddaughter of an earl. And if only your mother had made a push to cover up that silly episode, which was after all little more than a bit of a girlish scrape, rather than giving in to her horrid husband's determination to banish you, you would have received such invitations years and years ago.'

Cassy's heart swelled. Dear Godmama. She'd promised she would restore her reputation, but somehow she'd never truly believed it would happen.

'And you will be so proud of me,' Godmama added with a glowing smile. 'Bearing in mind how you feel about such things, I did not utter one single untruth! I may,' she added, with a slight lessening of her smile, 'have stressed certain facts, while leaving out others, but...'

Cassy didn't wait to hear any more. Swept forward on a tide of affection, she simply dashed across the room and flung her arms round Godmama, the one person who had gone out of their way to do something about the mess she'd made of her life.

There was nothing, she decided there and then, that she wouldn't do for her in return, no matter how this Season turned out.

That evening, Godmama's son, the Marquess of Devizes, had invited them to join him at the theatre, where he'd taken a box. Before setting out, Rosalind and Cassy went along to Godmama's boudoir so she could inspect their outfits, as she routinely did. But before she could say anything, Rosalind, who was still learning about the way aristocrats inherited their titles, had asked, rather rudely, how come Godmama had given birth to a marquess, but not a duke. "It is a courtesy title," Godmama explained. "Younger sons, as I have already explained, don't normally have any title at all. But it was just typical of my late husband," she said bitterly, "to grant that, and all the land that goes with it to Nick one day, and then evict us from our house practically the next. But enough of that…let me look at you. Ah, you look fine as fivepence,' she said to Cassy for the first time since bringing her to London. And for once, Cassy rather thought she did. The bodice of her muslin gown was covered all over in fine embroidery, with a similar border around the hem. She'd tied a peach-coloured sash beneath, so that the ribbon points fell to her knees. Best of all, though, was the satin amber pelisse with the chocolate chenille border she had draped over her shoulders. It was trimmed all the way round with swansdown and was the most decadent confection Cassy had ever owned. To top it off she had bought a white satin hat, turned up at the front in the Spanish style, which boasted an ostrich feather dyed amber to match the pelisse exactly.

'And you, too, Rosalind, well done.' That second statement met with less enthusiasm from its recipient, since, after only a few days under her care, Godmama had hired an extremely strict dresser who'd soon put a stop to Rosalind's penchant for an abundance of ruffles and ribbons and ropes of jewels.

However, both girls now looked as pretty and as elegant as it was possible for each of them to look, considering they had access to Mr Mollington's apparently bottomless purse.

'Now, Rosalind,' Godmama said firmly as she picked up her own elbow-length evening gloves. 'And you, too, I dare say, Cassy, if you haven't attended the theatre before. Have you? Anyway, as I was saying,' she warbled on, without waiting for a reply, 'you should know that nobody goes to the theatre to watch what is happening on the stage. Except some of the gentlemen when the dancing girls come on. So you must not be surprised if you find a lot of gentlemen turning their quizzing glasses in your direction. And then, of course, they will come to our box during the interval, for an introduction. You see,' she said, placing one hand on Rosalind's cheek, 'very many men who cannot get invitations to the better sort of places can simply purchase a ticket to the theatre, then get a friend to effect an introduction. You *must* be guided by me in your reception of them. No matter how handsome the gentlemen are, or how much address they may have.'

Rosalind nodded. 'No flirting with anyone below the rank of Baron,' she said solemnly.

'Good girl,' said Godmama, turning the caress into a gentle pat. 'Not that there is any harm in flirting, of itself. Only I did promise your papa to find you a really good match and if you get a reputation for being *fast*...'

She turned to Cassy. 'The same applies to you, of course. People are starting to believe our version of events, at last, so naturally you won't want to give anyone any excuse for saying that there was no smoke without fire.'

'No. I mean, yes. I mean, of course I won't do anything to undo all your hard work, Godmama,' Cassy vowed. Particularly not after the Colonel had reminded her how horrid it could be when he'd flung it all in her face.

'Good girl. Now, if we are all ready, let us join Captain Bucknell, who is to escort us to the theatre tonight.'

'Why,' Rosalind murmured into Cassy's ear as they trailed along the landing in Godmama's perfumed wake, 'isn't her son escorting us, since he's the one who issued the invitation to join him?'

'Because,' trilled Godmama over her shoulder, making Cassy suspect she must have exceptionally good hearing, 'he is far too indolent to put himself out on my account, darlings. Inviting us to share his box for one night is an immense concession on his part, let me tell you. So do make sure you thank him properly. Oh…' She paused at the head of the stairs and frowned at Rosalind. 'I had better warn you not to waste your time flirting with him. And don't poker up like that,' she added sternly, when Rosalind's lips pulled into a mulish line. 'I am telling you this for your own good. So many girls claim to fall in love with him at first sight that he finds that kind of behaviour excessively tiresome. Besides which, he is so wealthy that he has no need to look for a rich wife, even if he were the kind of man to want to settle down, which he gives no indication of doing,' she concluded, before sweeping down the stairs to the hall where Captain Bucknell was standing, gazing up at them with that habitual look of dog-like devotion which made Cassandra feel a trifle queasy.

Cassy saw exactly why Godmama had warned them to beware of her son, the moment the golden-haired Marquess glided forward to welcome them to his box, took his mother's hand and raised it to his mouth for a kiss. He was extremely good looking. Extremely well dressed and positively oozed charm. When he turned to her, lowering his eyelids as he examined her slowly from head to toe, she felt the strangest urge to giggle and blush like a schoolgirl. She managed to stop at the blush, although Rosalind was not so strong-willed. But then Rosalind had already been showing signs of becoming rather overexcited from the moment she stepped out of the carriage and joined the crowds making their way into the theatre. She'd gaped at the plush decor, her head swivelling from the glittering chandeliers, to the marble columns, to the velvet curtains, until Captain Bucknell had brought her back down to earth by chuckling at her.

Captain Bucknell wasn't chuckling now. On the contrary, he was scowling at Marquess, who'd somehow managed to take up Godmama's attention to the point that she seemed to have forgotten all about everyone else. Cassy wasn't sure what the correct form was for a man who was entertaining his mother's lover, but while freezing him out entirely was perfectly understandable, she didn't think it was fair for him to exclude her and Rosalind, as well.

Although, on reflection, she recalled Godmama warning them both that Marquess was not at all interested in debutantes. Especially not ones who blushed and giggled. So she decided to put his rudeness out of her mind, and simply enjoy the experience of her very first visit to a London theatre.

'It's just as well Godmama warned us about the behaviour of people at the theatre,' Cassy said to Rosalind, in an effort to distract her and stop her gazing at the back of Marquess's neck with wounded eyes. 'Otherwise I would have wondered why so many people are staring at us in that rude fashion.' She indicated the space beyond their balcony, at the wall of similar boxes opposite, which were filled with people training their glasses in their direction.

'Now I know what the sideshows at the fair must feel like,' said Rosalind, lifting her chin as a florid-faced matron actually leaned right round a pillar to get a better view.

'Never seen such a pretty pair of faces, I don't suppose,' put in Captain Bucknell gallantly, tearing his eyes from the sight of Godmama and Marquess with their golden heads together, chatting away nineteen to the dozen. 'Definitely not when she looks in her mirror, anyway,' he added wickedly, causing Rosalind to giggle.

It was Captain Bucknell who helped them place their chairs so that they could get a good view of the stage, since Marquess continued to ignore everyone except his mother.

In a way, Cassy was glad he'd been so lacking in manners because it meant both she and Rosalind were in the mood to give someone a frigid set-down. By the time the interval came, bringing with it the predicted influx of visitors, Cassy at least had a whole list of suitable phrases to hand and the disdainful look Rosalind turned upon the first of them to approach was worthy of a duchess. But then the lanky, rather dishevelled young man who'd burst in before the actors had even quit the stage thoroughly deserved it.

'This the heiress you was telling us about, Devizes? Don't suppose,' he said, turning to Cassy, 'you'd settle for a mere Mr, would you? My pockets may be to let, but I promise you I wouldn't give you half the trouble some fellows would. Never meet a more amiable chap. Ask anyone! Besides which, I'd be so grateful to you I'd worship at your feet like a—'

'Don't be such an ass, Smithers,' Marquess drawled. 'That is not the heiress. That is her friend. *This* is the heiress,' he said, waving a languid hand at a by-now fuming Rosalind.

'Ginger,' observed the friend, with the owlish expression of the very intoxicated. 'Might have guessed,' he added, his face falling.

It was at this point, while Rosalind was quivering with affront and Cassy was trying hard to stifle a completely inappropriate fit of the giggles, that the hairs on the back of her neck began to prickle. As though some sixth sense was picking up a threat. And, since she'd been looking over her shoulder every few minutes since the last time she'd seen the Colonel, she was not a bit surprised to see him standing in the doorway to the corridor, scowling at her.

But at least this time she was prepared to face his anger. In fact, she felt as if she'd been awaiting this moment ever since he'd marched away from her the last time. Her breath hitched in her throat. Her pulse speeded up. And everyone else vanished from her consciousness, as completely as the actors who'd disappeared when the curtain had come down.

Chapter Six

Nathaniel knew the exact moment she became
aware of his presence. She stopped flirting
with her latest conquest, a boy whose interest
she'd clearly stolen from her shorter, plainer
friend, and lifted her chin, then, after only the
briefest hesitation, sent a mutinous smile wing-
ing his way.

It made him want to stride forward and tell
her, in no uncertain terms, that he was no
green boy to fall for her charms. Even if she
did look more enticing than last time they'd
met.

It made him want to plunge his fingers into
her hair as he ravaged the smile from her lips.

It made him want to…

He clenched his fists at his sides. He was in a
public place, for God's sake. He couldn't kiss the
defiance out of her. Or toss the drunken young

fool who was currently slavering over her into the pit below.

He was a man of discipline, which he had to exert over himself. And so, after running his fingers over the buttons of his waistcoat to make sure each one was done up securely, he approached her at a stroll and made the bow which etiquette demanded. Only then did he growl, 'Still here, I see. In spite of my warnings.'

Her smile became positively triumphant. 'As you see,' she said, waving the fan she held in one hand round the opulent box procured for her by none other than the son of her poor deluded benefactress.

'Have you no shame?'

She lifted her chin. '*I* have nothing to be ashamed of.'

Her implication caught him on the raw. No man ought to speak to a lady the way he'd just spoken to her.

Yet if he admitted that much, or softened his stance over this, what next would she have him confess? That he'd rather be kissing her than fighting her? That would be only one step from…from lying down and rolling over at her feet, belly up. Which would mean he'd be letting Issy down. Letting Gilbey down.

So he drew himself up to his full height and stepped closer, obliging her to crane her neck to look up into his face. He adopted his coldest, hardest expression, the one which had invariably made his subalterns quake in their boots. To demonstrate that *he* was in command of the situation. That *he* would be the victor in this, or any other encounter they might have. The manoeuvre worked, up to a point. Because her eyes widened. And she swallowed. But unfortunately that reaction drew his gaze to the delicate column of her neck, where a pulse was beating rapidly, and the creamy mounds of flesh which rose beneath, And fell, and rose again as she drew in several rapid, shallow breaths.

'You leave me no choice,' he managed to say, tearing his gaze from her magnificent bosom, of which there was surely more on display tonight than there had been last time, 'but to tell your benefactress what you are.'

'She knows it all. So there,' she said and snapped her fingers at him. Right under his nose, making him jerk away, his heart stuttering in his chest. He went no further than one step, although his legs were screaming at him to run. Far, far from here. Away from the noise, and the seething crowds, and the...hell!

He ground his teeth. He was not under attack. There was no danger in this theatre, not of the military kind. Yet he'd reacted almost as badly as if someone had just let off a pistol in his face.

He drew in a deep breath, which smelled of a woman's perfume, not black powder, and ran his fingers over the buttons on his waistcoat, one by one. With each one he touched, the roar in the background steadily resolved into the voices of men determined to enjoy themselves, not the shouts of the battlefield.

'Colonel Fairfax?' His vision fixed upon a pair of dark brows pleated in confusion, above concerned hazel eyes...

He forced himself to remember a different pair of eyes, the eyes of his sister, filled with tears, and then the glazed, open eyes of Gilbey, which enabled him to dismiss the look of concern Miss Furnival was manufacturing. It helped his mind to recall what she'd said just before she snapped her fingers at him, triggering some weird kind of waking nightmare.

'You claim,' he said, 'to have told the Duchess everything? And she has not sent you packing?'

'She saw no need.'

'Then you cannot have told her everything.'

'I can assure you I did…'

At that moment, the lady in question materialised at Miss Furnival's side, holding out her hand in that regal manner which always obliged a man to take it and bow over it.

'Colonel Fairfax,' she trilled. 'How lovely to see you here. It is so good of you to take time away from your busy life to renew your acquaintance with my goddaughter. I *do* hope,' she said with what looked suspiciously like a flicker of amusement, 'we shall be seeing more of you. You are most welcome to call, whenever you can spare the time.' She stepped away and headed for the crowd of young men who were starting to cluster round Miss Furnival's friend.

'Call?' Was the woman touched in the upper works? He had better things to do with his time, as she'd just acknowledged, than to hang round Grosvenor Square in the hopes of talking some sense into this stubborn, heartless creature…

Although he wasn't getting anywhere with her tonight, was he? They couldn't really remove their gloves and get down to the no-holds-barred kind of fight they would clearly need to have, not with so many people present. What he had to say touched on private matters that the Gilbey family would not want bandied about. And, while most of the other occupants of the box were taken up with gossiping, at least one, Marquess of Devizes himself, was leaning against a pillar, his arms folded across his chest, watching the antics of everyone else in his box with an amused expression.

'Actually, on second thoughts,' said Nathaniel, 'that might be a good idea. We do need to talk. Privately.'

'You can say whatever you wish to say right now,' said Miss Furnival mutinously. 'I have no wish to subject Godmama to a visit from a man with your appalling manners.'

Which raised a good point. What would he be able to say to Miss Furnival in the confines of a drawing room? Very little. It would be even more difficult to speak his mind than it was here, since they would not have the background roar of the crowd in the pit to mask their conversation from inquisitive ears.

'A fair point,' he conceded, making her blink in surprise. 'I shall call upon you tomorrow afternoon to take you driving, instead. You will inform the Duchess of my intent.'

She tilted her head to one side. 'Do you expect me to snap to attention and salute?'

'I expect you,' he replied calmly, refusing to let her rile him any further, 'to give me an account of yourself. And I, at least, have the sense to wish to do it in private so that we may shield the Duchess from as much unpleasantness as possible.'

'That,' she said crossly, 'was below the belt.'

'If you are determined to fight me, then you may as well learn that I do what I must, in order to win.'

She pouted. Then sighed. 'Very well. I will come out for a drive with you tomorrow so that we can keep everyone else out of the arena.'

Now it was his turn to blink. He would have expected her to carry on defying him, so she could lead him a merry dance. She could have done so easily. She could have hidden from him within crowds, or behind the screen of etiquette which shielded females of good birth, almost indefinitely.

So why hadn't she?

If he didn't know better he might think she was, indeed, willing to shield the Duchess from unpleasantness. But he did know better. So she must have some other motive for appearing to fall in with his wishes.

She was up to something. That must be it. Still, forewarned was forearmed.

'Until tomorrow then,' he said and turned on

his heel and marched out while he could still claim to hold at least the appearance of victory.

By the time Nathaniel drove his curricle into Grosvenor Square the next day, he was no longer convinced he'd been victorious at all. There was a mountain of paperwork on his desk awaiting his attention. The only good reason for abandoning it would be if he needed to visit a manufacturer of blankets, or tent canvas, or one of the thousands of other varieties of supplies necessary for keeping an army on the march. He'd learned that one man, on the ground, could not make as much difference to the outcome of a campaign as he would wish. But here in London he could at least ensure that Wellington's army in Portugal had enough boots and blankets and bread to keep them going until they drove Bonaparte's armies from the Peninsula.

Yet here he was, wasting an afternoon dancing attendance on a slip of a girl who would not simply fade into the background. Worst of all, a part of him was enjoying tooling his own cattle through the streets rather than relying on his grooms to exercise them, was noticing various trees putting forth a brave display of blossom with pleasure. Was savouring the warm, if damp, air filling nostrils that had been breathing in nothing but dusty parchment for months.

And, he admitted with self-reproach, was looking forward to seeing her again.

That was the part of him that had once believed that spring was a season for new beginnings, he reflected bitterly. And had assumed that people were generally decent and dependable, or at least tried to be. Had he really been that naive? he wondered as he drew his curricle up outside the Theakstone town house.

He eyed the facade with determination. It wasn't just his own inclination he was serving by shirking his work and coming here, he reminded himself. He'd given Issy his word that he'd do what he could to put Miss Furnival in her place. And his word, once given, was his bond. Moreover, he'd made that pledge because he'd sworn, after the retreat to Corunna, that unlike some of the officers, he'd never break faith with the men who'd fallen. At the time, he'd meant to devote his energies and organisational skills to ensuring that such needless waste of so many lives never took place again. But Issy had reminded him that Lieutenant Gilbey was one of those men. That he owed it to his grieving family to *do something* about Miss Furnival. Because they were all, apparently, devastated by the way she was *'flaunting herself when by rights she should be hanging her head in shame somewhere, wearing sack-cloth and ashes'*.

And he did owe Gilbey a great deal, if that latest nightmare had any foundation in truth. Whichever way he looked at it, he'd robbed the lad of a chance to find what comfort he could in the arms of his bride during the last weeks of his life.

Nathaniel tossed the reins to a boy who was loitering on the pavement looking for just such a chance to earn a few coppers, got down from the driving seat and trudged up the front steps. The door opened before he had the chance to so much as raise his hand, let alone apply it to the knocker.

'Her Grace is expecting you, Colonel,' said the unctuous butler.

'I am not here to see Her Grace,' he said impatiently, causing the butler to look affronted. 'I am here to take Miss Furnival out for a drive.'

The butler cleared his throat. 'Her Grace gave me to understand that she invited you to call today. Her Grace said that—'

He cut the butler off before he could really get going. He knew what kind of things Her Grace would likely have said. The same kind of thing that so many of these society women were always saying. Timewasters, who wanted him to sit about drinking tea and chatting about frivolous things as they thrust their marriageable daughters under his nose.

'I do not wish to keep my horses standing. If Miss Furnival is not ready to come out with me yet, I shall drive them round the square while I am waiting.'

'There will be no need for that,' came a melodious voice from somewhere above. He looked up to see Miss Furnival descending the staircase, pulling on a pair of tan kid gloves as she came. She was wearing the kind of outfit that probably cost a fortune, if the way it clung to her curves while still flowing about her lower limbs as she moved was anything to go by. All pale greens and yellows, she looked like the embodiment of this spring afternoon. Like sunshine and resurgent life. Like all the things he no longer deserved.

He supposed that, actually, she'd simply chosen colours that set off her dark beauty. Colours that made her skin look full of health, her eyes sparkle and her mouth look even more inviting than usual. What would it feel like, he wondered yet again, to take that full upper lip between his teeth and nip at it?

He checked his lower jaw to make sure it wasn't sagging, then congratulated himself on discovering that the sight of Miss Furnival, so gloriously arrayed in her determination to conquer any hapless male she got within her sights, hadn't slain *him* on the spot.

'As you can see, Colonel, I am ready,' she said, reaching the bottom stair where she paused, looking up at him with what looked like the light of battle in her eye.

'So am I,' he growled, reminding himself that it was his duty to resist her pull on him. That he was supposed to be persuading her to leave Town. That he must not retreat from that position simply because he found her so attractive, or make allowances for her because she was female and she roused his chivalrous instincts. He only had to remind himself what had happened last time he'd given her the benefit of the doubt when he'd escorted her back into the assembly, rather than yielding to the temptation to kiss her. Look what that had achieved. Nothing! For the next time he'd seen her she'd been in the process of eloping with Lieutenant Gilbey. Making him wish he'd kissed her when he'd had the chance instead of persuading himself she was an innocent, naive girl in need of protection from man's baser instincts.

The butler opened the front door and stood aside to let them pass.

Miss Furnival checked when she saw the curricle parked at the foot of the front steps.

'Don't bother complaining about the lack of a groom,' he said, before she could utter a word. 'Or the fact that going out driving in a two-seated vehicle with a man to whom you are not related is likely to cause talk.'

'I wasn't going to,' she said.

'Just as well,' he replied, flicking a coin at the urchin who'd been holding his horses' reins. 'Or I would have been forced to remind you that causing scandal is nothing new to you.'

She smiled at him as he handed her up on to the bench seat. 'Such a gentleman as you are,' she said sweetly, 'I am sure it would have pained you excessively to have been obliged to say anything so cutting.'

'Hmmph,' he observed as he unwound the reins and flicked them over the horses' backs to set them in motion. At one time he would never have spoken to a lady the way he had spoken to her, it was true. But things had changed. He had changed. Sometimes, a man had no option but to harden himself and do what was necessary.

'So,' he said, as she set her hand to the rail to

steady herself as they set off. 'You would have me believe that the Duchess knows all about your association with Lieutenant Gilbey and how it ended, yet she is still willing to sponsor you into society?'

'I don't really care what you believe,' she said, with a defiant tilt to her chin. 'But it happens to be the truth, yes.'

Cassy was glad she'd taken hold of the rail. She needed something to cling to. She thought she'd been prepared to face the Colonel today, but the very first sight of him standing there in the hall, glaring up at her, had very nearly made her turn round and run straight back upstairs. How ever did she think she could stand up to a man like this? A man who'd spent so many years fighting real foes? With real weapons?

Yet, if she didn't, if she turned tail and hid, or let him drive her out of London, then that would be the end of Rosalind's hopes and dreams. And that, in turn, would make it very difficult for the Duchess to continue the stance she'd taken against her stepson, because Rosalind's father would stop footing the bills. There was no way she was going to let either of those ladies down, not after the way they'd taken her into their confidence and trusted her, and believed in her.

So she reminded herself that there was nothing he could really do to her in a carriage driving through the streets of London. Apart from utter threats. Empty threats, as Godmama had reminded her last night, when she'd asked her advice about how to handle the Colonel during this drive.

Nevertheless, it did help to have something physical to hold on to. It reminded her that she was safe, really. As long as she didn't tell him too much about what was going on inside Godmama's house.

'Now, darling,' Godmama had reassured her, 'I am not going to suggest you make up any stories to fob him off, since I know how much you dislike employing such stratagems. But, Cassy, men can be…' she'd given an eloquent shudder '…unpredictable. We have no idea how he might use any information you give him. We do not know him well enough to trust him, do we? So, just be…cautious. Yes?'

Of course she'd said yes. Because she had to reassure Godmama and Rosalind that she would never betray their trust.

But, oh, how she wished she could simply make a clean breast of things, about her own past at least, so that he would no longer look at her as though she was some kind of…menace to society.

But if she trusted him that far, how much more might he be able to worm out of her? She could not share secrets that were not hers to tell, just because she wanted him to smile at her for once, instead of scowling all the time.

Which meant that her lips had to remain sealed.

About everything.

Chapter Seven

Colonel Fairfax fired his opening salvo as he drove the curricle out of the square.

'The Duchess of Theakstone,' he said, 'is known for not being very wise. Her friends don't want to see her dragged down by the likes of you and that friend of yours, who, I have discovered, is the daughter of a mill owner.'

'And where were her friends when—?' She pulled herself up short. Godmama had made it clear that she didn't want her telling him what had really gone on between herself and her stepson. She mustn't let him goad her into being indiscreet. 'That is,' she continued, 'I am sure the Duchess is well able to take care of herself.'

'Hah! She is about as able to withstand the wiles of a woman like you as a hen faced with a fox. She is entirely too trusting, besides having the brains of a flea.'

Cassy drew in a deep breath. She wasn't sure whether she was more insulted at being compared to a fox, or at his assumption that her godmother had no intelligence. Why, if he only knew the complex stratagems Godmama had formed to keep her stepson from evicting her from Theakstone House, the subterfuge she'd adopted to explain the presence of herself and Rosalind without so much as giving a hint that it was all done to thwart the Duke, he'd be more likely to compare her to a general planning a siege. For a siege was what was going on right under her stepson's nose in Grosvenor Square. No matter what her stepson threw at her, Godmama always came up with a way to defy him.

But of course she couldn't tell the Colonel any of it. She would rather die than betray her godmama. Or, to a lesser extent, Rosalind.

'I suppose that is why you latched on to her,' he observed bitterly as he manoeuvred the curricle round a dray that was taking up far too much of the road. 'Though how you came to get an introduction to her...'

'I didn't need an introduction,' she seethed. 'She is my godmother.'

Bother. She hadn't meant to tell him anything. Still, there could be no harm in telling him that, could there? He could easily find that out by asking anyone.

'Your godmother?' He frowned. 'I was not aware of that.' And he didn't look at all pleased about it. 'Although I do seem to recall her referring to her goddaughter last night...meaning you?' His frown deepened. 'How the deuce did that come about?'

'She and my mother became friends during the years when she lived apart from her husband, the Third Duke. Or, at least, renewed and strengthened the friendship they'd formed as girls having their Season, so I believe.' Godmama had been rather vague about the details.

'Your mother was on terms with a duchess?' His frown grew deeper. 'What sort of woman was she? I assumed...'

'What, that she was the daughter of an apothecary or something of the sort?'

From the way his jaw clenched, it looked as though she'd hit the nail on the head.

'Well, I'm sorry to disappoint you, but Mother was the third daughter of the Earl of Sydenham.' So there! 'Which is why it is perfectly acceptable for Godmama to launch me into society. And why even the strictest hostesses are not above sending me invitations to their balls.'

That was not completely true and to her consternation Cassy felt her cheeks heat at the exaggeration. Only a few people had been willing to accept her and Rosalind to start with. The ones who had younger sons who would benefit from marrying an heiress, for the most part. And even though Godmama's hard work had resulted in receiving invitations from those two ladies who'd been friends of her mother, and that probably because they were the sort who were ready to believe the worst of her stepfather, she didn't hold out any hope that they'd receive vouchers for Almack's. Not only was Rosalind not cut from the right cloth, but there was no denying the fact that Cassy had made that Fatal Error.

What was worse, though, was the fact that somehow, not two minutes after vowing she was going to tell him nothing, she'd told him rather a lot.

'So that was how you managed it,' observed the Colonel grimly, as he turned the vehicle in through the park gates.

Far from Cassy managing anything, it had been the Duchess who had breezed into her life and swept her along with her plans. But she wasn't going to let him know anything more about her private life. She was not! It was bad enough that she'd succumbed to correcting the assumptions he'd made about her background. Which were ridiculous, because the first time they'd met she'd been one of a party made up largely of members of Guy's family.

Although she supposed he might not have been aware of that. It had been a public assembly, after all. Anyone could get in if they bought a ticket. And she'd danced with not only the squire, but the grocer, and the blacksmith's son. She cast her mind back to the cheapness of the burly lad's Sunday-best suit. And the unfashionable cut of her own cotton gown. She had probably looked as though she belonged with him, rather than with the silk-and-lace-clad ladies of Guy's female relatives. And if he'd thought that, then perhaps it wasn't so surprising that he'd disapproved of the match she and Guy had been planning.

She glanced up at the Colonel's hard, handsome profile, seeing exactly why he might have made *certain* assumptions about her. Although she was not going to launch into an explanation of her circumstances. For one thing, it would take a long time. For another, it was too painful to dwell on how horrid her life had been back then. But most of all, she had to heed Godmama's warning that she couldn't be sure what use he might make of anything she told him. Not when he'd made it plain he was out to thwart her in any way he could. Besides, every word he spoke, every gesture he made, even the way his nostrils flared, reminded her that no matter what she said, he was determined to believe the worst of her.

'I suppose she thinks she owes it to the memory of your mother, or some such feminine nonsense,' he said, incorrectly assuming that her mother was dead. Although in some ways that might be easier to cope with. It still hurt to recall the way Mama had made no effort to defend her. On good days, she could believe that Mama was simply too afraid of Stepfather to defy him by so much as the changing of a facial expression. But sometimes she wondered if Mama was in agreement with him. Did she think he'd done the right thing, in driving Cassy away? Did she agree with all the harsh things he'd said?

They drove in silence for some time, both staring rigidly ahead, both sunk in their own gloomy thoughts.

But gradually Cassy began to notice that many of the other people out driving in the park were whipping their heads round to get a better look at them as they passed, as if checking to make sure their eyes weren't deceiving them. Apparently, her appearance at the Colonel's side, during the fashionable hour in the park, was creating something of a stir.

Just as she'd made this observation, she regained the presence of mind to smile at the occupants of the next carriage that was approaching, because she recognised the features of Mrs Doughty, a widow with three unmarried daughters, all of whom were squeezed into the vehicle with her. Mrs Doughty had been among the first people to recognise Rosalind's worth and had invited her and Cassy to her home on several occasions, since she also had two sons to marry off. She wasn't wealthy enough to host balls, but she certainly knew how to arrange parties that young people would enjoy, with plenty of foolish games to get them mingling in an extremely informal manner.

Cassy's smile, as she recalled some of the harmless fun she'd had in Mrs Doughty's home, was still in place when the next carriage passed, although this one contained a lady she wasn't aware of ever having seen before in her life. The lady smiled back, however, in a rather cat-like manner, after her eyes had flicked from Cassy to the Colonel and back.

'You think you can succeed in society,' Colonel Fairfax grated after the open carriage had passed, 'because you have received a smile from one of the *ton*'s most vicious gossips?'

Vicious? Oh, dear. What would such a woman make of Cassy driving without a chaperon with an unmarried gentleman? Oh, she *knew* she shouldn't have let the Colonel have his way about this outing. Why did she keep on letting him goad her into doing such foolish, reckless things? And saying things she'd sworn she wouldn't say? Why did she keep forgetting he was her enemy?

Because, she answered herself, she'd spent so many years thinking of him as her hero, and it wasn't easy to shake off a habit that old in a matter of days.

'And because you have managed to persuade your godmother,' he continued, 'that you are as respectable as your mother, I don't doubt.'

They reached the end of the carriage drive and he turned the horses' heads in the direction of the gate.

Cassy heaved a sigh of relief. Her ordeal was almost over.

'I can see that I arrived on the scene too late to prevent you from getting a toehold in society,' he said grimly. 'And now that I know about your background, how you have managed to achieve it. I can also see that I would be wasting my breath by approaching your godmother and attempting to enlighten her. You must have explained your episode with Gilbey in some kind of romantic light that has made her not only forgive you for it, but also made her think she owes you a Season.'

Cassy turned her head and glared up at his profile, taking a breath to object.

'But don't think,' he said, preventing her from voicing her objections to this latest assumption, 'that I will let you get any further. From now on I shall be watching you like a hawk. I will not let you drag that hen-witted woman down into any sort of scandal…'

Cassy promptly closed her mouth. Because if it came to scandal, Godmama was on the verge of creating at least two already. Not only was she embroiled in a feud with her stepson which had almost resulted in all the staff in the Grosvenor Square house losing their jobs, but she was also carrying on with a lover who was young enough to be her son. If either of those two facts got out, Godmama would be the talk of the *ton* for weeks. Possibly longer, if nothing more interesting occurred to set tongues wagging.

'Nor,' he carried on implacably, 'will I stand

back and see you get your avaricious claws into some other unsuspecting male.'

Avaricious claws?

Unsuspecting male?

Cassy could not have uttered a word to save her life, she was now so furious. Far from ever getting anything in the way of money from any man, the only ones she'd been unfortunate enough to tangle with, through the course of her life thus far, had left her penniless and homeless. Well, yes, for the sake of complete accuracy she had to admit that Guy had, eventually, remembered her in his will. But his bequest had come along too late to make any real difference. If it hadn't been for the generosity of her female relatives and friends, she would have been destitute.

Not that she was going to waste her breath telling him so. Why should she even *want* to make him understand? He was just like every other man she'd ever known. Judgemental and mean, and…and altogether horrid!

Which was an awful revelation. Why couldn't he be the man she'd thought he was? Why wasn't he chivalrous and dependable, and practical? A man she could trust with her predicament? The way he'd been when she'd first met him.

Unless…had she only imagined he was all those things? Because she'd been far more gullible back then, seeing the good in everyone…

The image of the Colonel Fairfax of her girlhood shimmered in a mist of unshed tears, leaving only the cold and implacably hostile man who was sitting beside her. A man, she acknowledged with a sinking feeling, she still found more compelling, more attractive, than any other man she'd ever met.

'And then he said he wasn't going to let any other poor, unsuspecting male fall into my clutches,' said Cassy, turning away from the window, and pacing back to the fireplace. 'Godmama, this isn't funny,' she snapped as she caught the Duchess pressing a dainty handkerchief to her lips to disguise the fact she was laughing.

'Well, dear,' said Godmama, dabbing at her eyes, which were streaming with mirth, 'it depends on how you look at it.'

'How can I look at it with anything but… indignation,' said Cassy, walking back to the window, twisting her hands together at her waist, 'when he said you had the brains of a flea and that he was going to watch me like a hawk so that I wouldn't be able to drag you down into whatever scandal I was planning to hatch?'

'As an opportunity, of course,' said Godmama through her giggles. 'For what do you think everyone is going to say when they see him following you about, driving every other male away?' Cassy turned yet again and stalked back in the direction of the chairs grouped around the fireplace. 'That you are the only person who has ever meant enough to him to drag him away from all those stuffy duties he has always, before you came to Town, used as an excuse to turn down every invitation sent to him. And,' she said, getting control of herself, 'I shouldn't be a bit surprised if they are right. It is what I am going to tell them, anyway, because I think there is more than a grain of truth in it. So I won't be telling any lies on your behalf, which I promised, you recall, I wouldn't do. No matter how inconvenient it might be.'

'What?' Usually, Cassy had no trouble following Godmama's line of reasoning, even if she did relay it in a rather disjointed manner. But this time she was at a total loss.

'What do you mean?'

'I mean,' said Godmama, slowly, with a delighted smile curving her lips, 'that he is pursuing you and saying all those nasty things because, in spite of wishing he wasn't, he is attracted to you himself.'

'He…what?' For the first time since returning from the park, Cassy felt the need to sit down. 'He…no, he couldn't possibly…' Although he had said she was up to her *pretty* neck in mischief.

She sank down on to the sofa next to Rosalind, who'd patted the cushions by way of invitation. 'But he is always so…rude. And has assumed the worst of me, no matter what I say…' Not that she'd really said enough to exonerate herself, not with any conviction.

'Yes, he thinks you perfectly capable of luring unsuspecting males to their doom,' crowed Godmama, as though it was the funniest thing she'd heard in ages.

Well, actually, comparing her to a siren was…ludicrous. For she had never exerted, or attempted to exert, any fascination over any man.

Yet Colonel Fairfax kept on insisting she had such power.

Which meant… She looked up sharply at Godmama. Could she be correct? Well, Colonel Fairfax must feel that she had some kind of…allure, or something, to keep harping on about it the way he did. But did that mean he felt susceptible to it?

Her heart thudded thickly in her chest.

Could Colonel Fairfax be attracted to her?

He'd said she was pretty, hadn't he, at Lady Bunsford's ball. And had accused her of being able to lure any man she wanted, by merely...

At which point her imagination failed her. She had no idea how to *lure* anyone. And had no wish to exert any kind of destructive power, even if she had the first idea how to wield it.

'As I said, he may not want to find you attractive, darling, but he does,' said Godmama, spreading her hands in a little gesture indicating she'd made her point.

'Your Grace is right,' put in Rosalind with glee. 'Now I come to think of it, he was positively devouring you with his eyes all the time he was with you at the theatre last night.'

Cassy's hand went to her bosom, at which, she recalled, he'd been glaring for much of the time, as though he was offended so much of it was on show, when truly her neckline hadn't been all that daring.

'You see?' Godmama's eagle eyes had noted the faint fluttering of Cassy's hand to her neckline. 'He thinks you are so alluring that any man who was not on guard could easily fall into your, how did he put it, your *clutches*? Which means he fears suffering such a fate himself. Oh,' she cried, clapping her hands. 'But this is delightful!'

'No, it isn't. How can you say that when he has such a warped notion of my motives?' she said, feeling close to tears again. 'You know I have no intention of getting any man to fall into my clutches. I don't even have any,' she said, looking down at her hands in bewilderment.

'Which,' said Godmama, 'is what makes it so delightfully funny! Do you know, I have just had the most delightful idea? I think I should like to…'

Cassy got a strange shrinking feeling in her stomach. If this latest idea was like any of the other ideas Godmama came up with, then it was more than likely to tumble her into yet more mischief and she felt as if she was already up to her neck in Godmama's current series of schemes.

'Please, Godmama,' she begged, 'don't make me try to pretend to be the kind of woman he suspects me to be. I wouldn't know how. I'd only make a colossal fool of myself, and bring scandal down round your ears, I shouldn't wonder. And then what would happen to Rosalind?'

Godmama's face fell, confirming Cassy's suspicion that she'd been thinking of asking her to do something of the sort.

'Well, yes, I do see your point,' said Godmama, glancing at Rosalind with resignation. 'Only…' She tapped her chin with her forefinger, a sure sign she was hatching another plot. 'It seems such a shame to let him get away with speaking to you like that, and threatening to hound you the way he has, when it would be so easy to spike his guns…'

'In what way?' Cassy couldn't help asking the question, Godmama looked so wistful.

'Well, to start with, I shall be telling everyone that I believe he is wildly attracted to you. Because it happens to be the truth,' she said defiantly. 'I do believe that.'

Cassy supposed she couldn't object to that.

'And the harder he tries to prevent you from interacting with any other eligible man, the more credence he will give to my position.'

Rosalind clapped her hands. 'Your Grace, you are a genius!'

Godmama made a small deprecating gesture with her hand, though she smiled at the same time, to show the compliment was not unwelcome.

But Cassy's stomach was squirming. On the

one hand, she had spent some sleepless nights, wishing there was some way she could make him…grovel.

'Oh, pish,' Godmama was saying to Rosalind. 'It just occurred to me that while he is watching Cassy like a hawk, for no reason other than that he's got a completely nasty notion of her in his head, we may as well make sport of him. And by simply repeating my suspicions about how attractive he finds her, we can make him look like a besotted fool. Which will serve him right.'

Only, Cassy wasn't sure she wanted to make him look like a besotted fool. She knew what it was like to be stripped of all dignity and she would never want to inflict that feeling on anyone, no matter what. Nor could she forget that he had played a significant role in rescuing her from her Fatal Error. He might not have done it for the reasons she'd assumed, at the time, but nevertheless he had dipped into his pocket and given her the money to go home. And arranged for Betty to go with her. If he hadn't done so, she would never have learned about her aunts and who knew where she would have ended up? Wouldn't it be rather shabby behaviour to repay that act of generosity by making him look like a fool in the eyes of society?

On the other hand, he had made *her* feel like a fool, hadn't he, for holding his memory in her heart as a shining example of what a man ought to be…strong, and capable, and organised, and trustworthy…when all the time he'd wrongly assumed she was scheming and grasping and immoral.

For that, yes, actually she rather *would* like to take him down a peg or two.

'Besides which,' said Godmama, as if she could see her wavering, 'we have to give people some reason to explain his pursuit of you. And if it is not because we believe him to be smitten, then what tale will they come up with, do you suppose? Might they even start digging into your shared past and expose your silly scrape? And make it sound ten times worse than it was? Don't you think my solution will serve our purpose better than allowing people to learn what he is really about? Hmm? And what do you suppose *that* would do for Rosalind's chances?'

'Please, Cassy,' said Rosalind, taking her hand. 'It's not as if you have to tell any lies. Only not contradict what the Duchess says about him. Which will all be perfectly true.'

Cassy regarded each of the sets of pleading eyes in turn and wondered why she was even

trying to thwart either lady. She owed Godmama so much. She had been the only person
connected to her family who had loyally stayed
in contact with her through all her years of
exile. And had brought her to London so that
she could restore her reputation.

True, she had done it to further her own
schemes as well, but still…

And then there was Rosalind. In the short
time they'd known each other, they'd become
closer, truer friends than ever she'd known before. Rosalind had never looked down her nose
at her for being penniless, the way Miss Henley had done, back in Market Gooding. She
hadn't turned her back when she'd confessed
to committing her Fatal Error, either, the way
Agatha had done, even though Agatha would
have become her sister had Guy's plans come
to fruition.

And Rosalind was always so generous. She'd
been glad when Cassy had agreed to start
spending some of her father's money, saying
she would enjoy shopping far more if Cassy
could join in, rather than just watching. When
Cassy had pointed out that it made her a touch
uncomfortable spending someone else's money,
she'd waved her qualms aside, pointing out that
Papa expected her to run up enormous bills in

Town and would be disappointed if she didn't. Even when Cassy had suggested he wouldn't expect to pay her bills as well as Rosalind's, she'd just waved a dismissive hand in the air, saying he wouldn't mind in the least. 'Because,' she'd said, squeezing her hands, the way she was doing right now, 'you have always treated me as an equal. You've never once made remarks about me smelling of the shop, or anything of that sort. And you are a true lady, even someone as ignorant as I was when I came to Town could see that,' she'd said as if that was the end of the matter.

Money truly didn't matter to Rosalind. She had never treated Cassy like a poor relation, which she could easily have done. After all, it was how Miss Henley had behaved, in spite of all her protestations of friendship. Miss Henley has bestowed that friendship on Cassy from a lofty height and fully expected Cassy to be suitably grateful.

Which was why she'd been able to swan off to London without so much as a word of thanks for all the work she and her aunts had done.

Rosalind didn't expect Cassy to be grateful for all the bills she was getting her father to pay. She just wanted Cassy to have as much fun in London as she was having and shopping was part of it.

So how could she deny her, deny either of them, what they wanted?

'Very well,' she said with resignation, and was rewarded with a pair of beaming smiles.

Chapter Eight

It took a great deal longer to prepare for the ball they were to attend that night than usual, because Rosalind and Godmama had decided to get involved.

'If you are going to make him appear thoroughly besotted,' Godmama declared, flinging open Cassy's wardrobe, 'then you need to look a bit more...' She paused. 'Well, I know you have started choosing much prettier clothes lately. Only they are still rather on the modest side.'

'I have no wish to parade around looking like a...trollop!' She'd never been comfortable with dressing for the express purpose of attracting a man's notice. She'd never been comfortable with the kind of attention that might follow. Her mind flew back to that assembly she'd gone to with Lady Agatha and her family. Agatha had been flushed with excitement to see so many scarlet-jacketed officers present and thrilled by the fulsome compliments they'd uttered as a prelude to asking for a dance, whereas Cassy had shrunk from them. For she'd known only too well how insincere such flattery could turn out to be. She'd watched her stepfather court her own mother with such smiles and protestations of ardent admiration, all of which had turned out to be false.

The only one of them who hadn't turned on the charm that way had been Guy. He'd simply carried on treating her with the same brotherly sort of manner he'd always done.

And Colonel Fairfax, who'd been stern, though polite, when he'd escorted her back to the stuffy, crowded ballroom after she'd foolishly gone outside on her own.

'You may trust me,' said Godmama in that regal way she sometimes adopted, as though to remind everyone that she was every inch a duchess, 'to know where to draw the line.' She turned back to her perusal of the contents of Cassy's wardrobe.

'Now, what about this?' she said, drawing out Cassy's latest purchase. Cassy relaxed at once. The dress was of filmy white silk, embroidered about the neckline and hem with white flowers. The gauze overdress that went with it was liberally sprinkled with spangles, making her look, she thought, both pure and untouchable.

'Blount!' Godmama summoned Rosalind's dresser, who'd been standing at a respectful distance. 'Is there anything we can do with this gown, before the ball, to make Cassy look a bit more…tempting?'

'Godmama,' Cassy protested, rather feebly, before turning an imploring look at Blount.

Blount tilted her head to one side and pursed her lips. 'We should start with the underpinnings,' she said, casting an assessing look at Cassy's figure. 'The style of corset currently employed by Miss Furnival, if you don't mind my saying so, does not make the most of her assets. Once those are better supported, this gown will provide a natural, and lovely frame, which is what I am sure Your Grace suspected.' She drew the innocent gown from Godmama's arm and draped it across her own.

'But it is still rather…virginal,' said Godmama.

'But I am a virgin!'

'Yes,' said Godmama with a touch of exasperation. 'But you are not exactly a debutante fresh from the schoolroom, are you? You could show a *little* more of your…assets without looking fast. And you could wear stronger colours, too.'

Blount nodded. 'I have a length of scarlet ribbon I could attach to provide that splash of colour. That, and a more flattering corset, and possibly just a snip and a tuck here and there, would make the world of difference.'

'Ooh,' said Rosalind, practically bouncing up and down on her chair. 'How about wearing some of my jewels, Cassy? I know it is vulgar for me to flaunt them,' she said, shooting a look tinged with resentment in Blount's direction. 'But if you no longer want Cassy to look as though she's straight out of the schoolroom that would be different, wouldn't it? And it seems such a shame for them to stay locked up in my jewellery box all the time. It would be lovely to see some of them getting an airing, even if it isn't on me.'

'I couldn't possibly…' Cassy said. But Godmama was clapping her hands and beaming at Rosalind as if she'd just recited a forty-verse lyric ballad off by heart.

'You have some gorgeous rubies in your jewel box, I seem to recall,' said Godmama. 'They would set off the scarlet sash that Blount means to use to replace this insipid white band of satin.'

Cassy looked from Godmama to Rosalind to Blount in stupefaction. All three were clearly bonding, in a way they'd never done before, in their enthusiasm for transforming Cassy into the very kind of woman the Colonel had accused her of being.

'He will think I look…' Cassy began saying.

'Do not tell me you mean to back down now,' said Godmama, indignantly. 'You said you would do whatever you could to distract him so that he will not be able to spoil Rosalind's chances of making a good match. But that sounds to me as if you are afraid of him. You are not going to let him intimidate you, are you? I never thought you lacked courage.'

'I did say I would do what I could, yes, and I am *not* afraid of him.' Of course she wasn't, no matter how many threats he uttered, or how angry he seemed, because he wasn't a cruel man, not at heart. He wasn't threatening her for his own twisted pleasure, the way her stepfather so frequently had, but because he really believed she posed a threat to his fellow man. 'I just don't want to look…cheap.'

'Don't you worry, miss,' said Blount. 'I have been turning out society ladies for the best part of twenty years. And never in all that time has anyone had any cause to think they looked cheap. And nor will you.'

'Not with my rubies round your neck,' chortled Rosalind.

By this time, Cassy was beginning to see that, if she kept on making objections, she was going to deeply offend all three of them. Which would be so ungrateful, considering how much they were enjoying attempting to transform her. And really, was there that much harm in adding a splash of colour to her gown? And making it a touch more daring? It wasn't as if Blount was going to be able to alter it all that much in the few hours remaining before they needed to set out. She wasn't going to end up with bared shoulders, or, worse, a neckline so low that her nipples became visible. And even if her gown did cause men to look, that didn't mean she needed to give them any encouragement, did it? A man could only really harm a woman if she fell for his charm, if she believed his lies. And she was too wise, now, to repeat the mistakes she'd made as a schoolgirl.

So she agreed to having a different style of corset fitted and Rosalind's maid, Hetty, promptly produced one from somewhere. Once it was fastened, the corset pushed her bosom

up so much that she looked far more gener-
ously proportioned than she'd ever imagined
possible so that, when Blount finally draped
the gown over her head, she wondered if she'd
made a mistake. Because the neckline, which
had looked so pretty and modest before, now
did, indeed, frame her assets in a rather provocative manner. Unless it was the splash of
scarlet provided by the sash which now drew
attention to those same assets from beneath.
For Blount had tacked on the length of crim-
son satin immediately below the bodice and
secured it in a rather saucy bow.

Meanwhile, Rosalind had run off to fetch her
jewellery box herself and she and Godmama
picked out a stunning necklace made from a
triple row of pearls, gathered up in the centre
by a single ruby, as well as some earrings and
bracelets to match. Hetty had supplied some
little artificial roses which she fastened into
Cassy's curls with pearl clips. By the time
they'd all finished with her, Cassy scarcely
recognised herself.

'Stunning.' Godmama sighed, just as Cassy
was wondering whether it was all a bit much.
Not that she looked the slightest bit like a trol-
lop. Blount did indeed know her business well.
In fact, if she was married, and had been out

for several years, there would be nothing the slightest bit remarkable in her appearance.

But she wasn't married.

'You will take his breath away,' said Godmama.

'Will I?' An image of Colonel Fairfax, gasping with admiration, flitted into her mind, swiftly followed by one of him casting aside his misguided notions and declaring that he didn't care what anyone else might think, he adored her. She fingered the necklace uncertainly. 'You don't think this is all…'

'You look beautiful,' said Rosalind. 'Never mind that old Colonel—'

'He isn't old,' Cassy protested.

'You won't sit out a single dance, looking like that,' Rosalind continued as if Cassy hadn't said a word.

'Do you really think so?' She did like dancing. And it would be lovely to be a success at Lady Bradbury's ball.

'I should have made a push to get you dressed like this from the start,' said Godmama, with a vexed expression.

'No, I don't think you should,' said Cassy. 'I mean, the aim was to restore my reputation, wasn't it? And show people that, far from being ruined, I am still innocent. If I'd gone about dressed like this, from the start, the rumours would have resurfaced with a vengeance and I'd probably have received all sorts of unpleasant attention from the worst kind of men.'

'That may be true, dear, but I could at least have dressed you to show off your dark colouring a bit better. But there,' she said, clapping her hands and nodding her head as though she'd come to a decision, 'some good has come of our plan to confound that silly Colonel already. From now on we shall dress you in colours to set off your striking, dark sort of prettiness, rather than trying to make everyone believe you are next door to being a schoolgirl.'

Cassy took one more look at her reflection. She'd never looked so…well, she wasn't sure what the correct term was. But there was definitely *nothing* of the schoolgirl about her.

She glanced round at Godmama, Rosalind and the two maids, who all looked jolly pleased with themselves. And from the fondness in their smiles, she could tell that it hadn't all been about trying to thwart the Colonel. They all, she realised on a surge of emotion so overwhelming that she had to gulp it back, wanted to help her cast off the cloud of shame and sorrow that had been hanging over her since the day her stepfather had slammed the door shut in her face. And wasn't it about time she stepped out from under it? Didn't she owe it to these women who had become her friends, and who had gone to such efforts on her behalf, to try?

And what, when all was said and done, did she have to feel ashamed about, anyway?

And so it was with her chin held at a defiant angle that she turned away from the mirror, swept out of her room and strode along the landing.

Captain Bucknell, who was waiting at the foot of the stairs, let out a low whistle.

'Turning this one into quite the beauty, ain't you, Your Grace?' he said to Godmama with an appreciative grin. 'No chance,' he then said, turning to Cassy and addressing her directly, 'of you fading into the background any longer, eh?'

No, she realised with a sigh, even though that was what she'd been trying to do so far. Because she'd only agreed to come to London to help Godmama in her quest to thwart her stepson. She most certainly hadn't wanted to find a husband for herself. After her experience at the hands of men, she had no wish to surrender her whole life to just one, who could easily turn out to be either as cruel as her stepfather, or as inept as Lieutenant Gilbey, or as…well, she couldn't think of a reason why no woman ought to marry a man like Colonel Fairfax. His hardness, perhaps. Except, she couldn't help thinking that, in certain circumstances, that rock-like hardness was a good quality. And what was more, if she wasn't the person he was persecuting, she would most definitely admire him for the loyalty he was showing to poor Guy's memory, even if it was more than a touch misguided.

However, it wasn't just the men who took more notice of her that night. When they got to the head of the receiving line, the hostess, Lady Bradbury, actually held out her hand, took Cassy's and gave her a welcoming smile, rather than looking straight through her and greeting whoever it was who happened to be next in the receiving line, which was what Cassy had come to expect.

'Miss Furnival,' she said, causing Cassy a moment of shock. She hadn't expected to be greeted by name, even though this lady had been, according to Godmama, a close friend of her mother's. 'I am so glad you have come. And looking so…' She ran her eyes up and down

Cassy's gown, pausing at the pearls clasped about her neck. 'I shall await developments with bated breath,' she said with what looked like excitement, before turning to Godmama and whispering something in her ear.

'What,' Cassy hissed out of the side of her mouth, the moment they stepped away, 'did she say? What did she mean?'

'I am not perfectly sure,' replied Godmama, equally softly. 'She did say she had arranged a lovely surprise for you. Though I cannot possibly imagine what it could be,' she said, her eyes sparkling. 'But I do so love surprises, don't you?'

Not really. Her heart began pounding with what felt like dread as they slowly advanced into the ballroom, greeting and being greeted by Godmama's friends. And it skipped a beat entirely when a portly, middle-aged man stopped directly in front of them, obliging them to stop altogether. Because she knew him. Even though she hadn't seen him since she'd been a little girl and he'd been much thinner then, and had a lot more hair, there was no mistaking the features of her mother's brother.

Uncle Henry!

'Evening, Your Grace,' he said to Godmama.

'Niece,' he said, according her just a single nod before continuing on his way to the card room.

Cassy gripped her reticule and fan tightly in an attempt to disguise the fact that her hands were shaking. He hadn't cut her. In fact, he'd gone out of his way to deliberately acknowledge her. Had even spoken to her, even though it had been but a single word. But that single word held a wealth of meaning.

And people standing nearby had understood that unspoken message. She could hear it, spreading out on a wave of murmured voices, the way ripples spread out after a pebble drops into a pool. Or, in this case, a whopping great boulder.

For he'd acknowledged her. In public.

Godmama had done it! She was no longer dead to her family. Or at least, not his part of it. And he was the head of the family now that he was the fourth Earl of Sydenham. Where he led, the others would follow.

'Darling!' Godmama suddenly cried, darting away with her arms outstretched, to where her son, the Marquess of Devizes, was standing before a mirror, adjusting the set of his cravat. Leaving Cassy standing, stunned, on the spot where her uncle had, publicly, acknowledged her.

'How lovely to see you here this evening,' she faintly heard Godmama coo to her son. 'I didn't expect you to bother with anything quite so jejune.'

'Blast it,' said Captain Bucknell, jolting Cassy out of her state of joyful stupefaction. 'She will be an age with that young fop now,' he growled, then sighed, then turned to Rosalind. 'How about I take you for a spin about the dance floor, Miss Mollington? No sense us standing here kicking our heels, what?'

Rosalind glanced at Cassy.

'Oh, that is fine, you go ahead,' she said, since she needed a few moments alone to bask in what had just happened.

'Thank you,' said Rosalind, giving Cassy's hands a brief squeeze. 'I do so love dancing with the Captain. I never feel as if I need to worry about stepping on his toes.'

'Well, no, since you have already done so dozens of times,' teased the Captain, 'when Her Grace was letting you practise on me.' Which was true. And, she reflected, it hadn't only been Rosalind who had needed practice on a real man before Godmama would let them loose in a real ballroom. Cassy had only been able to vaguely recall the figures of the simplest country dances and had never learned to waltz during her years of exile in Market Gooding. There had been no need.

She ought to remember how good it had been of Captain Bucknell to indulge the girls on his afternoons off and the good-natured way he had brushed aside all their ignorance and lack of expertise. Especially tonight, when she'd been so fortunate. It would be petty of her to keep on resenting and disliking him, simply because the idea of him and Godmama romping...

Ugh. No, she wasn't going to think about such things tonight. Not when she was glowing with such gratitude for all the effort so many people had gone to on her behalf to bring her to this point. Even Captain Bucknell, in his own way.

If he asked her to dance later on she would swallow back the revulsion that the touch of his hand normally induced and smile at him. Perhaps she would not be able to smile with the same evident pleasure that Rosalind was showing as she practically skipped to the dance floor. But smile she would. At *anyone* who asked her to dance. No matter who they were.

Although it wasn't as easy to smile as she'd thought, when none other than the Marquess strolled over and made a courtly bow.

'Mama has told me,' he said, 'in no uncertain terms, that I must make sure you get straight out on to the dance floor.' He stepped back, took out his quizzing glass, and eyed her from top to toe in such a way that she felt her cheeks blush hotly. 'I suppose she thinks,' he said, tucking his quizzing glass away, 'that once the other gentlemen here have seen you looking so…ah…delectable, you will have no shortage of partners.'

'Um…yes,' she said, for although that much was true, that wasn't the whole truth.

'Do not be alarmed,' he said, offering her his arm. 'I shall not ask if there is one, specific, victim of Mama's latest campaign. I find it far better to avoid becoming embroiled in her schemes.'

'Are you not, then,' she snapped, forgetting all her determination to smile at whoever asked her to dance, 'afraid to dance with me? Will that not *embroil* you?'

He shook his head in mock reproof. 'Dear me. What a sharp tongue you possess. No, I do not fear becoming embroiled with you after just one dance. Nor even after exchanging this small amount of conversation. I do, sometimes, dance with young innocents, you see. As a favour to a friend, or relative…' he cocked his head at his mother, who was beaming at him from the chaperons' bench '...but only once.'

'She knows better than to depend upon you for help, then?'

'She has no need of it,' he replied, Cassy's taunt appearing to slide off his indolent facade like water off a duck's back. 'She is, from what I can see, thoroughly enjoying herself this Season and so...' He finished with an elegant shrug.

And proceeded to dance with her with equal elegance. And a sort of indifference, as though he was barely aware she was his partner. He could not have made his lack of interest in her more obvious, without being downright rude. How could a man make a dance feel like a snub? Yet he did. However, even the Marquess was not going to put a dent in her good mood tonight. The more he snubbed her, the more she smiled. To anyone else, it must have looked as if she was having the time of her life. Still, by the time the dance came to an end, she fervently hoped he never deigned to *honour* her in the same way again. She was really looking forward to the moment when he'd restore her to Godmama's side. Until, that was, she spotted Colonel Fairfax, standing in the midst of the throng of young hopefuls jostling for introductions to Rosalind, glowering.

And her hand involuntarily clenched upon the Marquess's sleeve. For the Colonel's demeanour was so hostile that even the Marquess, the man she'd vowed to stay well away from in future, felt like a safer bet.

Chapter Nine

She looked stunning.

Nathaniel ground his teeth, reflecting that the glittering white of her gown was far too much like snow catching the dawn light in Spain, while all those rubies put him in mind of the blood that had sprayed across it. Which meant her radiance came at too great a price.

She faltered when she caught sight of him and clutched at her dancing partner's sleeve. But the Marquess melted out of her hold, leaving her standing to face him, alone.

She began to turn away from him, her eyes darting back and forth as though she was searching for some safe corner into which she could flee. But he was not about to let her escape that easily. As she took her first step in the direction of the open door of the refreshment room, he swooped over and seized her wrist.

She stiffened, but did not do anything as obvious as struggle. Instead she lifted her chin and looked down her haughty little nose at him.

'You are holding my arm too tightly,' she said.

'Hah!' He was not hurting her, but she could not run from him now without making a scene, so he relaxed his grip a touch.

'And you may not have noticed,' she continued in that same frigid voice, 'but we are heading in the wrong direction. If you are not careful, you will end up on the dance floor. With me.'

Better that than allow her to charm her way into some other man's heart. He'd warned her that he wouldn't permit her to get her claws into anyone else. But what did he find her doing? Working her wiles on none other than the Marquess of Devizes, a man rich enough to keep her in the kind of luxury to which she probably believed her beauty entitled her.

'I *am* going to dance with you,' he warned her. He'd denied himself the pleasure the first time he'd ever seen her at a ball. But perhaps, if he'd indulged himself back then, she wouldn't still be exerting this strange fascination. Because he would already know what it felt like to be her partner. He would know she was no different from any other woman.

'Oh? I should have thought it was the last thing you would wish to do.'

He spun her round to face him when they reached the edge of the area where other couples were gathering. 'Far from it,' he growled. 'Because if I dance with you, at least it will prevent you from sinking your claws into some other poor sap.'

She flinched, as though he'd slapped her. But after only the briefest of pauses her mouth curved into a cat-like smile.

'You can only dance with me twice,' she pointed out. 'And after that you will not be able to prevent me from dancing with anyone else. What will you do then, Colonel?'

He would think of something. During two dances he'd surely be able to come up with something other than heaving her over his shoulder, carrying her to his house and locking her in his bedroom.

His bedroom? Why was that the first place he thought of imprisoning her? He gritted his teeth as an image of her bound, naked, to his bed flashed into his mind. He thrust it forcibly away, because if he sank to that level, then she would have won.

He bowed to her as the orchestra struck up the opening chords to his first dance with her and performed all the necessary manoeuvres with as much dignity as a man could, who was scarcely able to tear his eyes from his partner no matter where in the figure she happened to be. A partner who twirled and smiled as though promising him delights he would never experience anywhere but at her hands.

If he would but surrender.

To hell with that! He would *never* surrender. Not to the likes of her.

'Well,' she said eventually, her face flushed and her eyes shining with triumph, 'your two dances are over. You must release me.'

'I shall do no such thing,' he snapped, winding her arm round his own and securing her to his side. 'We will now go to the refreshment room.' He began to tow her in that direction.

'But what if I want to carry on dancing?' she complained, as a hopeful-looking young buck stepped into their path with a smile and a bow.

One glare, accompanied by a warning growl, was all it took to send the coward running for cover.

'I cannot believe you just did that,' she gasped.

'Snarling at him like a...like a...well, you really frightened him.'

He hadn't scared her, though. Not now, nor at any time since they'd renewed their acquaintance. She *had* looked scared when she'd been clinging to Gilbey's arm. Though back then, he'd been convinced she was so timid she would not be a suitable wife for a soldier on active duty. But she definitely had a great deal of pluck nowadays, he had to concede. Enough pluck to chide him as if she were his equal. It gave him a strange feeling inside. A feeling that reminded him of what it had been like as a young officer. A time when he'd had friends still living.

'Good,' he said as they set off once more in the direction he wanted to go. 'A man who is scared off by a look and a snarl is not man enough for you.'

She gasped. 'I... What kind of man do you...?'

The kind of man who would not be so bowled over by her beauty that he became a pawn in her hands, that was what she needed. A man who would look beneath the surface and appreciate her strength of character.

'No, never mind,' she continued, breaking through his peculiar foray into the realms of imagination. 'The point is, people are staring,' she complained.

'Do you care? Really? I thought you were made of sterner stuff.'

She shot him a suspicious glance. 'What do you mean by that?'

'Exactly what I say. You are not some simpering miss to wilt under the disapproval of a few society tabbies, are you?'

'Absolutely not, but...'

'Wine,' he snapped at the waiter on duty as they reached the buffet. 'And lemonade for the lady.'

'I might not like lemonade,' she pointed out tartly as he was about to hand her the glass he'd taken from the waiter. But she was reaching for it. Some imp of mischief had him whisking it out of her reach and holding it high.

She huffed with irritation. 'I only said I *might* not like it, not that I didn't.'

A reluctant smile tugged at his lips. He knew she'd been arguing with him for the sake of arguing. 'If I refused to hand this drink over,' he mused, 'I suppose you would accuse me of cruelty. Protest that you were dying of thirst, or something...'

She pulled her top lip between her teeth. A gesture probably born of frustration at his teasing. But it created an entirely different form of frustration in him. For how many times had he wondered what it would feel like to suck that provocative upper lip into his own mouth? Nibble at it?

'Here,' he said, thrusting the glass of lemonade at her and taking a hasty step back.

She took it, rather warily. 'I would not accuse you of…that is, I have never once thought you a cruel man,' she said. And then looked up at him, all wide-eyed, as though pleading with him for something.

'That won't work on me,' he declared, as much to remind himself not to weaken, as to convey a warning to her.

'What won't work?' She looked baffled. And if Issy hadn't warned him that she was not the woman she seemed to be, he would have fallen for her innocent act, right then.

But she *had* warned him.

'Your pretence,' he told her. 'Your flattery. The way you act as though the last thing you want is my enmity, when you…when you…'

Or was it the other way round? Was it more accurate to say that he didn't want to have to maintain hostilities against her?

God, he wished Issy hadn't dragged him into this. He couldn't sleep, he shirked his work, and…oh, lord. Now she was licking a drop of lemonade from that pouting upper lip with the tip of her moist pink tongue…

'That won't work on me,' he repeated, in desperation, although he could feel his own mouth watering. His lips tingling. 'I know what you are,' he reminded himself. 'I know what you are capable of—'

'No, you don't,' she said, draining her cup and setting it back down on the buffet.

What did she mean? That, no matter how hard he tried, he would never be able to stop her? Or was it a hint that, should she choose to really turn her sights on him, she could bring him to his knees? Or worse?

'You dare to threaten me?'

'What?' She blinked up at him in a very convincing show of bewilderment. And then her lips quirked as though he'd just said something amusing.

'And now you are mocking me,' he said.

'No, truly,' she said, laying her hand on his sleeve. 'It is just ridiculous to suppose that a mere girl could threaten a man who has fought real battles. Especially a man like you, who I have…' She swallowed. Turned an interesting shade of pink. 'Well, to be perfectly honest, I sort of held you up, in my mind, as some sort of hero, in secret, for years. Ever since you rescued me from my folly, I...'

He took a step back, shaking off her hand.

'I have already told you that you are not going to wind me round your finger by laying on such patently false flattery,' he told her, then tossed back the last of his wine and slammed the empty glass down next to hers before grabbing her wrist, loathe as he was to touch her again.

'Colonel Fairfax, what are you doing? People are staring. Even more than they did when you dragged me in here.'

'What,' he said bitterly, 'don't you like people looking at you? Knowing that you've got me worked up into such a lather that I don't know whether to strangle you, or pin you up against the nearest wall and kiss you?'

'Wh-what?' Her own lips parted and she stumbled, artfully, against him, pressing one breast against his upper arm, making him instantly hard and yearning for more than just a kiss.

Which meant that he had to retreat from the field after returning her to the Duchess's side. Because there was no way he could stay and watch her dancing with any of her other admirers. Not when there was nothing he could do but glare at them and make himself look like a ridiculous, besotted fool. Especially when his tight silk evening breeches would leave nobody in any doubt about what he was thinking.

But it wasn't over. Not, he vowed as he marched away from the ball, by a long shot.

'Run along now, Captain Bucknell,' said Godmama, the moment they returned to Grosvenor Square. 'I have a *lot* to discuss with the girls. And it really cannot wait until morning.'

He bowed over her hand and kissed it. 'Whatever you say, Your Grace,' he said, with resignation. But as Godmama ushered Cassy and Rosalind into the drawing room she took a quick peek over her shoulder, and, just as she'd suspected, he was heading for the stairs, not the front door.

'Well, now, darlings, I have so much to tell you,' said Godmama, arranging herself on her favourite chair by the fire. 'Lady Bradbury has been very, very busy on your behalf, as I suspect you will already have guessed, Cassy, from the fact that she not only got your uncle to attend her ball, but actually to acknowledge you. In front of everyone!' She clapped her hands in delight.

Oh, yes. Her uncle. Funny, but since dancing with Colonel Fairfax, her joy at the momentous reunion had faded to the back of her mind. Well, how could she think of anything else after he'd told her he wanted to kiss her? And looked at her as though he wanted to devour her? The shock of discovering that Godmama had been correct, that he was attracted to her, but didn't want to be, had left her in a bit of a daze. She could not, now, say who she'd danced with after that, or what she'd talked about with her other partners, even though there had been a steady stream of them for the first time since she'd come to Town. All she could think of was the way her knees had buckled as she'd looked at that hard slash of a mouth, which he'd said he wanted to press to hers. In a crowded ballroom.

He might just as well have done, because once he'd put the idea in her head, she couldn't think of anything else.

'It was just as I'd suspected,' Godmama was saying. 'Your stepfather has made himself so odious that it only took a judicious word or two, here and there, to get everyone questioning his version of events where you are concerned.'

Her stepfather? Oh, yes, Godmama wanted to talk about her family, not the Colonel. She had to stop wool-gathering and pay attention.

'How has he done that?' Rosalind had asked the question Cassy should have asked if she hadn't had her wits addled by thoughts of kissing the Colonel. So Cassy reached out her hand and took Rosalind's, in gratitude, since they were sitting side by side on the sofa facing Godmama.

'Well,' said Godmama, leaning forward and lowering her voice, the way she so often did when descending to the level of gossip. 'It turns out that Cassy's uncle has had to practically adopt Frederick, who is Cassy's younger brother,' she explained when Rosalind took a breath to ask who he was, 'because the hateful man claims he is not going to throw his money away sending him to expensive schools when there is a perfectly good one in the village. And he hasn't brought your mother to Town for so many years everyone was already beginning to wonder if he was being tight-fisted with her, too. Is he?'

'Well, yes, he was when I lived with him...' Cassy thought of the darning and hemming she'd had to do. Hours and hours of it, rather than buying anything new for any of the household.

Which had, ironically, stood her in good stead when she'd gone to live with her aunts.

'Apparently, when Lady Bradbury spoke to your uncle about you, he said...' and she leaned even further forward, lowering her voice as though someone might overhear although there was nobody but Cassy and Rosalind in the room '...that your stepfather was refusing to waste his blunt on another man's whelp. Yes, those were his very words! Which she told me in the *strictest* confidence,' she said, sitting back again. Which meant that those words were probably all over Town by now. 'So your uncle decided he was going to have to sponsor Frederick to some kind of career, or who knew what would happen to the lad?'

Cassy felt a weight lift from her mind. She'd been wondering how Frederick was going to survive. She'd wondered if her method of escape had been used as a cautionary tale to frighten him into submission, or whether it had made her stepfather act in some other way to increase his iron grip on her mother and brother.

But Frederick was clearly going to do far better than she, if their uncle had stepped in.

'And, of course,' Godmama continued, 'when Lady Bradbury reminded him that you have been living in straitened circumstances, too...' She spread her hands as though the conclusion was obvious.

'You mean...' Rosalind wriggled her bottom and screwed up her nose '...that this uncle of hers will now look after Cassy, the way he's doing for her brother?'

'Oh, no, nothing like that!' Godmama clucked her tongue as though Rosalind had said something stupid, which made Rosalind flush. 'He has done enough, don't you think? Speaking to her in public has let everyone know that he now accepts her as one of the family. Which throws into question every nasty rumour that her stepfather spread about her all those years ago. And from the hints he has already dropped about having to fund Frederick, because her stepfather is too mean to do so, people will probably put two and two together and start wondering if he simply turned Cassy out of doors so that he could get his greedy hands on her inheritance.'

'Oh. Do you have an inheritance?' Rosalind turned to Cassy, who was rubbing at her forehead where a feeling of pressure was building.

'Godmama, you know I didn't want to use that excuse. I told you at the start—'

'Yes, but I didn't, that's the beauty of it. All I did was listen to what everyone else is saying and told them that my lips are sealed!' She went off into a peal of laughter. 'Your future in society is assured. And, therefore, Rosalind's, too,' she put in quickly, before Cassy could raise any more objections. 'Because now, all the invitations you should always have had will come flooding in. You see if they don't.'

'Um, there is just one tiny problem, Godmama, in case you have forgotten.'

She frowned. 'And what is that?'

'Colonel Fairfax. He...'

Godmama flicked her fingers as though dismissing him. 'We don't need to worry about him. Unless...' She sat forward, her expression changing to one of concern. 'He didn't frighten you, did he? With all that...brutish display of jealousy and possessiveness tonight?'

Jealousy? Possessiveness? Before he'd talked about kissing her, she would not have believed that was what it was all about. But now she wasn't so sure. Even when he'd been dancing with her, she'd preferred the way he'd glowered at her the whole time to the way the Marquess had appeared to barely notice she existed. Why, Colonel Fairfax had practically shoved the other gentlemen in the set aside after they'd performed one of the figures with her. It might not have been an elegant display of dancing, but it had been, in a strange way, rather flattering. Because he didn't *want* to want her. It was far more satisfying than having a man pay her insincere compliments, because those, she'd learned from bitter experience, were often employed to try to deceive a woman. There was nothing deceitful about Colonel Fairfax. Everything was out in the open. Even, now, his unwelcome yearning to kiss her. Even if it was only a more law-abiding alternative to strangling her. It made her feel…irresistible.

'Frighten me? No, not at all. You forget, I lived with a *real* bully for many years. And not once has the Colonel ever frightened me the way my stepfather did. Yes, he is angry and breathing threats. But that is only because he believes the lies that have been told about me. Who do you think could have set him against me, do you suppose? Who could possibly hate me so much that…?' She shivered. 'Godmama, don't you think I could just tell him he has been misinformed? About the money I'm supposed to have extorted from Guy, if nothing else?'

She'd been on the verge of doing so over her glass of lemonade when he'd teased her, holding it out of her reach, and she'd glimpsed a lighter side of him. He was, she was becoming more and more certain, a fine man, deep down. Even the way he was misguidedly trying to prevent her from doing something she had no intention of doing was a sort of example of his deeply ingrained habit of protecting the vulnerable from predators. Just as he'd protected her from Guy's foolhardiness, thinking that he was protecting Guy from her.

Godmama shook her head. 'I may have humoured you by drawing the line at telling outright lies, but, Cassy, darling, the truth will not serve! I have told you, we don't know what he will do with it.'

That was, unfortunately, a fair point. She only had to remember the way he'd recoiled when she'd started to try to explain that he had nothing to fear from her, because she didn't want to fight with him and that really there was no need to be fighting in the first place.

'Besides,' Godmama continued, 'the other gossip I heard tonight concerns him. And you.'

'Oh?' Cassy sat up straighter. There was gossip about them?

'Most people think you are doing him the world of good.'

'I...what? How can that be?'

'Well, you see, darling, since he returned from the war, he has been something of a recluse. No matter how many invitations were sent to him, from the most determined society hostesses, he never accepted a single one. Not until that night he stormed into Lady Bunsford's rout and cornered you behind the potted palms. Well,' she said, clapping her hands, just once, 'that caused some speculation, naturally. But then he put in an appearance at the theatre and came to our box, and spoke with you in a most intimate fashion for several minutes before leaving. Never speaking to anyone else...'

'But—'

'And *then*, he took you out for a drive in his carriage,' said Godmama, denying Cassy the chance to say a word. 'And he *never* drives out in his carriage during the fashionable hour, let alone with a female up beside him. Nor does he waste his time doing anything so frivolous as going to the theatre, not even for a few minutes.'

'Yes, but it was all so that he could...scold me,' Cassy pointed out. 'Gossip is making it sound as though...'

Godmama waved her hand as though brushing aside a minor detail. 'Lady Bunsford has been crowing about her success in getting the Colonel to attend her rout, even though it was but for a minute or two, because it was the first such event he has attended for years. And she is such a jumped-up little mushroom, that none of the real leaders of society can bear it. They will do whatever it takes to have him grace their own events, too. Well, they don't want to be outshone by a creature like her, do they?'

'I thought,' said Rosalind, stiffening, 'you said getting an invitation to Lady Bunsford's rout was a coup.'

'Well, so it was. For you. I mean, for both of you, at the time,' said Godmama, waving her hand between the two girls. 'I know I told your papa that I could get you into the houses of the highest people in the land,' she said, looking a little shamefaced, 'but I'm sure you have realised, by now, that it was just the teeniest little bit of an exaggeration.'

'Because I smell of the shop and Cassy had committed that Fatal Error when she was younger,' said Rosalind grimly.

Godmama gave her a stern look. 'You know how hard I have worked to get you seen at lots and lots of places, where the kind of men who would want to marry you could put in an appearance without it looking *too* obvious. But now,' she continued, cutting Rosalind off when she took a breath to speak her mind, 'we really will be getting invitations to all the places I dare say your papa thought I meant, when I said the *best* houses. Because, not only have I repaired Cassy's reputation, but people are also starting to notice that if they invite Cassy to any party of theirs, the chances are the Colonel will show up, as well. Which would be a feather in any ambitious hostess's cap.'

'That's…' Poor Colonel Fairfax. He didn't *want* to go to balls and plays or driving in the park. 'It doesn't seem right to keep him on a string like this…'

'Pish! The man needs to get out more. His sisters and his aunts have been fretting about him for several Seasons, you know, because he really ought to be finding himself a wife. He is quite a catch,' she said, eyeing Cassy speculatively. 'The heir to an earldom, with a substantial fortune, several handsome properties dotted about the country, as well as his house in London, and connections to the most influential people in the land. Any woman who is lucky enough to marry him will become extremely important herself. Socially, I mean. So I wouldn't be a bit surprised if your uncle wouldn't provide you with a handsome dowry if you could somehow get the Colonel to turn all that thwarted passion into a proposal…'

'No! I mean…' She hadn't come to Town to

find a husband. 'And anyway, I must be the last person he would consider marrying.'

'Oh, I don't know. I think if you put your mind to it, you could easily make him forget himself. And then he would *have* to marry you...'

'No. Absolutely not.' There was simply no way she would stoop to such despicable behaviour. 'I am not so desperate for a husband that I would try to trap anyone. Especially not him.' She couldn't see him falling into any sort of trap set by anyone, not after surviving all that the French could throw at him. He'd only marry when he was good and ready. And for his own reasons, at that. Besides, he clearly thought of her as an enemy. He'd proved it tonight, when she'd attempted to negotiate a truce and he'd recoiled in horror. He would settle for nothing less than total surrender. On his terms. Which she could not give.

She still had *some* pride.

'As if she'd want to marry a bitter, bigoted man like that,' said Rosalind, hotly. 'Though I hope he does get caught by some woman who will turn out to be a suitable punishment for him,' she added, with verve. 'Someone who will make him miserable for the rest of his life.'

Cassy shrank from the vision of some woman

making him miserable for the rest of his life. She didn't think he deserved that. Besides, she couldn't really imagine him with anyone else without getting a horrid, wrenching sort of feeling inside. Not after being on the receiving end of all the heat blazing from his eyes when he'd threatened to kiss her, in full view of everyone in the ballroom.

'No,' said Godmama pensively. 'If Cassy won't make a push to secure him, it's unlikely he will make anyone any proposals this Season. He is only just coming out of the...well, whatever it is that has kept him acting like a hermit for the past few years. Next year, perhaps, or the one after...' She shrugged and sighed, and shook her head ruefully over what she was implying was a waste of an opportunity. 'You will not do anything to prevent him from appearing to dangle after you, though, will you, Cassy?'

'I don't think there is anything that would do that,' said Cassy. 'Apart from making a clean breast of everything.' Although would he believe the truth even if he heard it? She had the sinking feeling that he wasn't likely to believe anything that came from her lips.

'Which I hope you have no intention of doing,' said Godmama. 'Even if you don't want to get a husband this Season, we did promise to find one for Rosalind. And we are now just on the cusp of social success. Having the Colonel dangling after you is providing so much interest that we are bound to get invitations from even the highest sticklers, since they wouldn't be able to bear being the only ones *not* to have the Colonel visit their houses…'

'*I* wouldn't blame you,' Rosalind butted in, laying her hand on Cassy's, 'if you decided you'd had enough. You've got what you came to Town for, after all, haven't you? You got your uncle to welcome you back into the family and now you can take your rightful place in society again. And I can see how much you hate having that horrid Colonel persecuting you the way he did tonight. I can always write to Papa,' she said with a sigh, 'and tell him that his idea won't work, that no titled man is going to marry a girl from my background,' she said glumly. 'And we can both go home.'

Godmama gasped and placed her hand to her breast. 'But…he'd want his money back! And I've spent it all! There were debts, you know, and then the staff wages…'

Cassy looked from one crestfallen face to the other. Knowing she had the power to make them both smile again, she thrust her own qualms to one side.

'Nonsense,' she said with as much conviction as she could. 'I'm not ready to throw in the towel just yet. I've already told you, the Colonel doesn't frighten me. And it would be selfish of me to abandon you, Rosalind, before you've achieved your own goals.'

As the smiling faces of the two women turned to her, Cassy tried to draw comfort from knowing she'd made her friends happy.

And bade farewell to any hope she might be able to redeem herself in the Colonel's eyes.

Chapter Ten

Cassy shuddered as she looked at her reflection in the mirror the next morning. The puffiness of her eyes, and the shadows beneath them, bore testimony to the hours she'd spent weeping instead of sleeping.

What she really needed was some thin slices of cucumber to lay over her eyelids, to bring the swelling down before facing the world. Only to get some cucumber she'd have to face whoever was in the kitchen, which would rather defeat the object. For they would want to know what the matter was and if there was anything they could do. And since she couldn't understand the depths of the misery she'd gone through last night, how could she put it into words to explain it to anyone else?

So she went to the washstand and splashed her face with cold water instead. Hopefully it

would deal with the evidence of the bout of…
self-pity, yes, that was what had afflicted her
the minute she'd climbed into bed last night.

And while she repeatedly splashed her eyes,
she gave herself a stern lecture.

*You have no reason to feel sorry for your-
self, you foolish girl*, she told the wan creature
who stared forlornly back at her whenever she
raised her eyes to the mirror. *You live in luxury.
With a duchess, no less! You have a friend in
Rosalind. And a loving home to return to, when
this ordeal in London is over. And no more
need to hang your head in shame, because
the head of your family is no longer shunning
you. Why, there might even be an invitation to
Sydenham Hall this Christmas. So you should
be skipping around this bedroom singing, not
crying because…because…*

She leaned her hands on the marble top of
the washstand, letting water drip from her face
back into the basin. This was the nub of the
matter. It didn't seem to matter what anyone
else thought of her while Colonel Fairfax persisted in treating her as if she was some sort
of…Delilah, whose sole aim in life was to lull a
man into a false sense of security so she could
render him a slave to her evil plans. Yet she
was going to have to face his contempt, day

after day, until Rosalind finally bagged her titled husband, because she'd promised to stay in London until that happened.

Oh, but that day couldn't come soon enough. For only then could she go home. Home to Market Gooding and the house where she could…

A wry smile tugged at her mouth as she imagined the way her aunts would react if she went back to them, once again, broken-hearted because of a man. They hadn't allowed her to take to her bed and go into a decline the first time and they most definitely wouldn't do so now. In fact, they'd have less sympathy for her this time round, because last time they could tell that Guy had only been one part of the train of events that had led her to their door. He'd let her down, to be sure, but it was her mother's betrayal that had cut her to the quick. The way she'd stood by, refusing to defend her no matter how Cassy had begged, because she was so utterly cowed by Stepfather.

Well, *she* was not going to be cowed by a man. She reached for a towel and scrubbed her face dry. Letting a man have too much power, in *any* way, *always* resulted in abject misery. Even her darling papa, her real papa, hadn't done her mother any good, in the long run. Because Mama had rushed into marriage a second time with a man who had pretended to be just like him, probably so that she could recapture what she'd lost when he'd died. Well, also, because she hadn't wanted her children to grow up without any father at all…

Oh, if only Mama had stood up to Stepfather when he'd first started to reveal his true colours, Cassy wouldn't have turned to Guy. If Guy had more than the…the brains of a flea, he wouldn't have dragged her halfway across the country, before tamely allowing the Colonel to send her home when he *knew* what awaited her there.

Colonel Fairfax, she couldn't help reflecting, would never have done anything so corkbrained. If he'd set out to rescue a girl, he would have done it properly. He would have known all about licences and the age of consent, and all that.

Only he hadn't been interested in rescuing her, had he, back then? He'd been rescuing Guy. From her.

Even now, when he talked about being tempted to kiss her, he made it sound as though doing so would be to sink to the depths of depravity in a way that appalled him. Which made her feel like a…worm, rather than being able to rejoice in what Godmama had achieved for her.

She wasn't going to let him, or any other man, rob her of anything else, she vowed, striding to her wardrobe and yanking it open. She would remember where her loyalties lay, which was with Godmama, who'd worked so hard to free her from the chains of shame Stepfather had clapped on her. And Rosalind, sweet, generous Rosalind, who'd offered to put aside her own ambition because she could see that the situation was making Cassy uncomfortable.

And she would show everyone that she was perfectly happy with her lot, by dressing in the pretty clothes that Rosalind had bought for her. And she would go to whatever event Godmama decreed, and dance and smile all the time so that *nobody* would be able to guess that he had the power to make her feel...

Nothing! She was *not* unhappy. She'd never been so happy in her life. Or at least if she wasn't, then she jolly well ought to be.

'I need,' she said later, at breakfast, 'to buy some trimmings for my bonnets. No, Rosalind...' she held up her hand the moment Rosalind took a breath '...I am not going to let you buy me half-a-dozen new ones. The ones I have can be made far prettier with the addition of some ribbons and silk flowers, and so forth.'

Rosalind pouted. 'Anyone would think my money isn't good enough for you.'

'Rosalind, no! That is not it! I just don't want to take advantage of your generosity. You have bought me so many dresses and things already. That new carriage dress is due to arrive any day, don't forget, and that scarlet velvet opera cloak which is a positive extravagance. And I...' She paused to gather herself for the confession she could not withhold any longer. 'I have ordered far more material than I need for my own use already. I was planning to send what was left over to my aunts at the end of the Season. So you see, I don't feel I can keep on taking from you...'

'Oh, girls,' said Godmama, raising her head from a letter she'd been perusing. 'I don't think we can go shopping this morning, much as I would love to see you get some new bonnets.'

Trimmings for bonnets. Not new bonnets, Cassy wanted to protest. Although there was little point since it sounded as though she was not going to get either.

'You see, I am expecting to receive rather a lot of callers this morning. Ladies who will be wanting to ensure you will be attending their events and explaining why it is that they seem to have forgotten, so far, to put your names on their guest lists.' She smiled at them. 'I cannot wait to see what excuses they come up with for snubbing you,' she said, her eyes alight with merriment.

Cassy exchanged an appalled glance with Rosalind, for it sounded like a perfectly ghastly way to spend the day.

'Do we really have to sit through that, Godmama? We really would enjoy going shopping much, much more.'

Godmama stared at her, a slice of toast halfway to her lips. 'I keep forgetting how squeamish you can be sometimes, darling. Oh, very well. As long as you take Hetty with you, and Gordon to carry your parcels. And my town coach, too, to lend you respectability, I can see no harm in it.'

'Thank you, Godmama,' she said, rising from her chair to give the kind-hearted lady a kiss on her perfumed cheek.

'Enjoy yourselves, girls,' said Godmama, smiling at them as they scurried away, leaving her to the remains of her breakfast.

'It seems ridiculous to have to drive the length of one street to reach the shops,' grumbled Cassy as they were waiting in the hall, a little later, for the carriage to be brought round from the mews. 'We could have walked there by now.'

'Are you mad?' Rosalind shook her head as Dawes opened the front door to reveal the shiny barouche standing at the foot of the front steps. 'When we drive through Town with the hood down, in a carriage with a ducal crest on the doors, everyone knows we are *some-body*. And anyway,' she said, digging Cassy in the ribs as a footman opened the aforementioned door and let down the steps, 'I know you have written home to tell your aunts about how grand it makes you feel.'

Cassy felt her cheeks heat. 'Yes, that's true,' she said as Gordon gave her his hand to help her climb in. 'But you know I was only funning about me puffing off my consequence by never walking anywhere and always having at least a maid,' she said, nodding at Hetty as she took her place facing them, 'and a footman in attendance. And warning them that they will have to employ a score of servants when I go home because I will probably have become so pampered that I shall faint away at the prospect of carrying my own shopping home the length of the High Street.'

Rosalind giggled, which lifted Cassy's spirits no end. Especially as they carried on joking and giggling over nothing much until the moment Godmama's carriage drew up outside the modiste the Duchess patronised.

Cassy and Rosalind exchanged a look. 'She wasn't listening when I said I only wanted trimmings, not new bonnets, was she? Or she'd have told them to drop us off outside Grafton House.'

'No, but now we are here,' said Rosalind, looking at the shopfront with longing, 'we might just as well go in and see how they are getting on with our orders. And see if they have any new patterns, or material in for us to look at.'

'Very well,' said Cassy, 'and then we can walk on to Grafton House and see about trimmings for my bonnets.'

Rosalind grinned as she hopped down from the carriage.

The girls spent the next half hour or so browsing happily, before setting out along Bond Street in the direction of Grafton Street.

'I shouldn't be a bit surprised,' said Rosalind, linking her arm through Cassy's, obliging Hetty to fall behind, 'if you couldn't get some artificial cherries to decorate one of your bonnets. Don't you think that would look a treat, with your scarlet opera cloak? Especially if you added some scarlet ribbons and an ostrich feather or two.'

Cassy flinched. 'Er...well, possibly just one ostrich feather. If it was a small one,' she said.

'Well, well,' said a female voice in a rather arch tone. 'If it isn't Miss Cassandra Furnival.'

Cassy looked up to see Miss Henley standing a few feet in front of her, arm in arm with a young lady who was a total stranger to her. A very expensively dressed young lady, Cassy noted with her professional eye.

'Miss Henley,' said Cassy, smiling and stepping forward. 'What a lovely surprise,' she said, feeling a flash of guilt for having forgotten all about her being in London as well, because she'd been so busy with her own concerns.

'I must say I was surprised, for a moment, to see you coming out of such a very exclusive establishment,' said Miss Henley, waving a hand at the door of the modiste's some yards behind them. 'Although I suppose you in the trade all know each other. And you will have been able to pick up all sorts of useful tips you can employ when you go home. Miss Furnival, you know,' said Miss Henley to her companion, who was gazing at Cassy and Rosalind with distinct reserve, 'is my dressmaker, at home in Market Gooding.'

'Really?' The girl's expression turned from reserved to downright disdainful. 'Then I am surprised at you acknowledging her.'

'Oh, Market Gooding is such a small place,' said Miss Henley, while Cassy sucked in a short, shocked breath. 'We are on friendly terms with *all* the tradespeople.'

'Yes, in Market Gooding that may very well do,' said the haughty young lady. 'But this is London. The same manners do not apply here.'

Miss Henley made a rueful face. 'You see how it is, Miss Furnival,' she said. 'You understand.' And with that, she turned and strolled off in the direction of Brook Street.

'What a cow,' Rosalind remarked, without any attempt to lower her voice. Though for once Cassy had no wish to chide her for her manners, since she'd only said what Cassy had been thinking.

And then, as they both turned to eye the two girls who were walking away with their noses in the air, Cassy noted that Godmama's coachman had used the time they'd spent in the shop to turn the carriage round. And that it was now facing in the very direction that Miss Henley and her top-lofty friend had gone. And all of a sudden Cassy could see *exactly* why people might want to drive about Town in a shiny, open carriage with ducal crests on the doors and a driver and footman in smart livery on the box at the front.

'Let's not bother with Grafton House,' said Cassy, nodding at the coach.

'No. Let's not,' said Rosalind, seeing exactly what Cassy had in mind. Both girls hitched up their skirts and ran to the carriage, clambering in with more haste than dignity, lest the two ladies who'd just given Cassy such a set down had time to go into a shop and miss the sight of them driving past with *their* noses in the air.

Nathaniel took the pouch of papers General Fewcott pushed across the desk and stood to take his leave.

'I will look into this and work out a solution within the week,' he vowed.

The General pursed his lips. 'You are not going to get distracted, I hope?'

'Distracted?'

'By that Furnival chit. I've been hearing some very…interesting rumours.'

'Oh?'

'Is that all you have to say? Oh?'

Well, what else was there to say? He wasn't going to admit that he had, to his shame, allowed the *Furnival chit* to distract him from his duties. Especially since he'd managed to steer clear of her ever since that last, disastrous night when he'd succumbed to the temptation to dance with her and very nearly to the temptation to kiss her. He had only tried to intervene, in the first place, for Issy's sake. But he was finding that the cost to his peace of mind was too great.

The General's mouth relaxed. Almost formed a smile.

'Totally understandable, of course. A man must have his…outlets. And I don't believe you have mounted a mistress since you began to work with me, have you?'

Take Miss Furnival as his mistress? She wouldn't have him now, after the way he'd treated her. And, dammit, he didn't *want* to take her as his mistress. He glowered at the General for putting the notion in his head.

'I fail to see, with the greatest respect, what business that is of yours. Sir.'

The General huffed out a laugh. 'None whatever. Only that…well, since clapping eyes on her myself, at Lady Twickenham's last night, I'm not a bit surprised.'

Lady Twickenham's? First he caught her dancing with the Duchess's son and now he learned that she was running tame in the house of her oldest married daughter.

'If I were ten years younger...' General Fewcott mused, with a rather wistful look in his rheumy eyes. 'Although,' he continued, with a frown, 'it is rather odd the way so many rumours are flying around concerning her. I mean, first of all there was...' He waved his hand as though batting at an invisible gnat. 'Though the Earl of Sydenham scotched that one by recognising her at the Bradburys' ball, so it must just have been one of those family rifts that blow up over nothing and die away just as inexplicably. But this latest one...' He shook his head. 'Preposterous! As if the Duchess of Theakstone would take a seamstress into her house and try to pass her off as her goddaughter. I know she's a pea goose, but not know her own goddaughter? Besides, can't be true, or Sydenham would never have acknowledged her.'

'Seamstress? Are you speaking of Miss Furnival?'

'Yes. The latest on dit,' said the General,

leaning forward and clasping his hands on the desk, 'is that some other chit is putting it about that she hales from the same town where Miss Furnival works in a shop. Claims she made half the gowns in her wardrobe.'

'No, there must have been some mistake.' Miss Furnival had, according to his sister, who'd had it from Lieutenant Gilbey's sister, been living in some style, on the money she'd wheedled out of the lad. 'People must have got her mixed up with that ginger friend of hers. She *does* come from trade…'

'Hmmph,' said the General. 'I don't suppose it makes any difference. She's still just as pretty. And probably…' he leaned further forward, with a leer '…more amenable to accepting a business proposition if the rumour is true and she's a working girl, what?'

'I have no intention of making her *any* sort of proposition,' he said, through gritted teeth. Not that it was any of the General's business what he did on his own time.

'No? Well, she probably won't accept one from you now, anyway. Not now she's got two extremely rich viscounts and an elderly marquess dangling after her.'

Two viscounts and a marquess? Who would give her the option of becoming either rich, or of high status? How the hell had she managed to get that far in the space of four days?

No, he knew how. She'd only have had to smile at them and they would have gone weak at the knees. His pulse began to thud in his temples. And even though he'd just sworn he had no intention of making her any kind of offer, the thought of her in some other man's arms, some other man's bed, left him feeling distinctly queasy.

'Which will make whoever is spreading those tales about her livid. In fact,' said the General, sitting back and sucking on his moustache, 'shouldn't wonder at it if that isn't what started the whole thing. Jealousy. Miss Furnival is trespassing on someone's matrimonial ambitions, so they've decided to put a spoke in her wheel by making up this faradiddle. It's the kind of warfare women wage, you know. Since they don't have...' he nodded meaningfully at the packet of documents he'd just handed over '...more *important* matters to occupy their time.'

'Sir,' he said, recognising the note of dismissal. Tucking the documents under his arm, he made for the door.

He supposed he must have marched along the usual corridors and crossed the familiar lobbies on his way out. But he didn't notice his surroundings until he was blinking at the brightness of the watery spring sunshine.

A seamstress? No. Impossible. Issy had said...

But the girl who'd come from her hometown had claimed...

And *that* girl must have known it would be easy enough to check up on her story...

The conclusion was obvious. Someone was lying. Deliberately.

Which was a vile thing to do, considering what the consequences could be. Such as, his conscience muttered grimly, having a powerful man threaten to expose her alleged crimes and drive her from polite society.

His stomach roiled.

Even if she deserved it...

No! Nobody deserved to have their reputation deliberately ripped to shreds. Nobody. No matter what they'd done.

And now he came to consider it, although there was no denying she'd run off with Gilbey, she'd been so young. He hadn't, at the time, thought she'd been guilty of more than being taken in by the Lieutenant. Because he'd seen the way she'd behaved at the assembly in the back room of the White Hart. She'd been shy of all the officers, except Lieutenant Gilbey, who she clearly knew already, as a friend of the family. When Nathaniel had followed her outside she'd accepted his reproof with a start of guilt, as though it hadn't occurred to her she ought not to move out of sight of her chaperon. And had gone back inside with him without making the slightest push to engage in any form of dalliance.

He'd held her image like the pure flame of a votive candle in his heart until the very day she'd turned up on the quayside, clutching Gilbey's arm. And even though that had snuffed out his own flickering, tentative hope, he hadn't seen anything of the seductress about her. She'd been wearing clothes that belonged on a schoolgirl and staring about with huge, frightened, bewildered eyes, as though she'd never dreamed such a big bad world existed outside her schoolroom. Which was clearly where she'd still belonged, not in the train of an army about to set out on campaign. Gilbey had been looking harassed, but also shamefaced. Which had convinced Nate that Gilbey had been the one to instigate that mad elopement. And all his anger, then, had been directed squarely at the lad.

It was only after he'd heard Issy's version of

events that he'd started questioning his judgement. It had made him go galloping into a confrontation with Miss Furnival, all guns blazing.

Even then, if Miss Furnival had bowed her head meekly, the way she'd done when he'd caught her outside in that stable yard, he would have acted exactly the way he'd done the first time round. He would have taken her aside, discreetly, and explained about his sister's concern. About how her return to society was upsetting Lady Agatha, who'd once been her friend. And then he would have made it possible for her to go back to where she belonged, quietly and with no fuss.

Only she hadn't acted meekly. She'd changed, utterly changed from the shy, timid schoolgirl who'd had to cling to Gilbey's arm because she was unable to stand on her own two feet. She'd defied him. And *laughed* while she did so. As if she hadn't a care in the world, when his own experiences had left him…

And he'd seen red, that was what he'd done. And all the anger and bitterness which had been simmering for years had spurred him to go charging into a headlong confrontation, practically yelling a full-blooded war cry.

Which made him no better than the nameless female who was starting rumours based on spite.

He wiped his hand across his face. It was shaking.

That was the trouble with letting feelings loose. They exploded in unexpected directions, like Congreve's rockets. He needed to get a grip. Suppress them. Kill them. Stamp on them.

And then, when he could be cool, and calm, and collected, he needed to find Miss Furnival and explain himself. The way he should have done from the start.

Chapter Eleven

Colonel Fairfax gave the correct password to the hostess, ran the gauntlet of the more ruthless of the matchmaking mamas who were waiting to ambush unmarried males and made it safely to the tea table. Though by then he wanted something much stronger than tea.

He took a deep breath and started numbering the buttons down the front of his waistcoat. Only a weak man, a man who couldn't deal with the reality of his life, would attempt to obliterate his nightmares by numbing his brains with strong drink. And he would never succumb to that type of weakness. He was *not* going to go down that road. He was not going to become one of those men who needed that kind of crutch to get through their days. The kind of man who made a fool of himself in public because he'd addled his mind, and therefore his self-control, with strong drink. He would take just the one glass of wine. A glass which he did not need, but which gave him something to do with his hands and would help him to blend in.

Once the footman in his hostess's livery had poured it, he stood with the full glass in his hand, surveying the assembled guests.

It wasn't long before he spotted her. Standing at the edge of the dance floor, as she'd been doing the first time he'd seen her this Season. Although this time, she'd attracted a court of the type of men the General had warned him about. Respectable, titled, wealthy men on the lookout for a wife.

And he could hardly blame them for considering her. She stood out among the insipid debutantes on offer, in a gown of cream silk with splashes of scarlet here and there. It was not the least bit daring, yet something about the cut of the bodice made a man want to bury his face in all that luscious creamy flesh it framed.

He put the glass down, the wine untasted. Even one sip would be too much. He was barely in control of his wayward thoughts just through looking at her. He was *not* going to give her any further advantage in this encounter. He'd come out badly on every other occasion they'd clashed.

No. Not every other occasion. The first time he'd met her he'd been courteous and in full command of the situation.

But that had been before Corunna. Before...

His hand went to the buttons of his waistcoat again, checking they were all fastened tight, before setting out round the edge of the dance floor, to where she was standing. Waiting for him. Oh, she was still pretending to listen to the simpleton who was ladling out the compliments, but she'd been aware the very moment he entered the room. Probably the house. There was that invisible silken cord connecting them again. He was absolutely certain that she could feel its pull, too, though he could not have explained to anyone how he knew. He just did.

'Good evening,' he said, cutting right through the current spate of flattery one of her court was spouting.

'Why, Colonel Fairfax,' said Miss Furnival, batting her eyelashes as she turned to look at him over her shoulder. Where had she learned that trick? She'd never employed it before. Was she doing it for his benefit, or to try to make her other admirers jealous? 'How delightful to see you.'

'Is it?' The moment he'd barked the words he reprimanded himself. Hadn't he vowed that, tonight, he was not going to lose control of his temper? How could he have been on the edge of doing so the minute he got within speaking distance of her? Or was it because he could smell her perfume? Or because now that she'd turned round to face him, all that tempting, creamy skin was in touching distance?

'That is,' he corrected himself, 'it is delightful to see you, too. Looking so...' He couldn't help letting his eyes trace the edge of her neckline which was embroidered with a red motif. It made him think of the luscious flavour of sun-ripened wild strawberries. With cream. His mouth watered as he imagined sinking his teeth into...

'Lost for words, Colonel?' She shook her head at him. As though she knew exactly what he'd been thinking.

'I am a man of action, not words,' he said, taking her arm and propelling her out of the midst of her court, to a chorus of complaints.

'Really, Colonel,' she said.

'If you can convince me that you'd rather stand there listening to that bunch of libertines proposition you than take a walk with me, then I will gladly return you to them.'

She pulled her lips together. 'What makes

you think anyone has been making the kind of propositions you so clearly think I deserve?'

'For one thing, you have left them all behind to take a circuit of the ballroom with me, when so far I have done nothing but berate you. It is almost as if you would rather face that than listen to any more of what they have been dishing out.'

'If that is true, then it must contradict your opinion of me,' she pointed out. 'Surely, those kinds of propositions are the very thing I came to London to receive?'

Her statement gave him an odd feeling. Because it was true. If she was the kind of woman who'd come to Town to get her claws into yet another victim, she *should* be revelling in all the attention she was getting now. Yet she'd turned her back on it the moment he'd offered her the chance to leave them all behind.

Another inconsistency between what he'd thought he'd known and what Issy claimed about her. Though now was not the time to dwell on that.

'I did not come here tonight to resume hostilities,' he reminded himself, as well as making her aware of the fact.

'Really?' She looked up at him through narrowed eyes.

'No.' He sighed. 'I had intended to explain why I feel obliged to…make amends…for…'

'Make amends?' She shot him a look of incredulity, swiftly followed by one of suspicion. 'What, *precisely*, do you think you need to make amends for?'

'For the rumours which are circulating about you. For, possibly, making you the butt of gossip, by the way I have singled you out. There may be other reasons why fresh rumours have started to circulate about you. It is possible that someone simply has matrimonial designs on one of those fellows circling round you. And whatever you may have done in the past, you don't deserve to suffer from this kind of sneaky, underhanded campaign to blacken your name.'

'I…' She looked up at him in a bewildered fashion. 'I don't understand why you are suddenly so concerned with my reputation, now, when you have had no hesitation in flinging it in my face at every opportunity…'

'It was not well done of me,' he admitted. It had been shocking, the way he'd lost all self-control, merely because she'd been laughing. He hadn't been able to understand how she could have had such an effect on him. Could still not understand it. Although he hadn't exactly spent a lot of time attempting to work it out. Instead he'd pushed it aside, the way he'd pushed so many other distasteful things aside. Concentrated his mind on things he could actually do something about...

Which brought him back to the reason he'd sought her out tonight.

'But it is one thing, confronting you, privately, about things I know have happened—' and there was no denying the fact that she had attempted to elope with Gilbey, even if he wasn't totally sure about the rest of it any longer '—quite another to spread false tales about you behind your back. That kind of cowardly attack sickens me.'

She made a derisive sound halfway between a snort and a laugh. 'Look, Colonel Fairfax, I don't know what you hope to achieve by trying to persuade me you hate the effect that rumours may have upon me, but let me tell you, I am well used to being the butt of gossip. And I learned long ago that there is nothing I can do, or say, to make people change their opinion of me. So I just have to ignore it. Apart from taking note of what it says about the person who is spreading it. My true friends,' she said, giving him a pointed look, 'won't listen to it. And as for everyone else...' she tossed her head '...you may think what you like. I,' she said with emphasis, 'do not care.'

'That's as may be. And while your strength of character is, in this instance, an admirable quality...' And it was. And now he could see just how the years had altered her from that timid schoolgirl into the woman who stood her ground as she related, in just a couple of sentences, what she'd had to endure. 'Nevertheless, I shall do what I can to counter the latest rumours, by telling everyone I can that there is absolutely no truth in the rumours about you being merely a seamstress. Because if people start to believe that, they might go on to assume you are attempting to invade society under a false guise and those eager swains who were paying you such fulsome compliments to your sparkling eyes would instead start turning on you like ravening wolves round a shorn lamb. They'd gobble you up, Miss Furnival,' he said, coming to a halt by some open terrace doors.

'Oh, no, they wouldn't,' she said bitterly. 'I have had to put up with that sort of attention ever since...' She waved her hand in a way he interpreted as referring to her unsuccessful elopement.

And yet she hadn't taken up any of those offers. Which meant...well, he wasn't sure what it said about her, except that it was all of a piece with the way she'd leapt at the chance to escape the suitors who'd been surrounding her, just now.

'Besides, if you went around denying I am a seamstress you would be making a fool of yourself, which is the last thing I want.' She closed her mouth, and flushed, as though she'd admitted something she didn't want him to know.

'But—'

'But nothing,' she said firmly. '*Those* rumours, at least, are not untrue. I am very much a seamstress, or at least, that is how I was earning my living when Godmama—' She cut herself off, once more, as though regretting admitting so much.

Which of course roused his curiosity.

'Explain,' he said.

'Why should I?'

Because if she didn't, he'd push her out through those terrace doors, drag her into some dark corner and kiss the truth out of her defiant little mouth.

No, he wouldn't, though. That would be giving in to the kind of behaviour he most deplored.

'Indeed, why should you? You owe me nothing. And given the way I hounded you when you first came to London…' He drew her away from the terrace doors, back in the direction of the people thronging the ballroom. It was high time he started employing his brain, rather than letting his body do all the thinking for him. 'I suppose,' he mused, 'you must have run through the money Lieutenant Gilbey left you and found yourself in reduced circumstances.'

'No, I have not run through it. Not that you have any right to enquire into my financial circumstances. Really,' she said with exasperation, 'I don't know why I'm telling you this much.'

'But if you still have his money at your disposal,' he mused aloud, 'then I don't see why you could possibly have been working as a seamstress. Unless…was it a ploy to get the Duchess to feel sorry for you, so that she would bring you to Town where you could have the Season your family never gave you?'

'It was nothing of the sort,' she said, coming to a halt and rounding on him. 'For heaven's sake, use your head!'

That remark came so close to what he'd just been thinking he needed to do that it had about the same effect as if she'd slapped him.

'I took you for an intelligent man,' she continued, scornfully. 'So why have you overlooked so many pertinent facts? Hmm? Such as, for instance, the fact that Guy was only a younger son, who needed to go into the army, or find some other career, because he had no fortune of his own.' Her face was flushed with indignation, her greeny-brown eyes sparking with anger. He shouldn't have noticed, but the way she was breathing was making her bosom tremble as it rose and fell, rose and fell...

'Just how much money do you think a boy in those circumstances could possibly have bequeathed me?'

He tore his eyes from the sight he had no business enjoying quite so much and bent his mind to what she'd just said.

'How much?' He repeated what she'd just said to pull his mind back to the topic they were discussing and away from where it had been straying. But she took it as a question.

'Eight hundred and thirty-two pounds, that's how much,' she said, reminding him they'd been talking about money. 'Which my aunt's man of business invested for me. I draw the interest on a quarterly basis. Do you wish to know exactly how much *that* amounts to, if you must keep dwelling on pounds, shilling and pence?'

'No,' he said, appalled. If she was telling the

truth, and he could not imagine she could have plucked such a precise figure out of thin air at such short notice, then it made perfect sense for her to supplement it by working with her needle.

Only…if she *was* telling the truth, which supported what that other girl had spread about her, it was two to one against what his sister had told him. A cold fist formed in his stomach. Why would she have lied to him? Unless…she had some personal grudge against Miss Furnival? Was that it? Had she deliberately primed him with a lot of black lies so that she could use him as a weapon against an innocent woman?

No, no…he desperately scrambled for some other explanation. One that would exonerate his sister from blame. Had she, perhaps, been misinformed herself?

'I am not ashamed of earning my living by doing honest work,' Miss Furnival was saying, with a militant tilt to her chin. 'And I never asked Godmama for a Season in London. She took me completely by surprise when she came to me,' she ground on, while his conscience withered and twisted under the suspicions that were starting to form. 'And the reason I accepted her invitation to come to Town was because she made it sound as if it would be fun. Fun!' She looked round the ballroom in a haunted fashion. 'If I had not promised to—' Once again, she pulled up before telling him exactly what she'd been thinking and squared her shoulders. 'You are not going to hound me out of Town. And nor is anyone else. So what if people suddenly decide I'm an impostor, just because I've had to work for my living for the last six years? So what if they do think that it could blight my chances of making a so-called brilliant marriage?' Her lips curled in scorn. 'I didn't come to London in search of a husband in the first place. Now, if you would not mind returning me to my godmother's side, I believe this conversation is at an end.'

Yes, he supposed it was. Because he could not press on with it, with her, until he'd discovered just why his sister had told him that Miss Furnival had swindled Lieutenant Gilbey's family out of a fortune they claimed should have gone to them. And since she wouldn't have been working as a seamstress if Gilbey *had* left her a fortune, he was going to have to ask Issy some very searching questions. Because eight hundred and thirty-two pounds was nobody's idea of a fortune.

Chapter Twelve

'Well,' said Cassy, the moment she, Godmama, Rosalind and Captain Bucknell got into Godmama's coach to go home. 'Not only have I got Colonel Fairfax trying to ruin my enjoyment of the Season, but now I find that someone has been so busy spreading the story about how I've had to earn my living over the last few years that he thinks people will assume I'm an impostor and that nobody would ever want to marry me!'

Oh, he hadn't said it outright. It had been what he believed, though. Otherwise why would he have assumed someone had started rumours to *spoil her matrimonial ambitions*?

Rosalind turned to look at her with a puzzled frown. 'But you've got a handful of titled men dangling after you now…'

'Which could just mean they have not found out yet,' said Godmama, thoughtfully.

'But I thought,' said Rosalind, 'that now her uncle has acknowledged her...'

'Yes, but that is all he has done,' said Godmama ruefully. 'He has not invited her to his home, let alone got his Countess to call upon us. So it is all still a bit...tenuous, given that, you know, she *did* elope with a soldier, out of the schoolroom, and *has* had to work in a menial position for some years.'

'Are you telling me,' said Rosalind, 'that you got Cassy to town, knowing that her reputation was so bad you might never be able to mend it?'

'Oh, dear me, no,' said Godmama. 'I thought I could easily deal with a scandal that happened *that* long ago—'

'Well, it looks as if you were wrong,' said Rosalind, interrupting very rudely. 'And what is more, it sounds to me as though you deliberately duped Papa into parting with his money so you could fund a Season for *her*,' she said, eyeing Cassy with resentment. 'Since she's the one they're all interested in. There was never any chance of getting me married to a title, was there?'

'No, no, it is not as bad as that,' said Godmama, twining her fingers together in her lap. 'I mean, I managed to fire off both my daughters very successfully, without a penny to back them, so I thought if I did have a lot of money at my disposal I was bound to do as well, even for someone like…'

'Someone like me, were you going to say?' Rosalind was quivering with what looked to Cassy like the beginnings of serious temper. Captain Bucknell appeared to think so, too, because he started sliding deeper into his corner. 'And you didn't deny you were using Papa's money to try to restore Cassy's reputation, did you?'

'Well, no,' Godmama admitted. 'But then I really didn't think of that to start with. You know that I only wanted to find some way of preventing my stepson from forcing me to return to Theakstone Court. And the only success I have ever had was seeing my daughters marry well, in spite of all the disadvantages I had to work against. So I thought I could do the same for another girl. Truly, Rosalind,' she said, stretching out her hands again, 'it was only once your papa and I reached our little agreement that I saw we needed a pretext as to why I was launching you, without it looking as though I was doing it just for the money. And *that* was when I thought of bringing Cassy into it.'

'I don't believe you,' said Rosalind, making Cassy gasp and Captain Bucknell wince. 'I think this is a deliberate swindle,' she declared as the coach came to a halt outside the mansion in Grosvenor Square. 'You are forever trying to gammon people, then laughing at them behind their back once you've done it. If it wasn't for Cassy trying to rein you in, you wouldn't scruple to tell barefaced lies!'

'Well, really,' said Godmama. 'How rude!'

'And how could you think she would deliberately set out to swindle you?' said Cassy, as the coach came to a halt.

'It's all very well for you,' said Rosalind to Cassy, as Captain Bucknell, who'd been looking increasingly uncomfortable as the argument heated up, shot out of the carriage like a bankrupt pursued by creditors. 'You're one of them, even if you have got a tarnished reputation. And I'm going to write to Papa tonight,' Rosalind ploughed on, shooting Cassy as well as Godmama a venomous look as she gathered her skirts. 'He will know how to deal with the likes of you,' she snarled over her shoulder as she got out.

'Oh, dear,' said Godmama as Captain Bucknell leaned back in to offer her his hand to help her alight. 'Whatever shall I do if she writes to her papa and the man demands his money back? I have spent most of it. At least, I handed a lot over to Dawes to settle my outstanding debts and deal with the staff wages,' she twittered as they all began to mount the steps to the front door.

'He can demand all he likes,' said the Captain with an amused expression, 'but he cannot get back what's gone, can he? And what will he do? Sue you through the courts?'

Godmama let out a little shriek. 'No! I mean, yes! That is exactly the sort of vulgar thing a man like that would do! Oh, Bertram,' she said turning to him and laying both hands on his chest. 'What am I to do?'

He squared his shoulders. 'This is my fault, in part, I know that. So I will—'

'No, no, it isn't. You have been a rock…'

'But if it wasn't for your refusal to give me up, my angel, your stepson would never have started waging war on you, would he? Don't think I don't know it.'

Cassy, who'd grown increasingly suspicious of Captain Bucknell ever since she'd heard him tiptoeing along the bedroom corridor instead of going out the front door, began to think that he could not be all bad if he could look at Godmama that way, as though he'd take on the world to keep her safe. If a man looked at her like that, she supposed she might be tempted to defy the world to keep him in her life, too.

'You just leave that girl to me,' he said.

'But what can you do?'

'Well, for one thing, I can advise you to leave her be, tonight. Let her cool down.'

'But she might write to her papa...'

'So what if she does? How is she going to get a letter out of the house without involving one of your staff, who will do nothing without your say-so?'

'That's true,' said Godmama with admiration.

Cassy's opinion of the Captain promptly did another about-face. Was he really suggesting that they denied a guest the right to contact her relatives when she was in distress? And could Godmama not see how unethical that was?

No. As Rosalind had pointed out, and as Cassy knew only too well, Godmama never did have a very firm grasp on the principles of right and wrong.

'And tomorrow,' said Captain Bucknell, 'I will call round and take the girl out. To somewhere like Astley's and Gunter's for ices. Turn her up sweet.'

'Yes,' said Godmama. 'If anyone can do it, you can.'

'While you,' he said, tapping her on the nose, 'will go round all the society tabbies, explaining about Miss Furnival's family connections.'

'Oh, they know all about that!'

'Well, then, you must think of something else to salvage the situation. And you,' he said, turning to Cassy, 'you could always try to see what you can do on the girl, overnight. She might listen to an appeal to her heartstrings, if you can fashion one.'

She would do no such thing. Rosalind had every right to feel duped. Nothing about the Season was what she'd been led to believe it would be.

However, this was no time to start an argument with him. Not with Godmama gazing up at him as though he was the fount of all wisdom and the source of all her happiness.

'I will go and talk to her,' she muttered, heading for the stairs. Though she had no intention of making *an appeal to her heartstrings*, in the way Captain Bucknell meant. Because she felt that Rosalind had every right to be angry. For the men from whom Colonel Fairfax had unwittingly rescued her had all of them snubbed Rosalind, which was one of the things that had made her dislike them.

They'd also made her cringe as they paid her increasingly extravagant compliments, which were more to do with besting each other than impressing her. And they'd all put her in mind of her stepfather, who could put on a caressing manner when it suited him. The Colonel, for all his rudeness and prejudice against her, had been like a gust of fresh air, blasting away all the cloying falseness that had been practically choking her.

The truth, however hard, was always better than make-believe.

And so she would tell Rosalind the full truth, about how she'd been drawn in to Godmama's schemes. Surely Rosalind would understand how she'd felt when she'd seen all those gowns she'd worked so hard on drive past her cottage in Miss Henley's coach? Especially now that she'd met Miss Henley and seen what she was like? And how, when Godmama had turned up, not ten minutes after she'd wished she could go to London, and dance at balls, and all the rest of it, the temptation to go along with her plans had been too great to resist?

She could also remind Rosalind that the Season hadn't turned out the way Cassy had hoped, either. She certainly hadn't bargained for the Colonel and his hostility.

She sighed as she trudged up the stairs. Rosalind was so angry it was unlikely she'd be in a mood to listen to anything she had to say. She probably wouldn't even let her in her room. But at least Cassy would have tried.

Chapter Thirteen

Nathaniel pushed aside the papers that General Fewcott had given him the day before. He'd promised himself that he would attend to them before he investigated the matter of Miss Furnival's fortune, or lack thereof. But it was useless. The columns of figures wouldn't add up, no matter how many times he started again. Not when the amount of eight hundred and thirty-two pounds kept on going round and round in his head.

Could his sister really have believed such a sum amounted to a fortune? Or could her friend, Agatha, who was Lieutenant Gilbey's sister, have exaggerated the importance of it? The family *could* have resented Lieutenant Gilbey having made *any* sort of bequest to Miss Furnival, he supposed. Although surely, that money had been Gilbey's to do with as he saw fit?

Or had Miss Furnival told him a barefaced lie?

But if she had, then why had she been working as a seamstress? Or was that a lie to make him feel sorry for her? But then where had the rumour started? Unless she'd started it herself...

But why would she do such a thing? What did she have to gain?

He flung his pen aside with irritation and got to his feet so swiftly that his chair toppled over backwards.

As he reached the study door, it swung open, revealing the startled features of his butler.

'Is there something amiss, sir? I thought I heard...'

'I overset the chair, that is all, Dasset. In my haste. I am...' He frowned. Just when had he ever felt the need to explain his movements, or the speed at which he made them, to his staff?

'My hat and coat, Dasset,' he barked.

'Yes, my lord,' said the butler, snapping his fingers for a footman to run and perform the errand. 'And might I enquire as to whether you will be returning for dinner?'

Nathaniel glanced at the window to see that the sun was already on the wane. He must have been sitting in his study, accomplishing precisely nothing, for almost a whole day. By this time, his sister would be...well, he wasn't sure exactly how his sister filled her days. But many people would be parading about the park soon, he supposed. If he was quick, he might catch her before she went out. And if he could compel her to speak concisely, he would be back well before it was time to dine.

Concisely? Isabella?

'Probably,' he grunted. 'If my business goes smoothly.'

'Very good, sir,' said Dasset, helping him into the coat which the footman handed him before handing him his hat.

In less than fifteen minutes he was knocking on his sister's front door.

'Lady Fritwell,' her butler informed Nathaniel with a suitable expression of regret, 'is on the point of going out. But I shall enquire if she has time to receive you before doing so.'

It crossed Nathaniel's mind to simply march into whatever room his sister was in, preparing to go out, and demand answers.

Which stunned him. When had he lost his ability to remain detached from the kind of issues which preoccupied his mind so much, of late, that he couldn't even tot up a few columns of figures? Let alone consider storming the boudoir of a married lady to shake some answers out of her. Even if that married lady was his sister, whose pigtails he'd pulled when he'd been a lad?

He stalked back and forth in the hall as he awaited his sister's decision, half wishing there was a stool lying about so that he could kick it out of his way.

Perhaps he'd been spending too much time at desk work, lately. Perhaps he'd built up a store of energy that needed release in a bout of stool-kicking. He should visit a boxing saloon more often. Or a fencing academy. If he'd got to the stage where...

'Nate! How lovely to see you,' cooed his sister from the top of the stairs. 'Do come up. I am, as you can see, in the midst of titivating,' she said, waving her hand at her outfit as though he would see exactly what she meant by the word. 'But I am sure you won't delay me by more than a minute or two, will you?'

He was not in the habit of wasting more than ten upon his sister, on the few occasions he had paid duty calls to her house since she'd married Fritwell, so he supposed he could see why she might think this time would be no different. And he wasn't about to disabuse her of her assumption, not if it meant she would grant him the interview he sought.

'And I am sure,' she said as he began to mount the stairs, 'that you must have something very important to tell me, if you are visiting at such an hour.' Her eyes were gleaming with curiosity. But she did not look at all alarmed by his impromptu visit. Nor the slightest bit guilty.

What, he wondered as he reached the landing and she leaned forward to kiss him fondly on one cheek, did she think he might have come to tell her that would put such a beaming smile on her face?

He waited until they'd reached the sanctuary of her sitting room before saying anything.

'I have come to ask you for some information,' he said.

'Oh, yes?' Isabella folded her hands in her lap, though the smile on her face did not dim. On the contrary, it took on a cat-like quality. But then there was nothing his sister liked more than gossip. And this was the first time he'd actually asked her to tell him what she knew, rather than informing her he didn't care for tittle-tattle.

'It concerns Miss Furnival.'

'I rather thought it might,' she said, primming up her lips as though trying not to laugh.

'Yes. Some weeks ago you came to me with

some tale about her wheedling a fortune out of the family of Lieutenant Gilbey and urging me to *do something* about her. Something to the effect of stopping her before she got some other poor man into her clutches. You told me that your friend Lady Agatha was so cut up about her brother's fate that she could not face staying in Town in case, and I think I am quoting you accurately, she came face to face with the *designing baggage* who'd cast her spell on her poor deluded brother.'

Isabella shifted slightly. Her fingers, he noted, were no longer lying lax in her lap, but had twined into a sort of knot. 'Yes, that is correct. What of it?'

'Do you happen to know exactly how much Lieutenant Gilbey bequeathed Miss Furnival, in the event of his death before he was able to marry her?'

Isabella spread her hands wide. 'I am sure it must have been an awful lot, for Agatha to have carried on the way she did…'

'Are you?' He stared directly into her eyes, which slid away from his.

Guilty!

'Did you never wonder,' he said, slowly and with a hint of menace, 'how Lieutenant Gilbey came to be in possession of such a large amount of money that the prospect of losing it caused his family so much distress? Or if, since he had it, he chose to go into the army, as though he needed to earn his living?'

Isabella pouted. 'We didn't go into details, it's true...'

'I should like to give you the benefit of the doubt, Issy. I should like to believe that your friend lied to you, and put you up to this, for some reason of her own. However...' he got to his feet '...I cannot believe that, being so close to Agatha as you've been over the years, you did not have a pretty good idea of exactly how her younger brother was circumstanced.' She lowered her head. Picked a tiny piece of fluff from her sleeve and flicked it to the floor. Which evasive action removed all further doubt from his mind.

'So all that remains to learn is, why did you lie to me? What did you hope to gain? And I want the truth this time. Not some made-up tale about the family losing a fortune, or Miss Furnival being a grasping witch. Because I have it on good authority that she has been obliged to make her living as a seamstress, these last few years. And if she was the kind of creature you made her out to be and she'd managed to work her way through this vast fortune you claim she had, she would have been in Town long since, trying to sell her wares to the highest bidder.' As the words came out of his mouth, he realised something. She had a good deal of pride, did Miss Furnival. So much pride that she would rather work with her own hands at some honest trade than sell herself to a man. No wonder she'd been so indignant when he'd accused her of doing precisely that!

'So tell me, Isabella…' he leaned over her, bracing one hand on the arm of her chair '…what possessed you to come to me, with tears in your eyes, and beg me to destroy a woman who has never done you any harm?'

'Destroy her? No… I never meant that. I just…' She looked up into his face, with tears in her eyes. And then, to his utter shock, she reached up and stroked his cheek. 'I couldn't bear it any longer.'

He flinched away. She let the hand drop to her lap.

'Bear what?'

'The way you were. Ever since you've come back from the war you've been…' She waved both hands as though trying to grasp the right words. 'Like a dead man, walking. You've always been a touch serious, about some things, but you used to enjoy life, too. At first, we just thought we needed to give you time. That you'd recover from whatever it was that had made you go…' She made the vague gesture again. But she didn't need words to tell him what she meant. He knew exactly what she meant.

He was numb. He'd had to numb himself, or he would have cracked wide open under the pressure of all the things that had been churning around inside him, after Corunna.

'At least you weren't drinking yourself into an early grave,' Issy continued, 'like some men who came back from that dreadful campaign that Moore botched so badly. So we waited…'

'Who? Who is this *we* you keep talking about?' Issy had frequently irritated him in the past, but he'd never have believed she could stoop to the level of discussing him with her friends as though he was some…cripple who needed their sympathy.

'Bonnie and Dody and I.'

His sisters. He heaved a sigh of relief.

'And then later Aunt Charlotte, and Aunt Susan, and Aunt Meredith.'

'Good God.' He could imagine them all sitting about, like some coven, pulling his reputation to shreds over the teacups as though he were some tender lamb shank.

'And we all agreed that we had to take drastic action. Because,' she said, lifting her chin defiantly, 'you showed no signs of improving. You turned down every invitation you ever got to go anywhere. The only time anyone saw you go out was to the War Office. Or to some vile manufactory, or warehouse, or something equally tedious. And instead of showing any signs of healing, you're, well, we think you've been getting steadily worse. More...' She made a cutting motion with her hand. 'The crisis for us came when you stopped even visiting Cranbourne.'

'I can run my estate perfectly well from London,' he retorted. 'There is no need for me to keep on wasting time idling about down there when Greaves has everything in hand. But I do need to be here to make sure the army gets the funds and the supplies it needs. Wellington needs allies here, at the seat of government, to back him—'

'It's all very well,' she interrupted, 'saying Greaves has everything in hand, but he's only your steward. What about all the other estates you will inherit when Uncle George dies? What if you should die before you have an heir? And Cousin Sebastian steps into your shoes? Never mind what Greaves can do about Cranbourne, nobody will be able to stop Sebastian gambling it all away and leaving your tenants *starving*.'

That had the ring of Aunt Meredith about it. She was forever telling him to remember that he would one day step into his uncle's shoes, and become the next Earl of Crashaw. Or she had done until he'd given Dasset strict instructions to deny her admittance to his house. Which had been all the more reason for avoiding society gatherings where he was in danger of running into her.

'It is your responsibility, Nate,' Issy insisted. 'Your duty to marry and provide an heir to run things after you've gone.'

'I know that,' he said impatiently. As if he could ever forget, with the trio of aunts continually plaguing him to think of that duty. Not that he had any intention of shirking it. When the time came, of course he would marry and get on with the task of filling his nursery. He was just too busy to consider it yet.

'But how are you ever going to meet someone to marry if you won't take part in the Season? Suitable brides don't just fall into your lap!'

No, but then taking part in a Season wasn't exactly his idea of a sensible way to pick out a bride, either. A man was allowed a few fleeting, chaperoned meetings with girls who said all the right things so that he'd have no idea what she was really like until it was too late to do anything about it. Besides, he hated dancing.

Not when your partner is Miss Furnival, a wicked little voice reminded him. *You enjoyed it then, right enough. So much that you did it twice.*

'I fully intend to do my duty by the estate and the family, and marry and produce heirs,' he said. 'At a time of my choosing. Not at the bidding of you, or my aunts, or anyone else.'

She gave him a scornful look. 'And just when will that time be?'

'Once the army is on a better footing...'

'Oh, pish! The army is never going to be anything other than an immense muddle.'

'And just how have you deduced that?'

'You've written to me about your campaigns and I read the newspaper.'

He raised one eyebrow. Her cheeks flushed.

'Oh, very well. Fritwell reads the newspapers and tells me all about whatever he thinks I ought to know,' she amended. 'Which is always anything to do with your old regiment, or any campaign he thinks you have dealings with, or any speeches in Parliament about the horrid war,' she said with a moue of disgust.

'And we all think that until Napoleon is utterly trounced, you will always be able to claim you are too busy with army affairs to see to the equally important task of finding a wife.'

He considered her statement. 'You are correct. I shan't. After that…'

'And what happens if nobody *ever* defeats him? Are you going to continue to pour all your effort into equipping the army to resist him until you are so old and gouty you have to have half-a-dozen footmen carting you about in a chair? How do you hope to attract a wife then? Or get heirs by her?'

'It won't come to that,' he said irritably. 'Besides, what has this got to do with your campaign against Miss Furnival?'

'I have just been telling you. It isn't about Miss Furnival at all. It's about *you*. About making you get into the ballrooms while London is full of eligible young ladies.'

'By telling all those lies about a poor defenceless female? Have you no compassion?'

'Not when it comes to your happiness and the future of Cranbourne, no,' she said defiantly. 'Besides, we had to come up with something that would shock you out of your hermitry.'

'Hermitry? That is not even a real word!'

'It's real enough to describe the state you've been living in,' she said with a sniff. 'And because you are so obsessed with the army, and your fellow officers, and the men, and all that, we thought it would be the thing most likely to do it. An appeal to your duty to a fallen officer. We asked Agatha, naturally, if we could make use of her poor brother's name, in case she had any objections…'

'So it wasn't her idea? The family weren't baying for Miss Furnival's blood?'

'Oh, no, on the contrary, they all feel a bit… responsible for the way Guy sort of ruined her…'

'*Sort of* ruined her?' She'd lost her home and her good name. She'd had to work as a seamstress for six years. 'No,' he said, shutting his eyes for a moment as Issy took a breath to explain. 'Never mind that, for now. What I want to know is why did Lady Agatha leave Town, if not for the reason you stated?'

'Because she is increasing and has been rather unwell, and her doctor thought she might do better in the country than racketing about to balls and parties and the like.'

He got a strange, spinning sensation in his head as he considered the lengths to which Issy had gone to further her cause. And it occurred to him that this was precisely why he'd been able to give credence to her accusations regarding Miss Furnival. All his life, he'd watched the women in his family getting their own way by adopting stratagems of this sort so sneakily that his male relatives rarely realised what they'd been about. So it had seemed perfectly feasible for Miss Furnival to behave that way. Even without the benefit of a single, solitary scrap of hard evidence.

But it had been just another one of Issy's ploys to get him to behave the way she thought he should. Why hadn't he been more cautious? How on earth could he, knowing exactly what Issy was like, have fallen for her trap? Because she'd baited it so cleverly, he answered himself on a flash of insight. She'd not only tweaked at his sense of duty to his former comrades, but had also appealed to a part of him upon which she'd always been able to rely. When she'd been a girl, he'd never turned her away when she'd come to him with a problem, be it a broken doll, or a spoiled piece of schoolwork. And those few weeks ago she'd treated him the same—as though she considered him her all-powerful big brother who could do anything he set his mind to. Even unto making inconvenient females give up their ambitions and flee from London. So that he'd not just fallen into her trap, he'd positively *leapt* into it, pursuing Miss Furnival like a hound who'd caught the scent of a fox.

Though he couldn't recall the face of any of the young ladies that might have been present on any of those occasions whom Issy would consider eligible. He'd been too focused on Miss Furnival. Miss Furnival laughing. Miss Furnival defying him.

Miss Furnival staring at his mouth after he'd threatened to kiss her, as though it wasn't a threat at all, but a promise. He gave a silent groan. He had never wanted any woman the way he wanted Miss Furnival. Was that another reason Issy had used her to bait the trap? Had she somehow known?

He supposed it made no difference. Not now that he'd treated her so unfairly. She must despise him for a fool, if not a bully. Though she couldn't despise him any more than he despised himself right now, for falling for Issy's ploy.

'You admit,' he said, 'that you don't care what becomes of her? That, in effect, you deliberately sacrificed her to your cause? That you trailed her in my path the way a huntsman would drag a dead fox behind his horse, to get the hounds slavering for blood?'

'It's not as bad as that. It isn't as if she's defenceless. She is with the Duchess of Theakstone. Besides...'

'Besides what?'

'Well, it worked, didn't it?' She smiled. A triumphant sort of smile. 'Look at you. So... angry...'

'You think making me angry is some kind of victory?' That anger had caused him to humiliate himself, time and time again, in Miss Furnival's eyes.

'Yes. Because it shows you still have feelings. That you are not dead inside. That you can come back to us. Be like you were before.'

He could never be the same as he'd been before. For one thing, he never used to feel so angry that he wished for stools to kick. Or so disgusted by the behaviour of his female relatives that he was ashamed to be related to them. Ashamed of the ease with which they'd deceived him and the way he'd subsequently behaved.

'You sicken me,' he grated, before turning and storming out of the room. Out of the house and into the street.

Chapter Fourteen

Nathaniel couldn't decide who he was angriest with—Issy, or himself.

Issy, at least, had the excuse that she was acting from concern for him and what she perceived as his dereliction of duty to the family name.

But what excuse did he have? He knew what Issy was like. He'd had a feeling that there was something decidedly smoky about the tale she'd spun about Miss Furnival. Yet what had he done? Instead of discreetly investigating the matter, to find out how much truth there was in it, he'd gone storming into that ballroom and accosted Miss Furnival as though she was guilty of committing every single sin of which Issy had accused her.

And to think, he groaned, she'd smiled so warmly when she'd first seen him, as though she was really pleased to see him again.

It could have been the start of...

No! No, it couldn't have been the start of *any*thing. He'd ruined her chances of happiness with Gilbey, or *his* chances of happiness with *her*, whichever way you cared to look at it. He didn't deserve a chance with her, not under any circumstances.

It served him right, the way it had all turned out. He'd wiped the welcoming smile from her face and turned her into an adversary with a couple of blistering insults.

She'd never smiled at him that way again. Whenever he'd approached her after that she'd braced herself, expecting the worst. And regarded him with defiance, or mockery, or scorn.

Which he deserved. Completely.

Yet he couldn't help noticing that every time they'd met she'd looked more beautiful than the last. It wasn't his imagination. She'd definitely started wearing clothing that suited her better, in some mysterious way he couldn't have accurately described. That first night, she'd looked as though she'd been hiding behind dull, modest clothing as if she didn't want anyone to notice her much. Then she'd gradually begun wearing the kind of gowns that made a man's mouth water. As though she was no

longer cowering behind some sort of camou-
flage, but standing out in the open, with pride
as well as defiance.

So his influence on her hadn't been all bad.

She was no longer hiding. She was more...
herself. Even if it was a self that played down
to his assumptions about her.

By God, she was a plucky little thing. She'd
taken everything he'd flung at her and turned
it to her own advantage. Which was impres-
sive. Not many people had the courage to stand
up to him.

At least there was some consolation in knowing that he hadn't been able to drive her from
Town, no matter how badly he'd treated her. He
would never have been able to forgive himself
if he'd succeeded in destroying her chance at
happiness for the second time. He could only
hope that *she* could forgive him for attempting to do so. She might, if he went cap in hand
and... His hand went to his head. Where the
deuce was his hat?

He'd left it behind. Along with his coat.

Well, that explained the way people had
been looking at him since he'd left his sister's
house. He must resemble a madman, roaming
the streets without hat or coat, probably muttering to himself, as well.

Had he? Been muttering? Please God he hadn't sunk that low.

Though he'd sunk low enough to abandon just about every moral code in which he believed. It was his duty, as an officer, to defend women, not attack them. So why had he abandoned that creed with such alacrity? The moment Issy had mentioned Miss Furnival? Why had he been so eager to believe the worst of her?

Or was the truth that, the moment Issy had told him she was in Town, and where he might find her that night, he hadn't thought about anything but...but just seeing her again.

Though that was no excuse. And even if his sister's accusations had been true and the family were distraught at the prospect of her coming to Town and doing whatever it was they claimed they suspected her of planning to do, he'd had no business attacking her in such a public place. What had she called him, that night? He couldn't recall her exact words. Something to the effect of him bullying defenceless women...

Though she wasn't. Defenceless, that was. Which had nothing to do with the Duchess, as Issy had claimed. Miss Furnival herself was perfectly capable of defending herself.

She hadn't burst into tears, or gone off into a swoon, or created some kind of scene which would have made him look like a villain out of a badly written play. Because she was made of sterner stuff than the average society female. Had Lieutenant Gilbey seen that toughness in her, even all those years ago? Is that why he'd thought it would be perfectly reasonable to marry her and carry her off into the thick of the fighting? But then— He broke off, discovering he was halfway up the front steps of his house. His feet had carried him home without him having to think about it.

Though he had plenty of other things to think about. Such as, how was he ever going to obtain Miss Furnival's forgiveness? Telling her he'd made a mistake wasn't going to be good enough. He'd accused her of being the kind of woman who preyed on men, when she'd actually spent the past few years earning her living doing menial work rather than taking such a course.

Oh, Lord, he was going to have to grovel.

Just as that unpalatable truth bore down on him, his butler opened the front door and recoiled at the snarl emanating from Nathaniel's lips.

Nathaniel spun on his heel and went right

back down the steps. There was no point in going inside and coming up with a plan. There could be no plan. And the longer he put off the apology…or the grovelling for forgiveness…the harder it was going to be to make.

He dimly heard the butler shouting something about an umbrella as he set off in the direction of Grosvenor Square, but he wasn't going to stop for such fripperies now. He could not delay setting this matter right, or at least attempting to put it right, and it wasn't going to get any easier no matter how many umbrellas he was carrying when he did so.

It might have made it easier to knock on the glossy paintwork of the front door to the most imposing of the mansions that graced Grosvenor Square, though, he decided a few minutes later. And it would have spared him the raised eyebrow of a butler who was so superior to his own that, had he been in Nate's employ, he would never have dared exit his house without an umbrella. Let alone a hat.

'Her Grace is not receiving at this hour,' said the butler, as though Nathaniel really ought to have known it. 'But…' He stepped back and motioned as though inviting him to step inside.

'Perhaps you might care to come to the kitchen. I am sure Mrs Forbes could find you a towel.'

'Towel?' Oh, yes. It was raining. Quite hard. And his hair was wet. And so was his jacket. He'd scarcely noticed the rain, his mind had been so full of Miss Furnival, and how he'd wronged her.

'No, I had better… And it wasn't Her Grace I came to see.'

'Good heavens!' From halfway up the stairs came the voice of the woman he'd wronged. 'Colonel Fairfax!'

Miss Furnival came running down the rest of the stairs, her forehead creased with what looked like concern. *Concern*. For a wretch like him. 'Whatever has happened to you? You are soaked.'

'I…' Where to begin?

'Come inside out of the rain,' she said, taking his hand and dragging him over the threshold. How could she bear to touch him? She ought to be sneering at him and thrusting him back out into the rain, or ordering the servants to throw him down the front steps. 'Dawes, go and fetch the Colonel a towel,' she said, instead of taking her justifiable revenge. 'And some tea. Or perhaps brandy? He looks as if he's had a shock. Tea *and* brandy,' she said with a decisive nod.

He looked down at where their hands linked. She wouldn't be holding his hand and acting like a mother hen once she knew what he'd believed. Which knowledge made him, for some reason, grip it a bit harder.

'I need to talk to you,' he said. 'I have a confession to make. Can we…is there somewhere we could go and be…private? I know it is a lot to expect, given—'

'Of course we can talk in private,' she said at once, cutting off the rest of what he would have said. She frowned. 'Not the…but…well…' She looked at him as though weighing up her options, then her face cleared. 'Our sitting room should do. The one I share with Rosalind. Dawes, will you bring the towel, the tea and the brandy up there?'

'I don't think, Miss Furnival, that Her Grace would approve…'

'Well, you may tell her what I've been up to the moment she returns,' she said frostily. 'But in the meantime, anyone can see this man is in need of a warm room, and hot tea, and a bit of privacy. I have known him for…for ever. I have nothing to fear from him,' she declared.

Which made everything ten times worse.

'Miss Furnival, you are being too generous,'

he said as she began to lead him up the stairs she'd only just come down.

'Nonsense. The state of you! Anyone can see you've…suffered some kind of shock, or something.'

'A shock. Yes, it was a shock,' he said with a shiver, as he followed her along a landing on the walls of which were portraits of several people looking down their aristocratic noses, the way ancestors had a habit of doing. He stopped looking after the third sour face had sent another shiver down his spine. Instead he kept his gaze on Miss Furnival's profile. And wondered why he'd never seen just how compassionate she was. No wonder Gilbey had fallen headlong in love with her and hadn't been able to bear the thought of leaving her behind. Even if he had been getting cold feet by the time they'd reached Portsmouth.

She led him into a highly feminine sitting room. The kind of room in which his sister would not have looked out of place, with all its little tables and mounds of material, and half-finished sewing projects all over the place.

At the thought of his sister, he shuddered.

'Take off your jacket,' she said, pushing him in the direction of the fireplace, in which a mound of logs was blazing. 'You are soaked right through and shivering with cold.'

Was he? Or was it shame and the fear of what he had to speak about that was making him quake?

'That's the main reason I brought you up here,' she said, as he shrugged his arms out of his sleeves. 'The fact that I knew there was a fire going already. It would have taken an age to get any other room as warm and you need...' She trailed off, reaching out her hands as he looked about for somewhere to hang his sodden jacket. 'Here, let me,' she said, taking it and going over to an elegant and rather spindly chair, which she hooked up with her free hand, before carrying it to the fire. Once she'd set it down at a reasonable distance, she draped his jacket over the back.

She was so practical, seeing exactly what was needed and hang the consequences. She was the sort of woman who could turn the veriest hovel into a warm and homely place for a soldier on campaign.

'Do sit down,' she said, indicating an armchair set beside the hearth. 'Oh, I'd better just...' She bent and swept away the clutter of journals and lengths of material that had been hanging over the arms, so that he wouldn't crush, or soak, anything important.

'I should not sit,' he pointed out, 'until you do.'

'Nonsense,' she said briskly. 'Sit down while I fetch another chair. It won't take a moment.'

It didn't. But by the time she returned and had rearranged the furniture so that his armchair, and the chair on which his jacket was hanging, were as close to the fire as they could get without charring and had set her own chair a little further back, his jacket was starting to steam.

This, all this caring, was what he'd denied Gilbey. Perhaps he shouldn't have stopped her marrying the lad…

Only then she would have been caught up in that retreat across the mountains, too. And perhaps she would have…

He shivered convulsively and shook his head against the vision that invaded it.

'Colonel Fairfax?' Miss Furnival leaned forward in her chair. 'What is it? You look as though you've seen a ghost.'

He had. Hers.

'I *don't* regret stopping your marriage to that young idiot Gilbey,' he grated savagely. 'But it wasn't for the reasons you think. The reasons I told you.'

She sat back, all traces of compassion wiped from her face. She looked wary now, as well she might after the way he'd treated her lately.

'But I do owe you an apology. For…for the way I've…and the things I've said. For believing them… I…' He dashed his hand through his hair. His fingers came away wet.

He went to wipe them on his breeches, only they were wet, too. As were his boots.

'I should not have come up here in these boots,' he suddenly realised. He wasn't in some soldier's billet, even if his mind had been picturing her in such a setting. He was in an elegant sitting room in a ducal house in Grosvenor Square. 'I will ruin the carpet.' He shot to his feet.

'You will ruin more of it if you start striding about,' she replied tartly. 'You would do better to sit still and wait for that towel I ordered. Ah,' she said as there was a knock at the door. 'That will be it, now.'

It was. Not only the towel, draped over the arm of a granite-faced footman, but also a tray laden down with all the trappings for making tea. Along with a small carafe which looked as though it contained the brandy she'd ordered.

'Would you be good enough,' said Miss Furnival to the footman, as the maid set the tea tray down on one of the tables scattered about the room, 'to help the Colonel out of his boots. And then take them down and see what you can do about drying them before he has to leave?'

'Pardon me, miss, but I don't think…'

Miss Furnival quelled the footman's objections with a single look. And then, while the man knelt to tug off his boots, she set about stirring and pouring the tea. Without asking, she added a lump of sugar and a splash of liquid from the decanter.

'There,' she said, handing it to him the moment the servants had left the room. 'Drink that and then tell me what's troubling you.'

Warmth spread from his stomach outward as he took a sip of the hot, laced tea. But then she took the towel and draped it round his shoulders. And shame sent it curling back in on itself. 'You should dry your hair,' she said, 'as well. But the tea first, I think.'

'Yes, ma'am,' he said wryly. She would not only have done well as an army wife, but could have taken the place of many of his officers, with an attitude like that. He took another sip of the tea, hoping it would have the same effect as the first sip had done. It didn't. Nothing was going to be able to ease the burden of shame except his confession and her absolution. But at least he'd stopped shivering.

'Now,' she said, sitting on the chair on which she'd hung his jacket, which the servants had removed, along with his boots. 'Are you feeling up to telling me whatever it is that has reduced you to this state?'

He set the empty cup down at his feet, took hold of the towel and began to rub at his hair. 'To tell you the truth,' he said miserably, 'I think that this state is really all there is of me. This…shambling, scared man who no longer possesses the sense to take an umbrella to keep off the rain…'

'Nonsense,' she said again, though not unkindly. 'You are not scared of anything or anyone.'

'I am,' he said, flinging the towel away. 'I am scared of you. Of what you will think when I tell you…'

'Me?' Her eyes widened. She lay one hand upon her breast. A breast, he noted, that was decorously covered up because she hadn't expected to receive visitors. 'How on earth could a man like you be scared of a woman like me?'

'Because I am not the man you think I am.' Just as she hadn't been the woman he'd thought she was. *This* was more like her. With nobody to impress, she'd reverted to just being herself. The way anyone did at home, when they thought they weren't going to be disturbed.

'Once I stop hiding behind the…the… I don't even know what to call it,' he grated, dropping his head into his hands.

He was so close to falling apart completely. He needed…he needed…

His fingers went to the buttons of his waistcoat, a habit he'd got into increasingly of late.

Because he was starting to feel as if, in spite of all his precautions, he was finally starting to come undone.

Chapter Fifteen

'I found out, today,' he said, gazing up at her with an expression of pleading, 'that my sister lied to me about you.'

'Ah,' she said. 'Well, of course I knew that somebody must have done.'

She'd always known he could never have behaved the way he had unless he'd believed he was doing it for the greater good. Because his behaviour had been so very different from the stern, yet considerate way he'd escorted her back to the ballroom when she'd foolishly gone outside on her own. And the way he'd been even when he'd discovered her and Guy in the very act of eloping. He'd been angry, but all the anger had been directed at Guy. He'd even dipped into his own purse to ensure she had funds to reach home again.

Something inside her settled as she saw that

he really was the same inside as he'd always been. That he was the same man she'd admired so much all those years ago. Perhaps particularly because he still looked so troubled.

'It doesn't matter,' she said, hoping to soothe his conscience, which she could see was smarting.

'It does matter,' he countered, his features agonised. 'There is no excuse for treating you so abominably.'

'Well, no,' she conceded, since she could see he was devastated to learn that he'd broken the most basic code by which he lived. And needed absolution, not an argument about his deeply held creed. 'But you trusted the person who told you…whatever it was. I don't suppose you had any reason to suspect your own sister would lie to you about…another person.'

'It was what she told me that spurred me into action,' he said, a spasm of remorse flickering across his face, 'but I cannot pass the blame on to her. I don't want you to blame her, or be angry with her. She did it for the…for what she *thought* were the best motives.' He lowered his head, burying his face in his hands. But only for a moment or two.

'My family want me to marry. Well, it is my duty. But since I came back from that last campaign I have become...' He lifted his head. His eyes were so bleak, so utterly devoid of hope that it made her want to say she didn't need to hear whatever it was he was trying to say. Only something told her he needed to say it. That he wouldn't be able to forgive himself if he didn't make a full confession. So she kept quiet. And waited. Eventually, he heaved a sigh before continuing.

'I don't feel as if I have the right to go gadding about as though I haven't a care in the world, when so many others...' He grimaced. 'So I have been doing my utmost to prevent more needless deaths of the kind I witnessed on my last campaign. But they think...my female relatives think...that I have been neglecting my duty to the family. So they put their heads together,' he said bitterly, 'and came up with a ruse to *make* me attend balls and the like. They deliberately made me believe...' He looked up at her ruefully.

Ah, so *that* explained why he believed she'd inherited a fortune from Guy.

'Well,' she said, when he hung his head again, clearly struggling to find a way forward, 'I do know a bit about your reputation for being a recluse, because of the stir it caused when you came to Lady Bunsford's ball. And I can see that your sister, and the others, must have been at their wits' end over you.' And she didn't think it was all about him carrying on the family line, either. They probably cared about him, just him. The way anyone who knew him well couldn't help but do.

'You know, Godmama believes it worked to my advantage,' she said, hoping to relieve him of some of the guilt that was so obviously weighing him down. 'Because, once society's hostesses saw that you were likely to turn up to any place where I was, we started getting a lot more invitations than before.'

He grunted. 'That is a generous view to take. But I suspect it had more to do with the fact that your uncle recognised you.' He looked up at her then, with a searching frown. 'Was that why you came to London, after all this time? To try to heal the breach with the head of your family?'

'Well, yes, that was part of it. But it wasn't…' Now it was her turn to stop. It wasn't her place to reveal Rosalind's ambitions to snag a lord for a husband. And it would feel like betraying Godmama if she revealed the financial difficulties that had driven her to come up with the notion of finding a girl with a family wealthy enough to meet the expense of a Season for all of them. They were the ones to whom she should be loyal. They were the ones who'd always liked and supported her. Though, if she were totally honest with herself, since she'd met Colonel Fairfax again, he'd been at the forefront of her mind. She'd wondered what he would think of her in this or that gown, what he might say if he should be at this or that event and how she could answer him. She had to keep reminding herself that her main role in London was to support Godmama and Rosalind, and possibly scout out fashions for her aunts.

'It's no good,' he said wearily. 'I can see that the only way I am going to be able to make you understand the depth of my guilt will be to tell you from the beginning. Although it wasn't then that I…' He drew in a great shuddering breath and turned his head so that he was gazing into the flames. 'It was the horses, that was the last straw,' he said. His voice sounded thick with tears. Perhaps the threat of them was what had made him turn his head away, so that she wouldn't see them if he couldn't prevent them spilling over.

'You see, there weren't enough ships to bring them all back to England. Barely enough to cram all the troops on as it was.'

It took her a moment for her to perceive he

must be talking about the Battle of Corunna, the town in northern Spain from which British forces had taken ship home at the close of John Moore's ill-fated campaign.

'But we couldn't let them fall into the hands of the French. So we had to…destroy them.' He swallowed. 'You wouldn't have thought it would affect us so badly. I mean, during the course of our flight across the mountains, we saw far worse. Bodies of women and even children, lying frozen by the roadside…'

Cassy's stomach turned. She raised one hand to her throat. She'd known, of course, that there were a great many casualties during the course of that flight to Corunna. Guy had been one of them. But to hear of women and children dying, too, and their bodies left like that…

'I was fine, well, I coped at any rate, with the slaughter in the town…' he swallowed '…though it was the devil of a thing, having to shoot our own mounts. They looked at us with such trust in their eyes, even as we pulled the triggers.'

At this vivid description, tears sprang to her eyes. She wanted to do something…but what could anyone do to comfort someone who'd had to do such a terrible thing? There were no words to suffice.

'But then, as we set sail, there was one

horse…' he swallowed again '…which had somehow survived. And it started swimming after us. But there was no way we could get it on board, even if we'd had the room. Or the fodder to keep it alive during the voyage. Anyway, his owner, a hulking great Hussar, broke down. Fell to his knees, sobbing. And…it went like a wave through all the men. And when it reached me, that feeling of despair, I was afraid I'd drown in it.' His face suddenly hardened. 'But I was in charge. I could not permit a breakdown of discipline. I could not allow myself to break down. So I…' He ran his hands over the front of his waistcoat, in a gesture she'd seen him repeat often. 'The only way I can describe it is… I buttoned it up. Inside.' He ran his fingers over each of the buttons in turn. And she understood, then, that every time she'd seen him do that before, he'd been repeating a gesture that helped him control very strong emotions.

'And when that wasn't quite enough, I buttoned up an imaginary jacket over the top. And then a coat as well, to keep it all from spilling out.'

She could just see him, standing there, striving to remain unmoved at a time when anyone would be forgiven for breaking down and weeping. He was one of those people who couldn't bear to appear weak. Aunt Eunice was exactly the same, which made her come across, very often, as gruff, or even unkind. Though truly she was neither.

And nor was he.

'And I…got the men to bear up, somehow. I don't know what I said, but they listened to me.'

She was sure they had. Because she'd seen the way he'd been on the quayside, so many years earlier. She'd thought of him as a rock, round which all the others swirled. A rock she could cling to. Steady, reliable, dependable. It had been Colonel Fairfax who had provided her with an escape route from a situation she'd seen, by that time, was untenable. Even though it hadn't worked out the way he'd assumed, her life *had* become better, because of the way he'd stepped in. Even if he *had* done it to save Guy, rather than her.

Why, if he hadn't intervened, she might even have become one of those casualties who'd fallen by the roadside during that flight across the mountains.

'And by the time we reached England my men did at least resemble a disciplined unit. Which was more than could be said of some others. The only trouble was…' he thrust his fingers through his hair in a gesture that spoke of extreme vexation '...I couldn't unbutton again. I'd crammed all I felt, all the horror and despair, down so tight that I...well, to be frank, I was half afraid of facing it. There was so much, I thought that if I once even looked at it, it might burst out and completely unman me. So I didn't look. I left it all there, simmering, festering...' He rubbed at the front of his waistcoat as though there really was something lying coiled beneath. Something that only needed the slightest bit of encouragement to burst free and wreak havoc.

'That didn't bother me, to start with. I told myself there would be time enough to mourn and weep when we were all safe. Only, when we got back to England, I had new responsibilities. For my family, my tenants, my holdings. Besides which, I'd vowed that I would do whatever I could to try to ensure that nothing like that flight over the mountains would ever happen to our men again. I only ever stopped when I fell into bed at night. And that was fine, that was how I wanted it to be. If I exhausted myself, every day, then I wouldn't lie in bed at nights dwelling on—' his face contorted '—things. And if ever I did start to...

if anything ever reminded me of…that time, I squashed it down all the harder.

'But, anyway, my sister Issy, so she says, was growing steadily more worried about me. But she could see that I was trying to honour those who'd fallen and protect those yet to serve. So she made it sound as though I owed it to Lieutenant Gilbey to prevent you from destroying another man, the way you destroyed him. But you didn't, did you? Destroy him, I mean. That was the army. An accident of fate. But I believed her, because…it sounded convincing, because…well, for one thing, whenever he received a letter from you, he would become… I can't explain it, except to say he looked tortured. He would never talk about what you wrote, but I suppose it was hearing your family wouldn't take you back? And having to work as a seamstress?'

'Oh!' Cassy felt as if someone had stuck a knife in her heart. 'I never meant to upset him, let alone torture him,' she said, tears burning at her eyes. 'It was my aunts. They said he deserved to know what had become of me. That it was his fault and he should make restitution. I…perhaps I shouldn't have been… quite so frank with him. Did it…?' Her stomach clenched as a horrible thought crossed her mind. 'Did it make him reckless? Did it put his life in danger? Was that what you thought? Was that why you were so beastly to me? If it is true,' she whispered, aghast, 'then I deserved it.'

'No!' He fell to his knees at her feet, seizing both her hands. 'None of it was your fault. His unit was one of those fighting at the rear of the column, keeping the French at bay. He didn't fling himself into some forlorn hope, or anything like that. He was just doing his duty. And was unlucky.'

'But then, why…?'

'Was I so beastly, as you put it?' He gave a sad smile. 'I don't know. Truly. I don't understand where all the anger came from. I think…' He frowned. 'Possibly…it was because you had already disappointed me.'

What? How on earth had she managed that?

'The first time we met I thought you were so innocent, so in need of protection…but then not one month later there you were, eloping with one of my junior officers.'

And that had disappointed him?

Hah. He could not have been more disappointed in her than she'd been in herself. She had been stupid to believe Guy's assurances that she'd be happier with him than staying in her stepfather's house.

'So I thought I'd been mistaken. Instead of being the innocent, I thought you were...'

'What? No better than I ought to be?'

He winced.

'And then, when I saw you at Lady Bunsford's that night, you were laughing...'

'Is that a crime, now?'

He shook his head. 'No, but you were alive and enjoying life, and so untouched by all that the years had wrought, when so many others were...when I myself was...' He lowered his head. 'I know it was irrational. But it was... for some reason...' He lifted his head and looked deep into her eyes. 'The moment Issy mentioned you, your face kept on coming to my mind. I didn't want the distraction. Kept trying to thrust it away, the way I'd thrust so many other thoughts and memories away. But I couldn't. The harder I tried, the more memories kept intruding. It was as though she'd somehow opened a door to the past I believed was locked and bolted. And I couldn't slam it shut again. I kept seeing you as you were at that assembly, so shy-seeming and so wary of the officers, that I wanted to protect you from them all. And then as you were in the yard, in the moonlight, so trusting, as I thought…and then…' His face changed. 'That day, standing on the quayside, clinging to Lieutenant Gilbey's arm as though *he* was your only anchor. You, thanking me with tears in your eyes when I ordered him to send you home. And then the anguish on his face, every time he got a letter from you. The way he'd pace back and forth, berating himself. And the needless death of so many soldiers, not to mention the children and the horses…it all went whirling round and round in my head, and then…when I saw you laughing, against the background of all that horror, something inside snapped.' He shook his head, his face betraying both remorse and confusion. 'It all came spewing out…'

'Like when you shake up a bottle of ginger beer,' she said, seeing how it must have been. 'You had been holding so much back, for so long, that when you did lose control, there was no telling what form it would take. Just as you can never tell in which direction the cork is going to fly, when it does pop out, no matter how carefully you try to aim it.'

He gave a shocked gasp of laughter. 'You make it sound so…commonplace.'

'I'm sorry. I didn't mean to belittle your feelings…'

'No. No, it was a good analogy.' He gripped her hands a little tighter, his eyes losing some of their bleakness. 'Of being not quite in control of…of what I was trying so desperately to keep under control. I was right to have been afraid of what would spill out of me if I let down my guard, wasn't I? Although it didn't take the form I'd feared it would. I didn't think I'd become so…angry. At someone who had done nothing to deserve it. *Nothing.*' He reached up and stroked her cheek with such tenderness that it melted the last of her inclination to resent him.

'I'd thought I'd break down,' he said, his brows furrowing. 'And end up shaking and weeping in public like…like some of the men did. And then having to reach for a bottle to numb the memories.'

'Neither reaction would have been wrong, though, would they?'

'For others, perhaps,' he objected, looking affronted. 'But not for me. I needed to…' He frowned.

'You needed,' she said, turning her hand to grasp the one that he still held folded round hers, 'to stay strong for everyone around you. You are so used to providing for others, you dreaded becoming a burden on anyone else.

Even for the short time it would have taken for you to recover.'

His expression hardened. 'Don't make excuses for me. It was pride that made it intolerable to risk breaking down in front of others. And fear of looking weak.'

'Why are you being so hard on yourself?' As she said this, she suddenly recalled that, not so very long ago, she'd thought she would enjoy seeing him grovel. Yet now he was on his knees, instead of feeling triumphant, all she wanted to do was comfort him. Nothing else seemed to matter any more, not now she knew what had caused him to act towards her the way he had. 'You cannot be perfect all the time. You are just a man. A man who has been through a terrible ordeal.' She ran her fingers through his hair. He'd been coping with so much, alone, for so long. He was in such sore need of comfort and running her fingers through his hair was all she could think of to do. It was the kind of thing she'd often wished someone would do for her, when she'd been living with her mother and stepfather.

'You should be kinder to yourself.'

'I don't deserve any kindness,' he said grimly.

'Why? Because you survived? When others

didn't? You just told me that Guy's death wasn't my fault. That he was just doing his duty and was unlucky. Doesn't that apply to all the others who fell?'

'Yes, but I was in charge...'

'Not of who lived and who died. For goodness sake, only God has that kind of power. And if you lived, then it was because He decided to spare you.'

'If that is true, then all the more reason to work to prove myself worthy of such a great gift.'

She frowned. 'That *sounds* right, but...no, I don't think it is.' In spite of disliking the vicar of Market Gooding's sermons, listening to them week after week had not been without effect on her thinking. Because the minute the Colonel talked about why he didn't deserve any kindness, the vicar's exposition of the parable of the talents sprang to mind. He was always going on about how everyone ought to be cheerful, that there was always something to be thankful for, particularly the gift of life itself. So she felt confident in what she said next.

'Nobody is worthy of any of the gifts God gives. But to try to become worthy is...well, it's just silly. Because instead of showing any gratitude for what you call a great gift, you have buried yourself under a mound of work so never-ending that your family had to resort to shocking you away from it with all those made-up tales of my supposed wickedness.'

'But work is my only way to…'

'Prove yourself worthy of being spared, yes, we've already established that,' she said gently as she shook her head. 'Do you know what you remind me of? That parable about the man who buried the coin in the ground instead of using it to do some good. Oh, I don't mean that your work isn't doing some good. It is possibly doing a great deal of good. But the manner of your life…' She shook her head. 'Instead of treasuring the gift you have been given and showing how greatly you appreciate it by living your life to the full, you are burying yourself away as though you think it is worthless. And clearly, you are not worthless. Otherwise your family would not be so devoted to you. You need—'

'You,' he said, breaking in with such a fierce expression in his eyes that it almost stopped her breathing. It was so similar to the way he'd looked at her so many times before. Though there was an added ingredient now that made all the difference, as he repeated the words, 'I need you.'

'You…you need me?' Her voice came out in

a rush as she remembered how to breathe. For she'd admired him so much, for so long, believing it was impossible for him to return a tenth of her regard, that this seemed like a miracle.

'Your belief in me,' he said, both hands reaching up to cup her cheeks now. 'Your compassion.' His eyes roved over her face with what looked like hunger. 'Your strength,' he breathed, his eyes fixing, finally, on her lips.

'All of you,' he whispered. 'I've been fighting what I feel for you right from the first. *Then* I thought you were too young. But now—now you have grown up to become the strongest woman I have ever known. And I cannot fight myself any longer. I want *all* of you. Everything you are.'

Her heart was thundering. She was breathing fast, as though she'd been running, even though she was sitting still. And there were currents of something dark, and demanding, swirling through her veins. Through every single muscle in her body.

'I want you, too,' she finally admitted. In a way she'd never wanted any other man. Not even Guy.

He closed his eyes, sagging with relief against her breast.

She didn't push him away, although the position was highly improper. Instead, she started stroking his hair again, offering him the comfort he so clearly needed. Because it was obvious that the next thing he would do would be to ask her to marry him. So that she could be that source of comfort and strength that he'd just admitted he needed.

And for the first time in an age, she could see the point of marrying a man. When she'd eloped with Guy, it had been because she thought marriage was the only way a woman could escape an unhappy home. She'd thought she needed a man to take care of her. She'd also remembered how happy her mother had been with her father and had thought that Guy might be able to make her happy, too, because he'd promised he would do all in his power to make her happy.

But since then she'd seen her aunts living totally independently and being completely fulfilled in every way without a man in charge of their lives. And she'd come to think that was what she wanted, too. Apart from the fact that without a man, there would be no babies.

And even now, she didn't feel as if she needed a man to find happiness. It was just the thought of being needed…

Well, in that sort of marriage, she wouldn't

be the weaker, dependent partner. She wouldn't be a victim, as her mother had been.

Cassy couldn't have imagined that a day which had started out so badly could have ended up like this. She couldn't help smiling. She hadn't come to Town looking for a husband, but, oh, how glad she was that she'd run into Colonel Fairfax. Or, rather, that he'd run into her.

She put her arms round his bowed shoulders and hugged him. Rested her cheek against the crown of his head.

A shudder went through him. And then he made to lift his head. So she raised her own, giving him the chance to speak. And make his proposal.

He gazed at her for a few seconds, looking a touch uncertain. She supposed she shouldn't be surprised he was a bit nervous about what her response would be. After all, he hadn't exactly been the most charming of suitors, had he? Quite the reverse!

But she did admire him so. Even when he'd been at his worst, she hadn't been able to stop wondering what it would feel like if that harsh mouth ceased berating her and gave her the kiss he'd threatened her with instead. And, now she'd heard what he'd been through and understood what had made him treat her so unfairly, all she wanted was to spend the rest of her life helping him to recover. To be happy.

So she stroked his hair again and smiled at him encouragingly.

And, as if it was the sign he'd been looking for, he surged up from his knees, took her in his arms and finally, oh, finally, he kissed her!

Chapter Sixteen

Cassy had no idea how to respond because no man had ever kissed her before. Not like this, full on the mouth. But even though she felt unsure of herself, and what she was supposed to do, it was still by far the most wonderful moment of her life. The man she'd hero-worshipped, holding up in her imagination as the ideal man, for so many years, had not only grovelled at her feet, but was now still on his knees, kissing her as though his life depended on it. He'd realised she was innocent of all the things he'd flung at her. And thought she was, instead, exactly what he needed.

And, oh, it felt so good. Physically, that was, as well as emotionally. Who would have guessed that having a man's lips pressed to hers, with such fervour, would unleash such glorious feelings in totally unrelated parts of her body?

She was just starting to wonder if she might have the courage to try to do more than just sit there letting him do all the work, when, to her immense disappointment, he tore his lips from hers. But she didn't have time to do more than wonder fleetingly if she'd done something to put him off, before he began pressing hot, open-mouthed kisses to her jaw and then her neck, which made her spine turn to liquid. It wasn't long before the cocktail of relief and bone-melting sensation he was creating meant that she couldn't hold up her head, but had to let it loll back against the chair. At which point she realised that he must have undone some of the buttons at the back of her gown, otherwise he wouldn't have been able to tug down the modest neckline of her gown and begin trailing kisses along her collarbone.

'You have no idea,' he sort of growled into her skin, 'just how long I have been dreaming of running my tongue over this mole.' And then to her shock, he really did lick his way over not only the mole on the side of her neck, but right along the chain of moles that ran just below her collarbone. Licked her! If anyone had told her that a man might want to lick her, anywhere, she would have screwed up her face in disgust because it sounded so…animal.

But it wasn't disgust making her moan and plunge her fingers into his hair. It was…oh, lord, something equally animal springing to life inside her. Something that made her want to hitch up her skirts so that she could wrap her legs round his waist and rub up against him like a…like a…well, she didn't know what!

Fortunately, he was clearly in the same frame of mind, because he pulled her to the edge of her chair, ran his hand up her skirts along almost the entire length of her leg, then pulled her into almost the exact position she'd just been thinking was so shocking. She couldn't get either leg anywhere near his waist, because he hadn't pushed her skirts out of the way completely, but she could raise her left one and rub it along his thigh. Which felt good, though it wasn't enough.

However, she couldn't object to his lack of foresight too much when he didn't seem to be able to keep his hands focused on any one part of her. They roamed everywhere, as if he wanted to explore every inch of her. And not just his hands. His mouth followed the path his hands had travelled, kissing her shoulders, her face, her hands, her breasts, her chin, her ears…

And all the while he was undoing more buttons, pushing more fabric out of the way, as though he simply had to get his hands on skin.

Oh, but she knew exactly how he felt, because she wanted her hands on his skin just as badly. And, since she was such an expert on the subject of clothes, having made so many, for men as well as ladies, she had no trouble locating all the relevant fastenings.

The moment her fingers began working at the buttons of his waistcoat, however, he reared back, breathing heavily. And instead of simply getting the garment undone as swiftly as possible, she slowed down, knowing that this meant more to him than just disposing of a garment. He was letting her get closer to him than he'd allowed anyone for years.

In the same way that she was flinging all her own caution to the winds.

Once she'd slipped the last button through the eyelet, she slid her hand inside his waistcoat and laid it over his heart, which was pounding. He removed his own hand from where it had been kneading at her hip and pressed it over hers. Then raised it to his mouth and kissed the palm.

Did he want her to stop? Had this gone as far as he was able to go?

Or perhaps he was offering her the choice to

stop. Which made her all the more determined to demonstrate that she trusted him.

Or, at least, that was part of it. A small part, located in her brain. The rest of her was just clamouring for him to continue. For no other reason than that she *wanted* him. More than she'd ever thought it possible to want anything.

She searched his face for answers. But he closed his eyes as he placed her hand back on his chest and went totally still, as though he was awaiting her next move. As though he was surrendering to her will.

Well, if he was going to let her do what she wanted with him, then so be it. She wanted to get her hands on bare skin. After all, he'd touched her all over the place, so why shouldn't she do the same to him? And now that she'd undone his waistcoat it was relatively easy to tug his shirt free of his breeches and get her hands inside.

The moment she reached his skin, he shuddered. And moaned. And even though he kept his eyes shut, the expression on his face was one of bliss. Bliss that she'd made him feel. Which spurred her on to be even bolder. She brought her hands round to his chest, feeling the coarse tuft of hair at its centre, lowered them to the hard muscles of his abdomen...

He grabbed her hand to prevent her exploring any further. Opened his eyes to look into her face, with such naked adoration and longing, that her heart swelled. No man had ever looked at her that way before. As though she was special. As though nothing and nobody else existed. Just as nobody else existed for her, in this moment, but him.

And then he started kissing her again. And this time he somehow coaxed her lips apart so that he could delve his tongue into her mouth.

And now it was her turn to get the cork-about-to-pop-out-of-a-ginger-beer-bottle feeling. Only in her case it felt more like when she'd seen a mischievous lad take the brakes off a cart parked on the brow of a very steep hill. At first it had only slowly started to roll downhill. But it steadily gained speed until it was careering down the slippery slope until nothing, absolutely nothing, could have stopped it.

And, oh, she'd had the brakes fastened for so long, when it came to this man, that it felt positively glorious to let them off and just let this passion flaring between them carry her along wherever it might take her.

'Bedroom,' he panted, rearing back and tugging her to her feet. 'We cannot do this here, on the floor.'

She wouldn't have cared. But before she could say so, he'd lifted her up into his arms and was stalking across the sitting room to the door which did, fortunately, lead to her bedroom, rather than the corridor. For a moment a wave of hilarity at the prospect of him carrying her out on to the landing, with their clothing mostly undone and half-hanging off, made her want to giggle.

He smiled back down at her.

The smile transformed his face. She reached up in wonder to stroke his cheek. She'd always known that he could be like this. That all the angriness was a facade hiding something far better. And here it was. The man she'd met at the assembly at the White Hart. The protective man who'd later rescued her from Guy's folly. What was more, he was gazing down at her as though she was some sort of miracle.

And then they were kissing and panting, and clawing away any item of clothing that prevented their greedy hands from feasting on warm, naked skin. And it was the runaway cart all over again. A cart laden with so much need that anything getting in its way would have been flattened. She *had* to be naked, and horizontal, with his naked body pressed against hers. Nothing else mattered. Especially not when he seemed to be feeling exactly the same. When his need matched hers. He was as frantic to get close, and closer still, until their flesh merged at the point of greatest need, in a mutual cry of accomplishment, though hers was tinged with pain.

Not that it slowed either of them. They were careering to some kind of mutual, spectacular destination, she could sense it. Fortunately, he knew just how to steer them, with his clever fingers and the demanding thrusts of his body. Until, just as that cart had come crashing to its inevitable destruction against the bole of the elm tree at the bottom of the hill, sending bales and barrels bouncing and bursting in all directions, she shattered, her spirit soaring through the air, her wits gloriously scattered to the four winds.

And he was with her. Groaning, and shuddering, and clinging as tightly to her as she was clinging to him.

'Cassy,' he panted. 'Oh, Cassy, Cassy...'

'Cassy!' This voice, a shriek, came from the direction of the doorway, causing the Colonel to rear back and glance over his shoulder.

And there was Rosalind, standing in the doorway, her bonnet trailing from her fingers, her eyes and mouth wide with shock.

For a moment. Then she clapped her free hand to her mouth to stifle a giggle and ran from the room.

'Do not worry,' said the Colonel, peeling himself away from her sweat-slicked body. 'You can tell her we are to be married.'

'Mmmm.' She sighed, relaxing back into the pillows.

Then he went very still, his gaze fixed on where their legs were still twined together.

'Blood...there's blood on your thigh...' He looked back into her face, as though what he'd seen confused him. 'How can that be?'

'How can what be?' All of a sudden Cassy didn't feel so glorious any more. There was a chill creeping into her stomach. A chill of foreboding.

Shouldn't he be cradling her in his arms now? Talking about how soon they could get a licence? Discussing where to hold the ceremony?

Instead, he was backing away, not only emotionally, but physically. Reaching for his shirt and tugging it over his head. And all the while she was silently pleading with him not to say what she dreaded he was going to say.

'How can you have been a virgin?'

He'd said it.

'I should have thought,' she said, tugging the bit of quilt she wasn't lying on to cover what suddenly felt like shameful nakedness, 'that was obvious.'

'Not to me,' he said, hunting round the floor with a kind of desperation, until he located his breeches, as though he felt just as embarrassed as she now did. 'Or I would never have...' He looked at the rumpled bedding, the way she was clutching as much of the quilt as she could over as much of her body as possible.

And there she'd been thinking he believed in her total innocence!

'Your virginity is something special,' he said, thrusting one leg jerkily into his breeches. 'You should have saved it for your wedding night.'

How...how *dare* he find fault with her morals?

And what did he mean by *your* wedding night? Shouldn't he be talking about *our* wedding night? After all, he'd just told her she could tell Rosalind...

Oh! Oh, what an idiot she was. He hadn't said one single word about marriage until Rosalind had come in and caught them together. All he'd talked about was his *need*. By which he'd meant his physical need, hadn't he?

How many times had she heard her aunts talk, with revulsion, about the way men could bed any woman who was willing, while caring nothing for them at all, and put it down to their *needs*.

Whereas she could never have let him do what he'd just done if she hadn't been so sure love came into it somewhere. And the way he'd been talking, opening himself up to her in a way she was sure he'd never done with anyone else, had made her think she held a special place in his heart. That he trusted her with secrets he could never tell anyone else.

When all the time it had all been so much froth spewing from that imaginary ginger-beer bottle she was coming to heartily detest.

Just as she now detested what they'd just done. Strange, how, while she was in the throes of it, she'd thought it was glorious. But now it just seemed sordid. To let a man who'd never done anything but insult her into her heart and her body, in broad daylight, simply because he'd needed relief, release from that heavy burden he'd been carrying alone for so long.

She almost let out a bitter laugh when she thought of how Godmama had wanted to make him look foolish. For she was the one who'd been a fool. Because she'd let him do exactly what he'd threatened, from the first. He'd just made it impossible for her to marry anyone else. By ruining her. In *fact*, not just by reputation.

Just as she'd been on the verge of becoming respectable again.

She shifted up the bed and drew up her knees as he got his other leg into his breeches and buttoned up the fall.

'I will speak to Rosalind,' she said in a firm voice. Which was astonishing, considering it felt as if she was shattering all over again, inside, only not in a good way this time. 'She won't tell anyone about this if I ask her not to. So you don't need to worry about having to marry me.'

'Of course I do. You were a virgin. You cannot think I am the kind of man who goes round deflowering virgins and then walking away from them as though it was nothing, can you?'

So she'd been right. He hadn't been thinking in terms of marriage until he'd discovered her innocence. Or been caught in the act by Rosalind. Or both. So now he felt duty-bound to marry her. She drew in a deep breath. Well! She had no intention of letting him treat her as though she was nothing more than yet one more obligation he had to bear. She deserved better. If she ever did marry, which had never been likely, but was even less likely after this, then it would only be to a man who wanted to marry her because he couldn't bear the thought of having to live without her. Not because he'd been carried away in a fit of...whatever it was that had just had the Colonel in its grip...and was now suffering from the pangs of remorse.

And what was she doing, cowering against the headboard like some...timid little mouse? If she wanted to get dressed, then the fact that he was standing there staring at her was not going to prevent her from doing just that.

Indignation had her flinging aside the quilt and stalking across the room to where she could see her chemise dangling from the back of a chair.

'No, that's not the kind of man you are,' she agreed, shaking out the chemise with a snap, so that she could pull it over her head.

'Then...'

'You are a far worse sort,' she said, once she was covered to her knees, if only by a sheet of flimsy cotton. 'You are the kind of man,' she said, stalking over to where her gown lay sprawled on the floor, 'who persecutes innocent women in the hopes of driving them out of Town, without sparing a single thought,' she said as she bent to pick it up, 'to what brought them to Town in the first place.' She paused after straightening up, realising in the same moment that not only was she going to need the services of a maid to help with the fastenings, but that there was absolutely no way she could summon one to this room, right now, not with a half-naked, guilt-ridden man standing right next to her bed. Which made her even angrier than ever.

'I—' he said.

'The kind of man,' she interrupted, 'who believes the worst sort of gossip about a woman without a shred of evidence, then goes on to treat her as though she is that kind of woman.' She waved her hand in the direction of the rumpled bed. 'And then further insults her by acting as though it would be a huge sacrifice to marry such a woman!'

'It would not be a *huge* sacrifice…'

Cassy had not thought she was capable of getting any angrier. But that stress on the word *huge* proved she'd been wrong. It drove her to a whole new level of anger, something akin to what must happen when a volcano erupted.

'If you think I would ever consider marrying a man like you, then you must be touched in your upper works!'

'But we…' Now it was his turn to gesture towards the bed on which she'd just surrendered every scrap of her dignity.

'That,' she said, pointing in the same direction as him, 'was nothing more than a momentary lapse of good judgement. Which I not only regret, but have absolutely no intention of ever repeating, which I would be obliged to do if I was foolish enough to give in to your argument about the need to marry.'

He flinched, as though she'd slapped him. And she almost wished she had. Especially when he recovered in the blink of an eye and took a breath to begin a counter-argument.

She gripped her dress, the dress she couldn't get into properly without someone's help, in both hands. And thought of Rosalind. Rosalind could help her. She'd returned from her outing with Captain Bucknell and she'd already seen the worst.

And the Colonel couldn't follow her to Rosalind's room because his boots were still downstairs, being dried and polished by one of the menservants who knew how to do that sort of thing. And if she would find it hard to run about a house she knew extremely well, with hardly any clothes on, then it would be twice as hard for him. Well-nigh impossible, in fact.

So she put an end to his chances of carrying on with his argument by the simple expedient of darting to the door and running away.

'Cassy,' he snapped. 'What the devil do you think you are doing?' He followed her across the room and got as far as the doorway to the upper landing before his lack of boots brought him to a standstill. 'Cassy, come back here,' she could hear him yelling after her. 'We have not finished this discussion!'

Oh, yes, they had.

And if she had her way, they would never have any sort of discussion, about anything, ever again.

Chapter Seventeen

It didn't take much effort to persuade Rosalind not to breathe a word to Godmama about what she'd witnessed.

'She's your godmother,' she said, a bit ungraciously, as she buttoned up the back of Cassy's gown. 'It's up to you what you tell her or choose not to.'

'Thank you.'

Rosalind let out a bitter-sounding laugh. 'And to think she's always holding you up as an example to follow. Prim and proper, I always thought you. But you're as sly as she is.'

'Oh, no, I'm not! Truly.' Cassy whirled round as Rosalind fastened the last button. 'I didn't *plan*, er…*that*.' She waved one arm in the direction of her own room. 'I just…' She wrapped her arms round her waist. 'I got carried away,' she admitted, miserably.

'I must say you don't look too happy about it,' Rosalind conceded. 'Ain't he going to marry you, then?'

'Actually,' Cassy retorted, '*I* am not going to marry *him*.'

'Oh? Why's that? I thought you was keen on him.'

'I was.' Or she could never have let things go so far. 'But it turns out I was sadly mistaken in his character. No,' she said with a shake of her head. 'That's not quite right. It isn't his character that's lacking. It's what he thinks of me that I don't like.'

Rosalind looked down at her shoes. 'Yes, I know what *that* feels like.'

'At least,' said Cassy, 'after this, you are speaking to me again. I don't know what I would have done if you'd kept your door shut and refused to let me in today.' Her cheeks, already glowing, grew even hotter as she imagined running all over the house with her gown undone.

And Rosalind apparently was thinking the same thing, because she began to grin. 'You'd have shocked all the servants, who would have told the Duchess, and then you would have had to marry that old Colonel, that's what.'

'It doesn't bear thinking about,' said Cassy with a shudder of horror. 'So, thank you again.'

'No need. I'm sorry I wouldn't speak to you last night. Captain Bucknell said that wasn't fair. That you weren't ever in on the Duchess's schemes.'

'Well, certainly not deliberately to swindle your father, no,' said Cassy fervently. And then went on to explain the things she'd hoped to be able to say the night before.

By the time they had to go and change for dinner, Cassy felt she had repaired most of the damage done the night before.

She went back to her room with a bit of reluctance, almost afraid she'd find the Colonel still there. But there was no sign of him. Or that he'd ever been there. The bed was no longer rumpled, there were no clothes strewn anywhere they shouldn't be and...he'd even opened the window a bit, to let fresh air remove any lingering scent of their encounter.

She supposed she should be glad he'd thought of everything. That he'd expunged every trace of what they'd done. But she couldn't help feeling hurt that he'd taken the time to conceal what he'd referred to as if it had been a crime.

That he'd made absolutely sure he wouldn't get found out.

Of course, she didn't want to be found out, either. And she didn't want to marry the Colonel simply as a means to salve his conscience. But the two opposing reactions kept on struggling for supremacy as she got changed and neither had gained the upper hand by the time she went to the dining room. Instead, the fact that he could only regard marriage to her as a form of penance for sin robbed her of her appetite.

Fortunately Godmama was in such high spirits that she didn't notice that Cassy was only pushing her food round her plate rather than putting much of it in her mouth and swallowing it.

'My dears, I have had such a successful afternoon,' she said, beckoning one of the footmen to pour her some wine. 'It didn't take me long to work out that it must have been that awful girl from Market Gooding you ran into the other day who is responsible for starting the gossip about you having to work as a seamstress. But I have more than twenty years' experience of turning malicious gossip to good account. And this time I believe I have been particularly brilliant. In fact, I shouldn't be a bit surprised if I haven't destroyed that minx who dared meddle with me and mine,' said Godmama wrenching a bread roll in half with a sharp twist.

'Oh, no,' said Cassy, who couldn't bear the thought of anyone, not even Miss Henley, ending up socially destroyed. Because she knew, first hand, how awful that could feel.

'Oh, you need not worry, my dear,' said Godmama, slathering the roll with butter. 'I did not tell one single lie. No, I just laid the truth out in such a way that everyone will feel sympathy for you and dislike for your enemies. All I had to do was admit that I believed Miss Henley must be motivated by envy after seeing that you are being sponsored by a duchess—when the best she can do is a cousin of her mother who is a baroness—and by her fury to discover that you are far better-born than she could have guessed, and her spite after learning that her seamstress is invited to *ton* parties while she can only skirt round the fringes of society. I never once denied that you were obliged to work for a living for some years, merely expressed my sadness that your stepfather is so mean that it came to that at all.'

In short, she had made Cassy out to be some

poor maligned victim, with Miss Henley and her stepfather playing the role of villains.

'Godmama,' she protested, 'you haven't thought about the effect this might have on my aunts. For one thing, although I might be going to *ton*nish balls this Season, once the Season is over, I will have to go back to Market Gooding and take up my needle again.' It wasn't as if she'd ever expected to find a husband and, after what had happened this afternoon, the chances of her marrying anyone had reduced considerably. 'If society turns on Miss Henley and then her family decide to exact retribution, they could very easily prevent people from bringing work to my aunts. The Henleys do have a lot of influence in the area, even if they have very little in Town...'

'Pftt!' Godmama slashed her butter knife through the air as though cutting through her objections. 'You cannot persuade me that your aunts really need to work for their living. It's all a smokescreen, isn't it?'

'Godmama! Please, you cannot put them at risk by saying...' She shot a look at Rosalind. Fortunately, she was trailing her spoon through her soup with an abstracted air and didn't appear to have noticed the secret Godmama had almost let slip.

'Oh, very well,' said Godmama with a pout. 'I won't add any more fuel to that particular fire. Anyway,' she said, brightening, 'I rather think we've already cooked that girl's goose. Before long, if I'm not very much mistaken, she will come crawling to you...'

Godmama had a great deal more to say, but at the mention of having Miss Henley crawling, Cassy remembered how badly she'd wanted to make the Colonel crawl to her. How she'd felt when she'd got him to his knees. And how hollow her apparent victory had turned out to be.

She wanted to tell Godmama that she didn't want to make anyone crawl. That she never had. That she wished she'd stayed safely in Market Gooding. That she wished she could go back. Tomorrow. Only that would appear terribly ungrateful, considering all that Godmama had tried to do for her. And it wouldn't be fair on Rosalind, who couldn't very well stay on in London without the pretext of being Cassy's companion.

She picked up her spoon and dipped it into her soup.

It was bad enough that she'd behaved so badly, in secret, this afternoon. She couldn't compound her error by running away and leaving these two ladies in the lurch.

She would just have to endure London for as long as these two wanted her to stay. And during that time she could hopefully find a way to prevent Miss Henley from becoming a social pariah, before they all went back to Market Gooding.

Nathaniel had spent that same evening, and then the night, pacing back and forth in his room. Sleep was impossible, with all that he had on his mind.

She'd been a virgin.

She'd put her arms round him and told him she wanted him, had rubbed her leg up and down his flank, and had smiled at him, even giggled when he'd picked her up and carried her to her bed.

So how the hell could she have been a virgin? Virgins didn't put their arms round men and giggle. They didn't invite them up to their rooms and send for tea, but not a chaperon. They didn't get a man out of his wet boots and jacket, and put a dash of brandy into his tea, either. Those were the actions of a...

He turned on his heel. Those were the actions of a compassionate woman who trusted a man completely because she had no idea she was behaving improperly. In the same way that she'd had no idea she was behaving improperly that night at the White Hart, all those years ago. Because she hadn't had an attentive chaperon to guide her. Where the devil had her mother been? How could a woman allow her daughter to go off to a public event of that nature, to which any randy buck could gain admittance for the price of a ticket, without even warning her of the dangers of wandering off alone?

And why hadn't she learned any sense in all the years since then? Why hadn't she…?

No. It was not right to blame her. *He* was the one who'd behaved improperly. Indecently. And it was no use blaming that rush of emotion that had poured from him when he'd started talking about the horses. He shouldn't have mentioned them. He'd always known they were some sort of trigger, that if he ever admitted how he'd felt, had ever started to unbutton, he'd be lost.

Only he hadn't thought he would lose himself in that fashion. He'd thought he would have succumbed to feeble tears, or humiliating drunkenness. He'd never dreamed he would turn into some kind of…ravening beast and pounce on the very person who least deserved it…

He turned to pace in the other direction and

forced himself to examine everything, from her eager touch to her little cries, and gasps and groans which had been a genuine expression of the wonder she'd been experiencing.

Wonder. Because it had all taken her by *surprise.*

Though nobody had been more surprised than him when she'd turned down his proposal of marriage. Flat. Most women, when caught in such a situation, would have been relieved that a man was prepared to do the honourable thing. Instead, she'd acted as if he'd insulted her.

Though, he supposed, in a way, he had. His words had sounded clumsy and...not right, even to his own ears, as he'd been uttering them. No, not clumsy, *offensive,* his conscience whispered. What woman would not be offended when told she should have saved her virginity for her wedding night, by the man to whom she'd just gifted it?

He reached the bed and turned.

He'd never been much of a lady's man, that was part of his problem. He'd never acquired the knack of uttering smooth compliments. He'd been used to the world of men. Of being forthright. Honest. Only on this occasion, had he needed to be *brutally* honest? Could he not have...?

Hah. It was all very well looking back and seeing what he should have said. Or refrained from saying. Or said sooner. If he'd only proposed before kissing her, then she wouldn't have misunderstood his reaction to discovering he'd just deflowered her. Clumsily. With no finesse at all.

And even if he'd still blurted out those words of self-recrimination for losing control yet again when it was the one trait he prized in himself above all others, she might have been inclined to listen instead of running away and hiding. And he could have said that the blame was entirely his and beg her forgiveness for rushing her into a physical embrace that went so far beyond the bounds of acceptable behaviour...

That he'd wanted her so much, had wanted her for so long, that, when she'd responded to his kiss so sweetly it had been like a dam bursting.

Hell, why was it always like a dam bursting with her? He ran his fingers through his hair as he reached the window, before turning and pacing back again. Why couldn't he maintain any self-control the minute he got within two feet of her? No matter how sternly he lectured himself, or how many times he made sure the buttons of his waistcoat were fully fastened, why hadn't he ever been able to resist her? Or just stay away when he very first started to feel that magnetic pull she exerted?

Because he hadn't wanted to, he decided as he approached the bed. It was as simple as that. No matter what anyone told him she was, no matter what his mission in her regard had been, no matter how harshly he'd felt obliged to speak to her, the truth was he'd just been glad of any excuse to get close to her. No matter how poorly the encounter went. Because—he came to an abrupt halt as the truth struck him between the eyes—he was in love with her.

Almost at once, something else struck him, even more forcibly.

He'd ruined everything.

He breathed in, then out, fighting down a wave of nausea that rose on the thought that he might have driven her away for good.

But then he whirled away from the bed, his fighting spirit rising up with a roar, yelling *No*. He would not sit back and wallow in self-recrimination, whimpering that he might have lost her. Battles were not won by men who sat down and hung their heads in despair. They were won by men who refused to admit defeat, even when the odds were overwhelmingly stacked against them.

So, yes, he might have blundered, very badly, but he'd already taken steps to mitigate his error. He'd put the room to rights before he summoned a servant and demanded the return of his boots and jacket. Because she would not have wanted anyone to know what they'd just done. What she'd let him do. No, what *she'd* done. She'd enjoyed it, he was sure of it, right up to the point where he'd opened his big mouth and put his foot right in it. He must cling to that fact, for in it lay seeds of hope.

He reached the window and turned back.

He didn't want anyone to know what he'd done, either, if it came to that. God in heaven, he wasn't the kind of man who went round debauching innocents. He detested men who behaved little better than animals.

He was ashamed of himself. In so many ways.

Yet…he couldn't wish it hadn't happened. Because, thanks to Cassy, he'd spoken about his struggle, got it all out in the open and survived. He'd felt sad when he'd told her about the slaughter of the horses and the terrible deaths of the civilians caught up in the train of the army, but it hadn't cut him off at the knees. Because, when all was said and done, the retreat to Corunna had happened years ago.

While he'd been keeping his mind fully occupied, it appeared to have…healed up somewhat. The way a wound cut into his flesh would have healed. He thought of some of the men who'd almost died of their injuries. Carter, who'd lost an arm, or Barnes, who'd lost a foot to frostbite. Both men had gone through painful treatment and slow recovery. Had formed scabs and scars and struggled to get back to some semblance of normality. But they'd done it. Both of them were now leading almost normal lives. To look at them, it was almost impossible to tell what an ordeal they'd been through.

The bed was in his way again, so he had to do an about-face. As he did so, he recalled the jolt he'd suffered when she'd talked about the way he was burying himself away as though he wasn't grateful for being spared. It had… been like a shaft of light spearing through all the darkness that had been shrouding him.

It made him see that he ought to be more grateful for his life. And he was. He *was*. For having four functioning limbs and a solid roof over his head, servants to do his bidding, and work which enabled him to make a difference to the fate of those less privileged than himself. Hell, he was even grateful, at this moment, for his crazy, meddling sister. Because if not for her, he would never have found his way back to Cassy.

He wouldn't be standing here feeling as if he had his whole life ahead of him, to make of whatever he wanted. With Cassy, the woman he loved, hopefully at his side.

As he reached the window yet again he noticed with a shock that it was no longer completely dark outside. He could make out the outlines of rooftops against the pale grey sky. And it occurred to him that he, too, felt lighter than he had done for some considerable time. As though a great burden had fallen away.

It really was a new day.

Right then. Yesterday, and all the mistakes he'd made during the course of it, was over. He could start this day with a clean slate. And if his mind was truly healed, then it was about time he put it to good use. Come up with a stratagem to win Cassy round. Because he wanted—no, *had*—to marry her. There was no alternative.

But how to start? What was the etiquette for this type of situation? Had they danced together the night before, he could have sent her flowers. If he sent her flowers today, she'd probably rip off all the petals and then thrash the delivery man with the stems.

His mouth pulled up at the corners. Which stunned him. He…he couldn't be smiling, could he? At the vision of Cassy thrashing some poor defenceless florist round the head with his own bouquet?

He raised a questing hand to his mouth. Which had, of its own volition, smiled. At the thought of Cassy, proud, defiant, unconventional Cassy, taking out her anger with a bunch of flowers.

It would almost be worth sending some and hiding round the corner to watch her do it. He chuckled. Then blinked in surprise. When was the last time he'd laughed at something amusing he'd been thinking about? He cast his mind back, trying to capture such a moment. Then shook his weary head. His mind was too woolly with fatigue to think straight. As if to confirm that theory, a yawn took him unawares.

He still didn't have any idea *exactly* how he was going to make Cassy change her mind about marrying him, but change it he would. He was going to lay siege to her and not give in until she'd capitulated.

After he'd had a good few hours' sleep.

Having come to that decision, he yawned again, stretched his arms and finally lay down on his bed.

Chapter Eighteen

~~~~~~~~~~~~~~~

The next afternoon Cassy paid a call on the Henleys. For a couple of reasons.

For one thing, it was all very well God-mama saying her aunts didn't need to work, so it wouldn't matter if the Henleys *did* prevent people from giving them custom, because her aunts *did* rely on local goodwill. People could be so cruel to ladies who stepped beyond the bounds of social convention, for whatever reason. So, if there was anything Cassy could do to protect the ladies who'd been so kind to her from suffering that kind of ostracism, then she had to do it.

For another, she couldn't forget that Miss Henley was not very much older than she'd been when she'd run off with Guy. Girls of that age were easily led astray by glib-tongued so-called friends, and she had no doubt that it was that haughty female she'd seen her with who'd put her up to the spreading of rumours.

And also that it was in her power to rescue Miss Henley before things went too far.

Lastly, she could not condone what God-mama might have set in train regarding Miss Henley. And Godmama could protest all she liked about wanting retribution for Cassy's sake, but she couldn't help thinking that God-mama was far more concerned about herself in all of this. She might smile and call her *darling*, but Cassy had started to notice that she smiled more and became most affectionate when she was trying to get her own way.

'Miss Furnival!' Lady Henley got to her feet when Cassy entered her drawing room, her expression wary. It made Cassy wonder why she hadn't instructed her butler to deny her admission.

'I did not expect...' Lady Henley's face was pale. 'That is, I am sure you have no reason to...'

'Lady Henley,' said Cassy, cutting through all the stuttering and bluster. 'Thank you so much for agreeing to see me.'

'Well, I'm sure that this business will be better carried on behind closed doors,' she said defensively. 'But let me assure you, had we known of your connection to the Duchess of Theakstone we would have…that is…' She shot her daughter, who was sitting bolt upright on her chair, her hands clasped in her lap, her lips pinched, a dirty look. 'Although of course *now,*' she said crossly, 'I suppose it would be out of the question.'

So Godmama had been correct. Had they known about Cassy's connection to a lady of such high station, they *would* have beaten a path to her door. Which gave her hope that her offer of a truce would succeed.

'Not at all,' said Cassy, going to sit on the chair next to Miss Henley. 'In fact, I very much hope that you will come to call upon us, in Grosvenor Square, several times over the next couple of days. Just to show everyone that we…' she waved a hand between herself and Miss Henley '…are on friendly terms. Because if something is not done soon then I fear that remarks made by my godmother may prove fatal to your daughter's reputation.'

Lady Henley heaved a sigh of relief. 'There! What did I tell you, you silly girl?' she said to her daughter, who was looking more resentful than ever. 'Let this be a lesson to you to be more careful about your choice of friends.'

'I thought she was just a seamstress,' Miss Henley protested.

'Well, that just goes to show that you should treat everyone with respect,' returned her mother. 'You never know who anyone may be connected to!'

Cassy decided to intervene swiftly, before the Henleys launched into a full-blown quarrel.

'Do you have invitations to the Cardingtons' ball tonight?' Godmama had said they probably would, because Lady Cardington was one of those people who only considered their balls a success if people could scarcely squeeze into the ballroom.

When Lady Henley nodded, Cassy had to concede, once again, that Godmama knew what she was talking about when it came to society matters.

'Good. I shall make sure that Godmama comes to speak to you both and appears friendly.' She'd been very firm with Godmama about it, before setting out here, not wishing to arrive empty-handed, so to speak. Which had surprised everyone, not least herself. But she simply had not been able to stand back and allow Godmama to destroy a girl's reputation, apparently for the fun of it. 'I know,' she said grimly, 'what it feels like to be a social pariah. And I would not wish that on *any*one.'

Miss Henley bridled at that. However, that very same night, probably after much more talking-to from her mother, she smiled very prettily when Godmama approached her at the Cardingtons' crush. And Lady Henley became almost incoherent with gratitude when Godmama got Captain Bucknell to clear a path through the throng for all of them, so that the two older ladies could take places on the crowded chaperons' seats side by side.

Having succeeded in making Godmama behave, and putting Miss Henley in her place, Cassy suddenly found that she had the courage to say what she liked to *any*one.

She no longer cared if she gave offence, for some reason. Possibly because it no longer mattered what anyone thought of her now that she truly *was* a fallen woman. Which struck her as rather ironic, when she'd found it so hard to defend herself when she'd been innocent.

As the evening progressed, she began to enjoy coming up with increasingly quelling responses to all the insincere flattery that came her way. She'd always wished she had the courage to tell men what she thought of them and their ridiculously overblown compliments.

Now that she had nothing to lose she'd finally found it.

She'd never been desperate to find a husband, so what did it matter if she drove away all the suitors that Godmama insisted were the most eligible? She'd been minding her manners rather than speaking her mind for so long that it was like a…

She scowled. She would *not* think about the nature of ginger-beer bottles and popping their corks.

The scowl finished off what her tart rejoinders had begun. Before much longer she ended up all alone on the fringes of the ballroom with an empty champagne glass in her hand. But she didn't care. If she wanted another drink, she was perfectly capable of summoning a waiter herself. Or even walking into the refreshment room and getting one there. She had no need of a man to fetch and carry for her.

She didn't need a man for *any*thing.

No sooner had she come to that conclusion than a flurry of activity by the doorway drew her attention. Lady Cardington was going into raptures over the latest arrival—who was none other than Colonel Fairfax.

Cassandra set her empty glass down on a windowsill and turned her head away, but not before seeing him scanning the ballroom over his hostess's head and start heading in her direction.

Cassy's heart began hammering in her chest. It felt as if every minute of this day had been leading up to this moment. Even the men to whom she'd been so rude had only been in the light of a rehearsal for the main event. Because this was the man she was really angry with. This was the man she truly wanted to flay with her tongue and cut down to size.

His long legs ate up the distance rapidly, even though he didn't look as if he was hurrying. Even though she wasn't watching. Well, except for brief, sideways glances.

In next to no time he was standing over her, bowing. His eyes were bright, she noted with resentment, when hers felt so gritty through lack of sleep. He clearly hadn't spent the night weeping into his pillow. But then why should he? He didn't care a rap for her. Not a rap. Or he couldn't have done…what he'd done, thinking what he thought of her while he was doing it.

'Would you,' he said, 'do me the honour of joining me in the next set?'

'No,' she replied as stonily as she could, considering this was a public place.

'Not dancing tonight?' He smiled. 'I am glad

to hear it. I am not fond of dancing, as a rule.'
He glanced at the empty chair by her side. 'It
will suit me far better to simply sit and talk.
May I take this chair?'

'You may,' she replied coldly. 'Preferably to
the furthest corner of the room, where you may
sit and talk to someone else.'

He grinned at her. Grinned at her! If only
she had a handy...parasol that she could whack
him with. But parasols weren't permitted in
ballrooms. At least, nobody ever brought one,
since there was no need for them. As a rule.
Though perhaps debutantes should start carrying them everywhere, since it appeared there
was no getting rid of *some* men without them.

'I don't want to talk to anyone else,' he said,
sitting down beside her and turning the whole
of his upper body her way, making his interest
in her plain for everyone to see. From across
the room she saw Godmama's face light with
amusement. And Rosalind turned her head so
sharply as she galloped down the room that
she almost missed the outstretched hand of the
partner waiting to claim her at the bottom of
the set.

'Besides, I do need to explain why I spoke
the way I did, after you did me the honour of
allowing me to take your virginity.'

It was a good job Cassy did not have a drink in hand, because she would surely have spilled it. 'You cannot say things like that! Not in such a public place, where anyone could hear.'

'There are so many people here tonight that most of them are already having to shout to make themselves heard above the din. They aren't going to be able to hear anything that I might say. Particularly not if I lean close and murmur it into your ear,' he said, matching his movements to his words. 'Would you prefer that?'

Yes, oh, yes—having his mouth there, right by her ear, sending hot breath down her neck was…

She grabbed her willpower in both hands and leaned away. 'I would not,' she said primly. 'And if you don't sit up straight, this instant, I shall get up and walk away.'

'I shall only follow you,' he said. But he did sit up and adopt a more respectable distance.

'It all goes back to that business with Lieutenant Gilbey,' he continued in a conversational tone.

She had no idea where he intended to go with that statement, but at least it gave her the chance to get in a complaint. 'Ah yes, the poor hapless boy you assumed I'd seduced,' she said waspishly.

'That was only after Issy, that is, my sister, had filled my head with all sorts of lies. At the time you and he tried to elope I could see nothing lover-like about either of you. You looked scared and so very young, and he was treating you like a problem he had to solve, a problem that had landed in his lap like an unexploded shell which he heartily wished he could toss away, but couldn't.'

Well, yes, which was because by the time they'd reached Portsmouth they'd both realised they'd made a mistake. Guy hadn't taken into account just how much it would cost to transport a young lady right across the country, what with extra rooms in inns and the hiring of a chaise rather than just stabling his own riding horse. And she'd begun to see that she'd put her trust in an impetuous boy who had over-exaggerated his ability to take care of her.

'Why did you, as a matter of interest, take it into your heads to run away together?'

'I thought,' she couldn't resist saying, 'you assumed *I* seduced *him*.'

'I changed my mind.'

'Only after you discovered I hadn't!'

'Then won't you explain it now?'

'You have no right to ask about it *now*,' she snapped.

'Perhaps not the *right*, no. But I want to understand. Please, help me to understand that part of your past. I opened my heart to you. I told you everything. And once you understood why I'd behaved the way I did, you were easily able to forgive me. Don't you see how much difference it makes when you understand what makes people behave the way they do?'

Yes, but the difference was she'd seen that all his anger and bluster were on the surface. That he wasn't really that mean person who was trying to scare her by acting that way. That deep down he was a fine and noble man, even before he'd explained why he'd been acting the way he had. Whereas he'd never bothered to look any deeper into her.

'The moment I learned that my sister had lied about your financial affairs,' he pointed out, 'I came straight round to beg your forgiveness.'

Yes, but he'd believed that pack of lies to start with. He hadn't ever had any faith in her. She'd been so foolish to think that the way he'd looked at her, the tone of his voice when he'd said he wanted her...well, that had just been a man telling a woman he was attracted to the way she looked. That was all. He hadn't wanted her, the real her. He wanted the woman who went about in low-cut gowns shooting him come-hither looks. A woman who didn't really exist.

'And now I know that the other things people have assumed about you are lies, too. I want to know where those lies stemmed from...'

'Oh, please,' she said, finally losing her temper and thus her ability to maintain a stony silence. 'You know exactly where they stemmed from. They stemmed from the assumption that a girl could not possibly run away with a boy without getting up to mischief along the way. Not even if they'd always been more like brother and sister.'

'Was that how it was? Brother and sister? You grew up close to each other, I take it, if that is how it was.'

'Oh, for heaven's sake.' She turned to him. 'You aren't going to stop pestering me until you get an answer, are you?'

He shook his head and gave that wicked little grin again as though he was enjoying this. Enjoying baiting her.

'I'm not going to stop pestering you,' he said, lowering his voice to the merest murmur, 'until you agree to marry me.'

Her heart skipped. Several extremely inappropriate parts of her body thrummed, as if they were shouting *yes*. All the parts that no man but he had ever touched. Parts that wanted him to touch them again, damn them! Just when she thought she'd brought her reaction to him under control.

'I am not going to marry a man just because he accidentally took my innocence and feels duty-bound to atone for the crime. But I *would* have married Lieutenant Gilbey,' she told him, 'gladly. *He* treated me like a princess.' Which was because he suffered from the delusion that he was some sort of knight errant. As usual, when she reflected upon the fate of that young man, her spirits plunged.

'But how happy would you have been, if you felt for him the way a sister feels for a brother?' he mused. 'What is more to the point, what on earth could have happened to make you feel that it would be better to run away with him than stay at home?'

She flinched and turned her head away. She could tell him about her home life, she supposed. About the way her stepfather had bullied them into a state of perpetual anxiety. How he'd somehow driven wedges between them all so that nobody trusted anyone else. Until the only time she felt free was when she was out of doors, walking, walking, walking…

Which was how she'd come across Guy that day. He'd been sitting under a tree, a little the worse for wear after a night of heavy drinking. He'd leapt to his feet when he saw her approach, trying to be the gentleman, and winced. She'd told him he'd better sit down before he fell down and had sat next to him.

He'd put his arm round her, as though it was the most natural thing in the world. It had been so long since anyone had touched her to express affection that she'd leaned into him, buried her face in his chest and burst into tears...

'I know that your family would not take you back afterwards,' Colonel Fairfax was continuing. His voice turned remorseful. 'I have learned a great deal about your stepfather in recent days, and, had I known then what I know now, I would never have suggested that you go back to people who would not shelter you. But at the time, I thought you would be safer with them than sailing away with an army on campaign.'

'Well,' she said tartly, 'safety isn't everything. Or I wouldn't have agreed to Guy's mad scheme to run away with him. Only he...'

'Yes? You can tell me.'

She shook her head. 'You wouldn't understand.'

'I might.'

She looked down at the fan she held in her lap.

'Please. You will probably feel better for telling me. Especially if you haven't been able to talk about it with anyone else.'

She hadn't. Her family hadn't given her the chance to explain anything. Betty had been with her and so had simply understood how it was. Only her aunts had asked a few pertinent questions and that only when she'd first landed on their doorstep. They'd told her to let it be a lesson to her on the nature of men and encouraged her to put it all behind her. Since it had been by no means certain they'd let her stay, she'd done all she could not to annoy them by complaining about how she felt.

'I certainly feel better for talking to you,' he said, 'the other day.'

She flushed.

'In fact,' he said, leaning back in his chair and surveying the ballroom rapidly, before leaning back in, 'I would go as far as to say it was a very healing experience. Before that, as you know, I was buttoned up. Afraid of what would emerge if I let anything loose. But since then I have felt…' He shook his head and gave a soft laugh. 'Everything. It started with anger. The anger I felt every time I saw you, if you hadn't already guessed. And then yearning, then contrition, and grief, and…' he lowered his voice so that it rumbled down her spine '…ecstasy.'

'Don't refer to…*that*,' she bit out, her eyes darting frantically round the ballroom. It was making her heart beat and her blood pound, and her body remember the glide of his fingers, the rough texture of his legs, the heat and pressure of his mouth…

'Why not?'

'Why…because…' She was so…aroused that she was certain it must show. 'People will know what we are talking about.'

'No, they won't. They will just think I am making you blush by declaring my ardent love for you. They will simply think I am pressing my suit a little too warmly.'

She was blushing? She was. She raised her fan and began plying it vigorously, which made him chuckle.

'I wish you would go away,' she said angrily.

'No, you don't. You still want me. Even though I blundered badly. Once you have forgiven me, I will ask you to marry me again.'

'What makes you think I will ever forgive you?'

'You are not a vindictive woman.'

'I…how do you know that?'

His eyes slid across the room to where Lady Henley was sitting next to Godmama. 'You could have made things extremely difficult for the baggage who started spreading gossip about you,' he observed, just as Miss Henley went skipping past down the set in which she was currently dancing.

'She only told the truth. I...'

'Nor will you utter one word of condemnation against the man who led you astray and effectively abandoned you the moment I exerted the smallest amount of pressure. Nor even against the family who drove you away in the first place and who wouldn't take you back when you most needed them.'

Finally, he was showing signs of understanding what she was really like. It made her look up into his face.

'Do you know,' he said with a rueful smile, 'what I like about you the most?'

She shook her head. She hadn't thought he liked anything about her except the way she looked. Oh, please God he wasn't going to start wittering on about her limpid eyes, or her glorious hair, or some such twaddle. She'd thought he was different.

'I like the way you stand up to me. You have

never backed down, not even when I was at my worst.'

Well, that was certainly different. Only, he was wrong about her. She was timid and deferential, and...

Except, her eyes widened as the truth hit her, except with him. It was true. She'd never once attempted to placate him. Not even when he'd been at his most beastly.

Why was that?

He laughed. 'I am a soldier. I am used to fighting. And I am looking forward to our courtship, even if it is a long and stormy one. It will bring some spice to my life, which has been such a desert waste, for so long.'

'It must have been if you can talk about wearing me down with your proposals of marriage as something to look forward to,' she said, then found that she had to make use of her fan again to cool her suddenly burning cheeks.

Chapter Nineteen

Cassy didn't doubt he meant what he said. He'd made up his mind that it was his duty to marry her and he *never* shirked his duty.

And so she wasn't surprised when he came to call the next day, bearing a posy of red roses. Even though, strictly speaking, he need only have brought them if he'd danced with her.

It was a strange experience, having him sit next to her in a drawing room, attempting to utter pleasantries. He didn't seem to know where to begin. It didn't help that Godmama's other visitors were clearly drawing their own conclusions about his presence and kept darting him arch glances, which made him shift in his seat and clench his jaw.

'Oh, dear,' said Cassy with mock sympathy. 'I can see you are finding it terribly hard to think up something pretty to say. How much easier it is for you to hurl insults my way.'

'It's true,' he said tersely, surprising her. She'd thought he might at least have put up some show of gallantry, in the name of his current cause. 'I have never been much of a one for flirting. So I have not the experience with flattery that this situation clearly calls for.' He glowered round at Godmama's cronies, who nearly all nudged each other and tittered.

'How any man ever manages to conduct a courtship in such conditions has me baffled.'

'Yet last night you were so sure of yourself. Are you ready to throw in the towel already?'

He turned his glare in her direction. 'I shall never give up. You are mine,' he said, getting to his feet and marching to the door.

Leaving her all churned up inside. On the one hand she rather liked hearing that he found it hard to conduct the sort of banal conversation most men seemed to think suitable for a lady's ears. And she had really enjoyed watching him squirm under the scrutiny of some of society's most formidable matrons, but his parting shot had been so arrogant, it almost erased what pleasure she'd derived from the rest. How dare he declare she was his? Just because she'd yielded to the clamour of her body and her mistaken belief that he loved her? Or at least valued her?

That meant *nothing*.

As soon as the last of that day's crop of visitors left, she pulled all the petals off the posy he'd given her, before tossing them, and the remaining stalks, into the waste bin under her dressing table.

She was *not* his, she had muttered under her breath over and over again as she'd prepared for the ball they were all to attend that night.

She danced with him, when he asked, naturally, since if she refused him she would have to refuse all other offers. And she went into supper with him, but only because he thrust all other potential partners out of the way with such determination he didn't leave her any choice.

'I have to say,' she informed him, as he began to lead her to the queue that was lining up by the buffet table, 'that I do not care for your tactics. You are not,' she said, lifting her chin in an attempt to look down her nose at him, 'behaving like a gentleman.'

'I have never behaved like a gentleman where you are concerned,' he shot back. 'And that didn't stop you from letting me into your bed.'

'How dare you bring that up here?' she

hissed between her teeth, glancing wildly at the crowd jostling their way through the door to the refreshment room. 'Anyone might hear.'

He shrugged. 'Well, as you said, I am no gentleman, am I?' He gave her a half-smile. 'I am a soldier. Used to employing ruthless tactics to obtain my objective. To getting what I want. And,' he said, leaning down to murmur into her ear, 'I want you, Cassy.'

The words slid down her spine, turning her knees, and several points in between, almost liquid. She snatched a glass of champagne from the buffet and took a most unladylike gulp, feeling a sudden welling of understanding for her godmother's weakness for Captain Bucknell. When a man made your body feel like this, with just a few words, it was incredibly hard to resist him. The only part of her that wasn't straining to meld with Colonel Fairfax, right now, was her pride. If pride could be considered part of her body.

Actually, she worked out as she slammed the empty glass back down on the buffet, pride did not reside in the body, but in the mind, which was why it wasn't lying down and rolling over. Pride was, on the contrary, reminding her that this man had *humiliated* her. She'd often looked back on her younger self with disdain for allowing Guy to make a fool of her, but she was beginning to think she hadn't learned her lesson. She was just as susceptible now. Because, the last time Colonel Fairfax had said those very words about wanting her, or needing her... well, it made no difference, really...the point was that instead of taking them at face value, she'd bound them up with her own hopes and interpreted them as meaning something far different from what he'd intended.

And after she'd yielded to the urgings of her body, assuming that it was fine because they were in love, and would be getting married, he'd turned round and lectured her for...lack of morals!

That timely reminder of how he'd turned his reluctant proposal of marriage into an insult gave her the strength she needed to get through the rest of the evening, but she tossed and turned in her bed all night.

She rose the next day bleary-eyed, knowing he would be calling with another posy of flowers later on. When he set his mind on doing something, nothing would dissuade him, no matter how little encouragement she gave him. He'd told her so.

It was a matter of pride.

* * *

Sure enough, later that day, he marched into the drawing room clutching the regulation posy of flowers. They were pink today, rather than red. As though his enthusiasm, like the colour of the flowers he presented, was fading.

'You don't care for pink flowers?' A smile tugged his lips, probably at the expression of disappointment on her face. 'Did you prefer the red ones? Somehow, I didn't think it would matter what colour they were. I was so sure you would only tear all the petals off and stamp on what remained of the stems.'

That was so uncannily like what she'd done that she almost gasped. Yet, if he knew she would treat the flowers in such a way...

'I wonder why you bothered bringing me any more then,' she retorted, 'if that is what you suspect me of doing.'

'It is the done thing,' he said, presenting them with a flourish.

She took them from him, since to do anything else would have been unthinkable, under Godmama's watchful eye. Although what she really wanted to do was hurl them across the room. She didn't want his insipid flowers, especially not since he appeared to regard them as some sort of joke. Nor did she care for his dogged determination to win what he seemed to regard as a battle of wills between them.

'I wish,' she said, the moment they sat down next to each other, 'that you would leave me alone.'

'No, you don't.'

'Excuse me? Now you think you know better than I do what I want?'

'In this case, yes. Without me to put that dangerous sparkle in your eyes, you would subside into a tepid sort of ennui.'

'I…' She hesitated. Was that true?

'I am the only one of your admirers who makes your cheeks flush so prettily.'

'That's because you are generally so annoying. It is a flush of anger.'

'Nevertheless, the others never inspire anything more than boredom, do they? I've watched you stifling yawns behind your fan when I've been obliged to retreat for the sake of propriety.'

That was, unfortunately, true. She took a breath to say that if she yawned occasionally, it was not through boredom, but because she was tired. But she had a suspicion that if she mentioned tiredness, he would deduce that she hadn't been sleeping well and would somehow know that it was because of him.

So she took a different tack.

'You are not going to persuade me to marry you by annoying me, though, are you?'

He regarded her thoughtfully. 'What would it take? I should have thought... I mean, being caught in flagrante delicto would be enough, more than enough, to have most women dragging the man in question up the aisle by his... er...'

She shuddered as he floundered about for a polite way to describe what he was thinking. Because it reminded her so forcefully of God-mama's advice to use his attraction to make him *forget himself,* so that he would have to marry her. 'I am not so desperate for a husband that I would resort to such a low-down, sneaky trick as that.'

He gave her a searching look.

'You know, the more I consider that aspect, the clearer it becomes to me that we were both simply carried away by what we felt, against our principles, against our better judgement. How long are you going to keep on denying us what we both want, Cassy?'

Until he stopped talking about it as though it was an error of judgement. As though it was something to be ashamed of, even though it was. She *was* thoroughly ashamed of herself.

Most especially because whenever he alluded to what they'd done, the sensations she'd felt at the time came flooding back to her so vividly that she went weak with longing.

'As long as it takes,' she managed to grate, through a throat that was tight with shame, and longing, and increased shame at feeling such longing. 'And stop calling me Cassy. I have *not* given you permission.'

'You did not object before,' he pointed out, reminding her of the way he'd moaned her name, over and over, into her ear while they were pressed to each other completely naked.

'That was different. I was not in my right mind that day...'

'On the contrary. You were more your true self then because you were not fighting what you feel.'

'More fool me,' she hissed.

'Why don't you call me Nathaniel? I should not object. In fact—'

'Because it would imply an intimacy that does not exist.'

'Oh, but it does. Or it did. And it could again if you would only stop thinking of this as a siege.'

But that was exactly what it was, she saw in a flash of insight. He had every intention of sitting outside her metaphorical walls until she surrendered to him.

The moment he'd gone she bounded up the stairs to the sitting room she shared with Rosalind, her fingers itching to mutilate the posy he'd brought. Only that was exactly what he'd expect her to do. So instead she went to the window, flung up the sash and hurled the posy outside.

'Cassy,' cried Rosalind. 'Whatever are you doing?'

'I'm… I'm…' She gripped the windowsill. 'I'm raising the drawbridge,' she decided, turning round to face her friend. 'He's got some crackbrained notion of laying siege to me as if I'm a citadel he wants to conquer. Well, he's not going to do it with posies,' she said, slamming the window shut.

'I'd have him,' said Rosalind wistfully, 'if you really don't want him, if only he had the title Papa wants for me. He isn't, actually, as odious as some of the others. Nor as ugly…'

'Whether he has a title or not should have nothing to do with it,' she said, stifling the fierce jolt of revulsion she felt imagining him walking down the aisle to Rosalind. But not liking the thought of him marrying another was *not* the same as wanting to marry him herself.

'Oh? What would make you marry him then?'

'I would only marry *any* man if I thought it would be an improvement on my life as a single woman. No…that's not quite right. The only point in marrying someone would be if I felt as if I couldn't live without him. And if I believed he would make it his life's work to make me happy,' she declared with conviction.

'So, if some man came along and vowed he was so deeply in love with you he couldn't bear the thought of you marrying anyone else, that would be enough? You…you wouldn't care if he didn't have a title? Or any money of his own to speak of?'

Cassy's breath hitched. If Colonel Fairfax had ever said he was so deeply in love with her he couldn't bear the thought of her belonging to anyone but him, it would have changed everything.

Or would it?

'The title is certainly irrelevant. But so is what a man says,' she said bitterly. 'Men can say anything to get what they want.'

'Aye,' said Rosalind moodily. 'In my case, my money.'

'No woman,' Cassy declared, 'should ever believe a single word a man says when he is trying to get a girl to marry him. My stepfather, for one, was so charming before he got my mother up the aisle and within a week he'd turned into a veritable monster.'

'How can we choose a husband, then?'

'Lord knows.' Cassy sighed. 'Personally, I'd rather not get married at all. I'd rather be completely free. But…' she darted a glance at Rosalind, noting that her brow was creased in thought '…if I had to get married, then I'd choose a man that I thought was most likely to put me first, rather than his own selfish needs.'

As Rosalind nodded, Cassy went to the bell-pull and yanked on it. 'And while we're on the subject of men's selfish needs, it's time I added a moat to this citadel.'

'What?'

'I am going,' Cassy explained to Rosalind, 'to tell Dawes that I will not be at home to Colonel Fairfax, no matter how large a posy he brings, nor for any reason he might employ to attempt to gain entrance.'

'You won't be able to avoid him when we go out to balls and such, though.'

'No, but at least this will gain me *some* respite from his persistent attentions. Even citizens of castles under siege didn't spend all their time dodging the boulders being lobbed over the battlements.'

* * *

His reaction, when he found out what she'd done, was not what she'd expected.

'It will be a relief not to have to run the gauntlet of all those terrifying matrons every day,' he said with an infuriatingly cheerful grin as he took her arm to lead her for a stroll round the edge of the ballroom. 'Particularly as it wasn't getting me anywhere, not being a dab hand with polite chit-chat.'

For two pins she could have stamped her foot.

'And think of all the money I can save on flowers that you are only going to toss out of the window anyway.'

She gaped up at him in shock.

'Ah—you were not throwing them *at* me, then? I cannot tell you how relieved I am to learn that they only landed upon the pavement just where I was standing by the merest coincidence.'

'Of course I was not throwing them at you. I had no idea you would still be there...and what were you doing loitering outside all that time as you must have been doing if they narrowly missed you?'

He shrugged. 'I was in a brown study, I have to confess. Gazing up at the house, hoping I'd be struck by inspiration, rather than floral missiles. However,' he continued, 'I can't say that I am sorry that I shall not be wasting any more afternoons in that manner. I shall be able to get a damn sight more work done now that I can stay in my study, uninterrupted, all day.'

Cassy got the peculiar sensation that she was swelling up to twice her size with the effort of suppressing the scream of vexation she was desperate to utter.

'You won't win,' he informed her with nonchalance, 'by denying me admittance to your godmother's house, however.'

'Neither of us will win,' she said tartly, 'if I agree to marry you. Surely you are not so boneheaded you cannot see that?'

'Well, I must be exceptionally bone-headed,' he said affably, 'since I cannot see that at all.'

'Oh, for heaven's sake.' She stopped dead and rounded on him. 'For one thing, your family will be livid.'

'Why do you say that?'

'Because, well, because it is obvious. They think I'm the kind of woman who would dupe a young man into leaving me all his fortune. And if,' she said, holding up her hand to prevent him from objecting, 'if they didn't believe it, they were perfectly happy to lie about me and persuade you that I was that sort of woman.'

'Yes, but only because they could see you were exactly the right person to bring me back to life. I was, as they put it, like a walking dead man until the night I saw you at Lady Bunsford's ball. If I now declare you are the one woman who will bring all their plans to get me married off to fruition, they will...well, it wouldn't surprise me if they claimed that was their intention all along. Because they really don't care who I marry, as long as I marry someone and set up my nursery.'

The brief glimmer of pleasure that had flared up on hearing she'd brought him back to life sputtered out on learning that any woman would do for him and his family.

'Do you have,' she said resentfully, 'a clever answer for every objection?'

'I don't know,' he replied cheerfully. 'I don't suppose you have exhausted your list of objections yet.'

'I don't suppose,' she said darkly, 'I have.' Because she hadn't come to London to find a husband in the first place. Her aunts had a perfectly lovely lifestyle without having a man underfoot to spoil things. And she would gladly return to that way of life the moment God-mama released her from playing the role of friend to Rosalind. Which time couldn't come soon enough.

Anyway, all that aside, there could be only one reason for marrying a man. And that was if she felt she could not live without him. And if he could persuade her that he could not live without her, either.

The reasons Colonel Fairfax had for claiming he wanted to marry her were simply not good enough. She could see that he wanted to atone for all the horrid things he'd believed about her and protect her from possible scandal, if Rosalind should ever reveal what she'd seen. To pay the penalty for having done it at all. Oh, yes, he was a great one for atoning for things, was Colonel Fairfax.

But she didn't want to become his penance. She felt humiliated enough as it was. Why, all he'd had to do was admit that, in spite of believing she was the worst kind of woman, he wanted her, and she'd ripped his clothes off and dragged him to bed.

She still couldn't forgive herself for that. She lay awake long into that night, weltering in a stew of recrimination and self-loathing. Part of the problem was that it was *this* bed she'd dragged him to. *This* coverlet she'd writhed round on. *This* canopy she'd gazed up at over his shoulder as he'd thrust into her, over and over again…

She rolled out of bed the moment she heard servants begin to stir about the house, washed her overheated body and went in search of breakfast.

The dining room was deserted, which wasn't surprising at that hour.

What did surprise her, however, was the shriek which emanated from the region of Godmama's room not long after Cassy had sat down to her first cup of tea of the day. She'd slopped about half of it over the tablecloth when Godmama uttered a second, equally piercing shriek, which rose in volume until it could only be described as a wail. It made Cassy leap to her feet and go running to find out what on earth could have happened.

But Godmama came bursting into the dining room before Cassy could even reach the door, still wearing her night attire and with a lace nightcap tied under her chin.

'That girl,' she cried. 'That ungrateful, treacherous harpy!' She staggered to her place at the table and sank on to her chair. 'Brandy,' she said to the nearest footman, who happened to be Gordon.

Gordon cast his mistress an anxious look, but then, clearly as concerned as Cassy by her wan features, and the fact that tears were streaming down her face, went trotting off to fetch a bottle, in spite of it being so early in the morning.

'Do you mean Rosalind?' Cassy went to sit next to Godmama, passing her a napkin to blot at the tears. 'What has she done?'

'She's run off with Bertram,' sobbed Godmama. 'Eloped!'

'What?' Captain Bucknell? How could any woman want to run off with a loathsome specimen like that? 'But I thought she was determined to marry a man with a title,' said Cassy, in shock herself.

'That was just her father's wish, according to this,' said Godmama bitterly, waving a crumpled note she was clutching in one hand. 'Apparently she wanted *romance*,' she said with loathing.

Cassy recalled how interested Rosalind had been when she'd told her the little she'd been prepared to admit about her own elopement with Guy. How she'd thought it romantic and sighed, and looked impressed.

And then she recalled the amount of time Captain Bucknell had spent lately, taking Rosalind to places like Astley's and Gunter's, while Godmama was busy laying false trails of gossip all over Town. How happy Rosalind had looked every time he'd asked her to dance, which was at least once every time they went anywhere there was dancing.

And then she went cold inside as she recalled the conversation they'd had the day before, which she'd thought had been about her determination not to marry Colonel Fairfax, during the course of which she'd said it wasn't important if a man didn't have a title or any money, as long as he would devote himself to making his wife happy.

No wonder parts of that conversation had seemed a little odd. For Rosalind had been weighing up the pros and cons of a proposal she must have received herself from Captain Bucknell.

And, oh, no! Cassy had practically exhorted Rosalind to run off with him, in spite of her father's ambitions.

But then she saw something else. This was going to bring Godmama's whole charade to an end. Now that Rosalind had taken her fate into her own hands, there was no longer any need for Cassy to stay in Town. Which meant she would be free from Colonel Fairfax, too, because she could not see him pursuing her to the remote town of Market Gooding. He might claim that nothing would make him relent in his determination to get her to marry him, but the truth was that he wouldn't want to be away from the centre of government for any length of time. His first priority was, and always would be, the army. And serving his country.

'And as for him,' Godmama continued, 'oh, it is too humiliating. After all I've sacrificed on his account. The stand I took!' She reached out and grabbed Cassy's hand. 'I am going to have to admit my stepson was right about him. He told me I ought to break with Bertram, that he was no good. And I thought he was saying it out of spite. To spoil my fun. And when he reminded me who held the purse strings, and how difficult he could make things for me if he chose, I took it as a threat and invited that girl into my home so that I could defy him, when—' She broke off as Dawes himself came in, bearing a silver tray with a full decanter and a crystal tumbler on it.

'Allow me, Your Grace,' he said, pouring her a stiff measure. Godmama let go of Cassy's hand to reach out for the glass and took it with trembling hands.

'Thank you, Dawes,' breathed Godmama. 'At least I can rely upon someone. You will never betray me, will you? You will always stay by my side, no matter—' She broke off, her lower lip trembling.

'Of course not, Your Grace,' said Dawes staunchly. 'The very idea!'

'Oh, how glad I am to have such good friends,' she said, taking a most unladylike gulp of brandy. 'And you, Cassy, too,' she said, raising the glass in her direction. 'Thank goodness I still have you at my side. You won't run away once tongues start wagging, will you? I know it will be unpleasant, but you don't want for pluck. You can stand it, can't you?'

Cassy's heart sank. There was, as Godmama had just pointed out, going to be a lot of the sort of malicious gossip that was meat and drink to Godmama's set. And Cassy couldn't possibly leave her to face it on her own.

It felt as though the steel jaws of a trap had just snapped shut, tethering her here for the foreseeable future.

'Finally,' said General Fewcott as Nathaniel entered his office. 'Thought you were never going to show up with these costings.'

Although the General had every right to be

annoyed at the amount of time Nathaniel had taken over this particular report, he looked more amused than anything.

'Heard you haven't had much time for this sort of thing of late,' he said, tossing it on to a pile of similar-looking folders. 'Heard you have been dancing attendance on that Furnival girl. Heard you have outshone all your rivals and are now the clear front runner.' The General now looked positively amused.

'I...uh...'

The General slapped his hand on the desk and guffawed with laughter. 'About time you sowed a few wild oats. You've been making us all nervous, stalking about with that grim face, working so hard you make us all look like park loungers.'

Wild oats? Was that what everyone thought? Of course they did, because his sisters had blackened Cassy's name, which made it all the more imperative she agreed to marry him. Only his own family could undo the wrong they'd done her.

The trouble was, she was still determined to resist him. So determined, that he'd even started to hope he might have got her with child. She'd *have* to marry him, then.

Only, did he want her to marry him just because she felt she had no choice? Would she not resent him and embark on their marriage determined to hold aloof, inside, where it mattered?

'...which is what everyone could see from the very first,' the General was saying, making Nathaniel aware that he hadn't been paying attention. 'Scoundrel like that. Theakstone mismanaged that affair badly. Came the heavy with her. Reminded her of his father, I expect.'

'Theakstone?'

'The Duchess's stepson. Surely you know all about that side of the family, with you being so wrapped up in the goddaughter?'

'No, I...'

'Hah! Well, I'm not one for gossip,' said the General, leaning forward on his desk, his eyes lighting up the way all gossips did when imparting a juicy titbit. 'But we all think that is why she invited the Mollington girl to Town in the first place. To thumb her nose at her stepson's autocratic ways. He tried to break up the affair with Captain Bucknell when she grew a bit too indiscreet, don't you know? Should have just bided his time. It would always have ended up with something like this.'

Captain Bucknell? The big, bewhiskered guardsman who was always hovering about

in the background? What did he have to do
with anything?

'I'm sorry, I don't follow.'

'No? Well, it was obvious a fellow like Captain Bucknell was never going to warm the
Duchess's bed for long. And now he's run off
with that heiress…'

'I beg your pardon. Heiress?'

'The Mollington girl. Well, you know that
her father is some sort of mill owner. Latest on dit is that he wanted his daughter to
be launched into society as if she was a lady.
And the Duchess was totty-headed enough to
be the one to take her on. Probably to thumb
her nose at Theakstone, if I'm not mistaken.
However…'

Suddenly, a lot of things that had not added
up before made complete sense. Cassy had
never properly explained what she was doing
in Town, if it wasn't to find a rich husband.
But if the Duchess was at war with her stepson and had enlisted Cassy's aid to provide
cover for Miss Mollington…yes, that must be
it. He should have seen it before. Only Cassy
had been so close-mouthed about it all…but
then of course she would, wouldn't she? She
was honour-bound to keep her godmother's
secrets.

'And you say the girl the Duchess took into her home has run off with the Duchess's lover?'

'That's it. First thing this morning.'

'Good God.' How on earth had General Fewcott learned what went on, inside a private house, so quickly? He shuddered to think.

'I should like to see what's going on in Grosvenor Square today,' the General remarked. 'Hysterics, I shouldn't wonder. Gnashing of teeth and tearing of hair.'

How could the old man find all this so amusing? But then, that was the way of the world. Most people found nothing more entertaining than the misfortunes of others.

Cassy, however, would be devastated. No matter how scandalous her godmother's behaviour, Cassy had never once said a word against her because she was loyal.

Which gave him an idea. An idea of such brilliance that he couldn't wait to set it in motion.

'If you will excuse me, sir,' he said, 'I have to…' And without awaiting a word of dismissal, he turned on his heel and left.

Chapter Twenty

The butler at Grosvenor Square pokered up the moment he opened the door.

'I regret, sir, that I cannot…'

Nathaniel thrust him aside and stepped into the hall.

'I know what your orders are,' he said. 'But let me tell you that the Duchess will be very glad to see me.'

'Her Grace is not receiving,' the butler said.

'Because of that girl running off with the Captain, yes, I'm not surprised she doesn't want to see anyone else. But I have a solution she will want to hear,' he said by way of explanation.

'I… Colonel, please, I…' The butler might have made a token protest, but Nathaniel could not miss the way the man was gesturing with his hands to the upper floor. And then, as if being struck with a brainwave, he added, 'I really must protest. Gordon!' A young footman came trotting along the upper landing. 'Make sure this man does not disturb Her Grace. Bar the door if necessary.'

At that, the footman went trotting back along the landing and took up a belligerent pose outside one of the doors. Which told Nathaniel exactly where he would find the woman he was searching for. Cassy. She was bound to be at her godmother's side at a time of crisis, offering what comfort she could.

He pushed the faintly protesting butler aside, again, and stalked up the stairs, weighing the odds. On the one hand, the footman was a big, burly fellow who looked as though he was going to enjoy denying Nathaniel admittance. It was the same young chap with the granite jaw who'd given him such black looks the day Cassy had received Nathaniel alone. He'd been wanting to plant him a facer when he'd handed him back his boots. And now he had permission to do so he was grinning with anticipation.

On the other hand, Nathaniel had spent much of his adult life fighting real battles. Learned a lot of low-down tricks from men who'd grown up in the gutters. Tricks that had saved his life on occasion. Tricks that a domestic servant could not begin to imagine.

Nathaniel reached the landing and advanced to a point just out of reach of the footman's long arms. For a moment the two men stood eyeing each other. Then Nathaniel put up his fists in the traditional sparring pose.

The footman sneered.

Nathaniel feinted with his right.

The footman threw a punch that would have felled an ox. Nathaniel, however, was not an ox and so easily managed to dodge it, getting in a jab to his opponent's kidneys on his way past, because the energy that the footman had thrown into his punch carried him several feet beyond the point where Nathaniel had been standing. Several feet away from the door he was supposed to be guarding.

Nathaniel darted to the door and got it open before the footman had stopped his headlong rush. But with a bellow of rage, the young man turned, lunged and wrapped his massive arms round Nathaniel's upper body just in time to prevent him getting inside the holy of holies.

Nathaniel thwarted him by the simple expedient of letting his knees go soft, so that the footman's weight propelled both men forward into the room. They rolled over and over each other and landed in a tangle of limbs on a very fine, and thankfully soft, pale blue rug.

The Duchess—who, Nathaniel noted from under the edge of the footman's wig, was lying on a daybed, still clad in what he couldn't help noticing was some very fetching night attire—uttered a shriek and flung out one hand, rather in the manner of Mrs Siddons making her farewell address. The other hand kept tight hold of a decanter.

Just before the footman gripped him by the collar and hauled him to his feet, he saw Cassy was kneeling beside the daybed, bathing her afflicted godmother's temples with lavender water. She leapt to her feet as well, dropping both handkerchief and bottle, before grabbing the end of the daybed to stop herself overbalancing.

'What do you mean by bursting in here like this?' she cried, taking up a defensive position in front of the Duchess in dishabille.

'Don't you fret, miss,' panted the burly footman who still had his meaty hand in Nathaniel's collar. 'I'll soon settle his hash.'

'You might want to hear my plan first,' Nathaniel bit out, before jabbing his elbow into the footman's stomach so hard the man doubled over.

'I beg your pardon, Your Grace,' said the butler, stumbling into the room in almost as theatrical a manner as his mistress had just employed. 'I told him you were not receiving, but he would not take heed.'

'He says he has a plan,' said the Duchess, gazing at Nathaniel hopefully. 'Oh, put him down do, Gordon, and let him speak. It's not as if things can get any worse, is it?'

'They might,' cried Cassy. 'Don't listen to him, Godmama.'

'Now, sweetheart,' he said, shaking off the disappointed footman and turning to Cassy. 'I know you wanted to wait until Miss Mollington was settled, but really there is no point in keeping our news a secret any longer.'

Cassy's eyes widened. Her face paled as she saw what he was intending. 'No, you cannot mean to—'

He seized one hand and slid his other round her waist. 'Miss Furnival and I,' he announced to the room in general, 'are to be married.'

'Oh, Cassy, you foolish girl, you did not need to keep such news secret from me,' said the Duchess, her face lighting up.

'Oh, but…' But the Duchess didn't want to hear Cassy's explanation. Nor did the servants. The butler was smiling at her fondly and the footman had a look on his face that said *about time*. So she was not going to get any help from that quarter.

'The *Gazette*,' said the Duchess, swinging her legs to the floor. 'You must get a notice posted today, Colonel. Then nobody will be able to say I failed this Season, will they? Because I did find *you* a husband, at least, Cassy. And a ball,' she said, tossing the decanter aside carelessly. Thankfully it landed upright amidst the sofa cushions. 'We must have a ball. I will make it the most sought-after event of the Season. Well, naturally it will be. Everyone will want to see the *ton*'s most elusive bachelor finally tie the knot. And if they want to be present, they will not dare utter a word about that…' she screwed up her face '…double-crossing pair of deceivers. Not to my face, anyway, not if they want to get an invitation to your betrothal ball. And who cares what anyone may say behind my back?'

'You could let it be known,' Nathaniel suggested, 'that you were tired of Captain Bucknell anyway and effected the introduction to Miss Mollington out of the goodness of your heart. He may not have a title, but he does come from a very good family.'

'That's true,' said the Duchess, brightening even further. 'And even though he doesn't have a title at the moment, which is what Rosalind's papa wanted for her, there are only two older brothers and his father standing between him and a marquessate,' she said, ruthlessly disposing of all the Captain's closest male relatives, 'when all's said and done.'

'B-but, Godmama...'

'Oh, Cassy,' said the Duchess, surging to her feet, and flinging her arms round her. 'I knew I could rely on you. It was the best idea I ever had, bringing you to London, wasn't it?'

'Um...'

If Nathaniel had been less desperate, he might have felt sorry for Cassy, who was looking decidedly hunted. But he'd given her plenty of chances to forgive him and accept his proposal, and she hadn't made use of them. And didn't they say that all was fair in love and war?

'And now...' the Duchess sighed '...I may be happy.'

'Surely...' said Cassy, looking at the Duchess's beaming smile in a perplexed manner. 'It will not be *that* easy to put aside your grief...'

'Grief? Pooh,' said the Duchess, waving her hand in a manner expressing contempt at the very idea. 'You speak as if my heart is broken, whereas it is only my pride that has taken a battering. You cannot really think I was in love with that great booby, can you?'

'But…but…you said you took a stand when your stepson tried to make you give him up.'

'Well, what if I did? Do you think I was going to let that boy bully me, the way his father did?' She tossed her head, making the lappets of her lace cap flail wildly. 'I would probably have grown tired of him by now, anyway. He may have had his uses. Well, it was very flattering to have such a young, handsome escort for a woman my age. And he was exceptionally skilled in the…ah…well, we won't go into that,' the Duchess concluded with a positively naughty smile. 'Goodness, there is so much to do,' she said to Dawes, who was still hovering by the door. 'And I still in my dishabille,' she said, heading for that door. 'I must get dressed and start making lists. Cassy, I know you will come and help me, in half an hour or so. That is all the time I can leave you two lovebirds alone,' she said with an arch smile, before beckoning the servants to follow her, leaving them in sole possession of the room.

'You sneaky so-and-so,' said Cassy, rounding on him the moment they were alone. 'Telling Godmama we are going to be married when I've said no I don't know how many times!'

'You could have put her right,' he said, unabashed.

'No, I couldn't. As you very well knew when you said it! You deliberately backed me into a corner, didn't you?'

'Yes.'

'Don't you at least have the grace to pretend to be ashamed of yourself?'

'No. After seeing how easily you were able to withstand me when I laid siege to your heart, I could see that I was going to have to call in reinforcements. Which I did, in the form of the Duchess. I knew, you see, that you could not fight us both. You are so loyal to that woman that you would never do anything to hurt her, since she appears to be about the only person who has stood by you, through thick and thin. As I mean to stand by you,' he said, taking a couple of steps closer, 'in future, in sickness and in health, in good times and bad.'

'In short,' she replied, standing her ground, 'you just had to beat me, no matter the cost.'

'Cost? There is no cost. Not to me.'

'Good grief, do you really care so much for your image of yourself as an honourable man you will ally yourself to a woman you have never respected?'

'I do respect you.'

'So much that you lectured me about tossing my virginity away before my wedding night!'

'I… Cassy, I was not in my right mind that day. Could you not tell? I had just gone through an amazing… I don't know how to describe it. Almost like a rebirth…because of you. Your generosity, your compassion…and I felt as though I'd taken advantage in the most despicable way.'

She snorted in a most unladylike fashion. 'You don't need to marry me as some sort of act of atonement…'

'I won't be doing so. I will be marrying you because I love you.'

She blinked. 'No, you don't.'

'Don't presume to tell me what I feel or don't feel.'

'Don't get on your high horse with me, either!' They were standing toe to toe by now, glaring into each other's eyes. It occurred to Nathaniel that if anyone came in at that moment, they'd think they were enemies, not lovers. 'If you really loved me,' she spat, 'you would have come straight round here to beg my forgiveness, on bended knee. Not stroll, whis-

tling, into a ballroom two days later and tell
me I'd restored your sense of humour!'

Had he done that? He didn't think so.

'Look, Cassy, if I'd thought that begging
your forgiveness would have worked, I would
have done so. I did everything else I could
think of,' he pointed out. 'I did all the things
serious suitors are supposed to do. I called. I
bought you flowers…'

'You gave up the moment I put an obstacle
in your way, though, didn't you? You said you
were relieved not to have to bother with it. That
you were glad you needn't waste any more of
your precious time when you had far more important things to do!'

'Not…exactly those words. But, yes, I was
not very good at playing the part of a suitor…'

'Playing the part? See? I knew you weren't
in earnest.'

'Then you were wrong. I just needed to employ a different set of tactics. I could see it was
useless trying to behave in a way that was for-
eign to my nature. It wasn't even producing
results, was it? That was why I was so pleased
to learn about that girl's elopement.'

She gasped, looking horrified.

'Ah—that did not sound the way I meant it.'
He ran his fingers through his hair. 'I am use-

less with words. But, Cassy, don't you see? I knew it was my chance to make you lay down your weapons. I knew that you would rather keep your opinions of a man who has just announced he will marry you to yourself, than disappoint the Duchess when she has already been betrayed by two people who owed her just as much.'

Cassy frowned. 'What?'

He took a breath. That explanation had come out all tangled up. He had to focus on the nub of the matter.

'You are so loyal, Cassy. So honourable that you would rather let people believe a lie, than to reveal someone else's secrets.'

Something flared in her eyes at that. Something that looked a lot like a decrease in hostilities.

'What,' she said, in a voice that sounded curious, rather than furious, 'makes you think that?'

'Because I have spent countless hours going over everything I thought I knew, and comparing it with what I felt, in my heart, about you. I had been at war with myself over you from the moment I came to seek you out, because I reacted with such…longing…for a woman my head told me was unworthy. Because the only women I knew really well, my own female relatives, are so…duplicitous they will stop at nothing to get their own way. But it turned out my heart had been right all along. You are nothing like them. Or what I feared you might be. You are…' he took the risk of reaching out and taking her by the shoulders '…perfect.'

Her glower returned. But she didn't try to shake him off and she didn't immediately launch into a counterattack.

'I took a risk, I know, by ambushing you, just now, but I thought it was worth it. What did I have to lose, anyway? I hadn't been able to break down your defences by attempting a traditional courtship.'

She leaned back and peered up into his face, as though searching for some reassurance.

'I know you find it hard to trust men, too. So many of us have let you down. Your stepfather, Lieutenant Gilbey, your uncle, even your brother for all I know. And then me. Though I, at least, intend to make it up to you if it takes me the rest of my life. And also prove to you that not all men are selfish, short-sighted, untrustworthy…'

'Judgemental, greedy, parsimonious and stupid,' she supplied when he faltered for want of the right words and because she wasn't trying to pull out of his hold any longer. There was a softening to her features that was making his heart pound and, because they were standing so close, with every breath he took, he filled his lungs with her soft, sweet scent.

'I am guilty of being all of those things,' he said ruefully. 'And ruthless, as well. But in your case that is only because I cannot help but do whatever I need to do to keep you in my life. Because I cannot live…that is, I do not want to live without you. I…I need you, Cassy. I love you,' he finished, he felt, rather lamely.

'You love me?' She looked at him with those suspicious, wounded eyes again, but there was also something of hope faintly flickering to life.

'Yes,' he assured her. 'I love you. Do you think I could have admitted all that about the horses to just anyone? Or how hard I've struggled to keep it all in check, all these years? I'm far too proud.'

'No,' she said consideringly, then reached up to lay her palm against his cheek. 'I didn't think you could have told anyone unless you trusted them, deeply. At first, I thought that was what you meant, when you said you needed me. It was only afterwards that I…' Her eyes filled with tears. 'I thought I'd got it wrong. That you didn't love me. You only *wanted* me. That was what you'd said, after all...'

'I'm not good with words, Cassy. They come out all wrong at the most crucial moments. As you have learned to your cost. I need to show you what I feel. Which I intend to do by living it.'

And then, because he'd just promised to show her what he felt, he drew her closer, slid one arm right round her waist and lowered his head. Very slowly, so that, had she truly objected, she could have said so. Or slapped him.

She did neither. She simply sighed and gazed up at him with a longing that mirrored his own.

So he kissed her. Pouring all the love and respect he felt for her into it. And then, because she responded so sweetly, the passion.

Had the Duchess not burst into the room shortly after, that kiss would have ended up on the daybed she'd so recently vacated.

'Colonel Fairfax, you naughty man,' chided the Duchess, although she didn't sound the least bit shocked or angry. 'It is just as well I returned when I did to ask about who Cassy wants to add to the guest list, or you would have had to go and apply for a special licence,' she said on a girlish giggle. 'We cannot have your firstborn making his appearance until at least nine months and one day after the ceremony, can we? Or everyone will say I have been presiding over a scandalous household.'

Cassy went pale. Her eyes widened. Her hand flew to her stomach, then she peered up at him suspiciously again.

'Why didn't you use that very argument?' she hissed through clenched teeth as the Duchess turned to say something to the footman he'd been wrestling earlier, who was hovering at her elbow.

'Because I didn't want you to feel you had no choice,' he admitted. 'You might have ended up resenting me.'

'But you didn't scruple to use Godmama's trouble against me.'

'Not against you, sweetheart. For us. And that was different. You made a choice. And in offering you that choice, I showed you that I knew what kind of woman you really are. A fiercely loyal, compassionate one.'

Her face cleared. 'You did. You really did.' She smiled at him. And then turned to the Duchess. 'Actually, Godmama, I think a special licence is a *very* good idea.'

'What?' The Duchess looked from one to

the other in disappointment. 'But I wanted to throw a grand ball…'

'I think a small, select gathering will serve our purposes better,' said Cassy firmly. 'You will be able to exclude far more people. And only people who are your true friends and family, of course,' she added as though it was an afterthought, 'will receive an invitation.'

The Duchess smiled. A mischievous smile. Her eyes flickered from side to side as though considering all the people she would be able to slight by not inviting them. Then she looked at the pair of them.

'In that case,' she said, her smile growing even more wicked, 'there is no need for me to stay in this room one second longer.'

And with another of her girlish giggles, she slipped out through the door.

'Honestly!' Cassy stared at the door in annoyance. 'That woman has the morals of a—' She broke off, flushing.

'But a very generous nature to make up for it,' put in Nathaniel. 'That's why you cannot help loving her.'

She looked up at him with a wry smile. 'You really do know me, don't you?'

'I'm starting to,' he said, pulling her to his side. 'But I mean,' he said, kissing her jaw, 'to get to know you,' he added, lowering his mouth to the side of her neck, 'much, much better.'

'Oh,' she breathed, as he steered her to the daybed, proceeding to demonstrate what he hadn't been able to tell her with words and, to his intense satisfaction, she didn't raise one single, solitary objection.

The only word she said some time later, and it was really more of a sigh, was, *'Nathaniel...'*

* * * * *

MILLS & BOON

Coming next month

STOLEN BY THE VIKING
Michelle Willingham

'I am Breanne Ó Callahan,' she answered. 'My foster father is King Feann MacPherson of Killcobar.'

'I know who he is.' He turned at that moment, and his gaze fixed upon her. 'I recognised you the moment I saw you. And you are worth more than a slave.'

'How could you possibly know me?' she demanded. 'I would have remembered you.' Heat flared in her cheeks when she realised what she'd said. But it was too late to take back the words. Breanne tightened her grip upon the drying cloth, and in that heated moment, she grew aware of his interest. He studied her face, his gaze drifting downward to linger upon her body. There was no denying that he wanted her.

But worse was her own response. She was caught up in his blue eyes and the dark hair that framed a strong, lean face. There was a slight scar on his chin, but it did nothing to diminish his looks. The *Lochlannach* warrior was tall and imposing, his physical strength evident. Only the slight limp revealed any weakness.

'What do you want from me? A ransom?'

He reached out and cupped the back of her neck. It was an act of possession, but instead of feeling furious, his sudden dominance made her flesh warm to the touch. His blue eyes stared into hers as if he desired her, and she was startled by the unbidden response. Though she tried to meet his gaze with resentment, her imagination conjured up the vision of his mouth descending upon hers in a kiss. This warrior would not be gentle…no, he would claim what he wanted from her. Heat roared through her, and she thought of his hands moving down to pull her hips against his.

That might be what he wanted from her, after all. She was well aware of how female slaves were used as concubines. The thought shamed her, but another part of her was intrigued by this man. She could not deny the forbidden attraction, and she had the strange sensation that his touch would not be unwelcome.

As if to make his point, Alarr stroked the nape of her neck before releasing her. 'You will remain with me at all times, obeying everything I ask. If you do this, then I will remove your bindings.'

'When?' she demanded.

'When you have earned my trust. Not before.'

Continue reading
STOLEN BY THE VIKING
Michelle Willingham

Available next month
www.millsandboon.co.uk

COMING SOON!

We really hope you enjoyed reading this book. If you're looking for more romance, be sure to head to the shops when new books are available on

Thursday 20th March

LET'S TALK
Romance

For exclusive extracts, competitions
and special offers, find us online:

facebook.com/millsandboon

@MillsandBoon

@MillsandBoonUK

Get in touch on 01413 063232

For all the latest titles coming soon, visit
millsandboon.co.uk/nextmonth

MILLS & BOON
A ROMANCE FOR EVERY READER

- **FREE** delivery direct to your door
- **EXCLUSIVE** offers every month
- **SAVE** up to 25% on pre-paid subscriptions

SUBSCRIBE AND SAVE

millsandboon.co.uk/Subscribe